The Journey Somewhere

By Suzie Carr

Also by Suzie Carr:
The Fiche Room
Tangerine Twist
Two Feet off The Ground
Inner Secrets
A New Leash on Life
The Muse
Staying True
Snowflakes
Sandcastles
The Dance
Beneath Everything

Keep up on Suzie's latest news and projects:
www.curveswelcome.com

Follow Suzie on Twitter:
@girl_novelist

For you, Mom and Dad. Thank you for teaching me how to focus.

When you stop seeking perfection,
suddenly everything comes into focus.

Acknowledgements

I feel enormously grateful to so many people for the guidance they've provided me in writing this book. Kristen Leister, thank you for being there during my first draft woes. Within minutes, you helped calm my mind and reclaim my focus. I will always be grateful to you for saving me! Diane Marina, you are a treasure, a true friend, and one of the best role models. Angela, your kindness and support are much appreciated. Thank you for helping me discover the perfect book cover. Felicia, Bethany and Joni, thank you for putting your heart into this book project. You've given me a comfort that runs deep.

And finally, a huge thank you to my readers who continue to support my writing. I am blessed beyond belief.

Dear Readers,

Music has a way of touching the soul and reminding us how fragile, vulnerable, and beautiful life is when we surrender our fears and just be. Like most intangible things, music is magical. Even still, music can wreak havoc on our hearts. In one moment, we are captured by its sensual appeal, and in another, we are left tasting the bitter sweetness of its notes.

In The Journey Somewhere, I've woven these two dichotomies together with the journeys of former lovers, Kelly and Becca. We first meet folk musician, Becca James, and her then girlfriend, Kelly Copeland, in Tangerine Twist. Back then, Becca's newfound fame played its tricky hand on their relationship, and now, several years later, they are back facing new temptations.

For these two to move forward in life, be it together or apart, they must let go of past regrets, failures, and fears. To be truly happy and successful, they must acknowledge that stability is nothing more than a crutch, and that yearning for a picture perfect life is nothing more than an obstacle in the pursuit of purpose and ultimate joy.

Pull up a comfy seat, and escape into this melodic world to discover for yourself that it doesn't really matter where we start the journey, as long as we start it somewhere.

- Suzie Carr

Carr—The Journey Somewhere

Chapter One

November 2011

I had everything I needed to be happy and successful.

I was engaged to Bonnie, and I never had to worry about whether or not she loved me. We adopted our lovable husky, Zoey, and enjoyed snuggle time with her every night in front of the television. We lived in a cute condo with vaulted ceilings and a balcony that overlooked a river. My parents welcomed Bonnie into their lives, and her parents had done the same with me. Just a month earlier, our parents even instituted a new tradition of playing bridge together on Saturday nights. The icing on the cake was that Bonnie and I both worked for the same publishing company as assistant photographers. We commuted together and even ate peanut butter sandwiches and apples together in the cafeteria.

We just celebrated our sixth month anniversary as a couple.

We lived a picture perfect life.

Then the phone rang, and our happy life together experienced its first unraveling.

One phone call. That's all it took.

# #

I stood on the balcony and stared down at the calm river, dumbfounded, dripping chili cheese sauce from a spatula in one hand, and clutching my cell phone in the other. Just five minutes earlier, I had been happily stirring Pepper Jack cheese into my homemade chili. With a peaceful sway, I hummed along with the Aerosmith song on my iPod, inhaling the scent of the spicy chili cheese. When my cell rang, I couldn't answer because I needed to pay close attention to my macaroni boiling on the adjacent burner. So, assuming it was just Bonnie calling me on her way back from the liquor store to tell me she scored a bottle of the seasonal beer I'd been craving, I let the call go to voicemail. After I strained my al dente macaroni, I checked the message. Bonnie had not called to shower me with the good news that she would be delivering my favorite beer to go with our chili.

Nope. It was Becca, my ex-girlfriend, returning my call from earlier. A call Bonnie insisted I place.

Bonnie suggested we invite Becca out for dinner. She offered that suggestion without a clue that ever since the day I walked away from Becca, I fought to regain my footing in life.

I had asked Bonnie, "Why on earth would you want to put us through a dinner with her?"

"Because she sent us flowers and a basket of dog treats. We can't be rude."

I stood before my fiancée, trying my best to protect her from the residual emotions and weaknesses still climbing up the walls of Pandora's Box. "I don't think that's necessary."

"I'd like to invite her. It'll give us that last bit of closure." She squeezed my hands.

2

I stepped back from her, picked up the phone, and called Becca. Relieved when she didn't answer, I left a message, inviting her to dinner.

Now, a few hours later, my breath hitched in my throat as I listened to Becca's message. "Hey, Kelly. Hey, Bonnie. It's Becca. I appreciate the invite, but I'm going to have to decline. I've got so much going on. Thank you, though. I wish you both the best."

I shrank away from the counter. Her well wishes for me and my fiancée stung. I still wanted her to fight for me.

Dread filled my core, drowning me in deep regret for not being a strong enough person to stop pining over Becca, and for not appreciating the good life I already had.

I spent the next thirty minutes shivering on the balcony. At one point, I banged my chili stained spoon against the railing, wishing the repetitive action would quell the chaos in my mind. I looked towards Orion's Belt overhead and reminded myself that I was happy.

Becca's fame as a musician didn't fit into my life plan. I wanted stability, security, and the comfort that came from knowing I had someone to return home to at the end of the day. Someone who needed me as much as I needed her.

I had that with Bonnie.

With Bonnie, I was an equal, and never trembled in her shadow. I loved that I no longer had to stress about how much I failed to achieve in life. Bonnie didn't care whether my photos landed in prestigious magazines or if my body packed on a few pounds. She wouldn't care if I told her I never wanted to go out on the town again.

She lived a simple life, and I craved such simplicity. I never had to worry about what was hiding on the other side of that corner when I turned it. I liked a solid plan, a straight path, and knowing that at the end of the day, my life would be the same as when I rose.

Why would I ever want anything different?

I waited on my answer under a brilliant display of stars, confident I'd get one. Then I heard the front door and Bonnie's happy greeting that she did, in fact, score me some of that coveted beer. I looked up to the sky. "Thank you," I whispered.

I re-entered the kitchen with my dried up cheesy spoon in hand. I hugged Bonnie like I hadn't seen her in twenty years. "I love you so much," I whispered. I clung to her, hoping that somewhere in the comfort of that peaceful embrace I would find the powerful love I yearned for so I could forget about Becca James for good.

# #

About a week after Becca declined our dinner invite, I met my best friend, Margie, for lunch at McFadden's Pub. It was the place where Becca made her debut appearance as a musician. Margie walked in and was glowing with her golden mane of hair cascading past her shoulders. Her teeth sparkled and her cheeks appeared fuller. Even her eyes looked bigger. She was the only woman I knew who, at five months pregnant, could still fit into her size four jeans without unbuttoning them.

I sat across from her with my hands folded. "So how's life?"

She drummed her manicured fingers on the table. "How's life you ask?" She chuckled. "That sounds like a cliché amongst strangers, doesn't it? Then again, I guess we're sort of heading in that direction, aren't we? It's been what, like a month since you've answered my call?"

"Life is just so crazy busy right now. You run a day spa. You know how it is." I could never tell her the real reason I blew off her invites. How do you tell your best friend that your fiancée finds her annoying? What choice did I have but to ignore her calls?

"Yet, miraculously, I still shift things around so I can be here for my best friend."

Joe, the owner, popped up beside our table, saving me from further grief. He greeted us with two waters and a bowl of popcorn. "Hey, you're early. Becca doesn't go on until nine tonight."

The blood drained from my face. "Becca?"

"Yeah." He stood tall. "She didn't want any publicity so I haven't advertised it. It'll be a surprise for anyone who's here." A smile crept on his face. "I think she wants to get her feelers out there as a soloist before she tells her fans that she's back."

"We'll be coming back." Margie squeezed her lemon in the water. "Well, Marc and I that is. Kelly over here is too busy watching television with her new fiancée to get out anymore." Margie tossed the wilted lemon into her water and took a sip.

Joe offered me an understanding shrug then handed us a menu. "I'll be back around to get your order in a few." He walked back to the bar.

Margie sipped her water without a trace of compassion for how the mention of Becca's name might stab at my heart. "Do you think she'll do okay on her own?"

"Yep." She craned her neck, scanning the amber lit room and avoiding my eyes.

"Really? Without Kara?"

She snapped her gaze to me. "She's done with that fool. Our old Becca is finally back to normal. Tonight is all about her getting back on that stage by herself."

Jealousy stole my balance. "Fantastic for her."

5

Margie clasped her hand around my wrist. "Becca told me about the dinner invite."

I wiped some sweat off the water glass. "Bonnie suggested we invite her out after she sent us flowers and treats for Zoey."

"She isn't in a good place right now."

"And so she turned down our invite?" I asked.

"Out of respect for you both."

"Out of respect?" I rolled my eyes. "Let's just order some crab cakes."

# #

Later that night, Bonnie and I were discussing the color of our kitchen walls. She wanted to paint them chili pepper red. I wanted to keep them white. That erupted into a heated, one-sided debate from me about how we could never agree on the simplest of things.

"It's just paint," I said, dunking the spaghetti into the boiling water. Bubbles boiled up and over the pot's edge and onto the burner, creating a halo of steam to protect me from the hurt in her eye.

"Why not red?" she asked.

I stirred the spaghetti, avoiding her intense stare.

Why not red? Because red was one of those impossible colors to get right. Everything about red spelled trouble. It required layers of primer and even more layers of paint before it homogenized. The cleanup took hours, scrubbing and soaking the paint brushes, and covering up the mistaken strokes on opposing walls and trim. Before one paints a wall red, one has to be ready to love it regardless of the outcome because once that roller hit the wall, you can't unroll it. One had to suffer through the consequences of such a bold decision. If you hated it, too bad. You had to either learn to love it or become

6

adept at turning a blind eye to it and focusing on something other than its constant reminder of the massive flub created.

Red paint was permanent.

I stirred the marinara sauce. Some popped and squirted up at me, landing on my pink t-shirt. I jumped backwards. "This is why." I scoffed at the mess. "Red is messy. Red is irreversible. Red is disastrous."

Bonnie removed the red stained spoon from my hand and stared at me with the hesitation one might stare at a rabid raccoon. I hated when she did that, as if she never had a grumpy moment.

"Take it easy, Kelly." She put the messy spoon down and removed the sauce pan from the hot burner. Then, she turned back to me. "No problem. We'll keep it white." She braced her hands on my shoulders. "It's not that big of a deal. It's just paint."

I hated when she ended an argument as if she were the cool and collected among us. "You want red so badly? Fine. Buy the paint and we'll paint the wall red." I stormed down the hallway and locked myself in the bathroom.

She knocked on the door. "Why are you acting this way?"

I grabbed the counter. How do you tell your girlfriend that you're angry that your ex-girlfriend is moving on in life without you? "Just give me a few minutes."

I stared at my reflection and hated what I saw in myself, a woman still desperate to understand the inner workings of Becca James. I wanted to forget about her. I carried her memory around like a bag of wet cement on my shoulders, stumbling and crumbling under it. I needed to unload that weight back onto her so I could paint my walls red and be satisfied with it.

I talked to my reflection. "You're strong. You don't have to pine over her. You've moved on to bigger and better love. You have plenty of self-control. If she walked into the room, you wouldn't think twice about sending her a wave and getting on with your fun. You're not some rabid fan, falling at her feet in a weak mess. You are doing just fine on your own without her, and she needs to know this."

I exited the bathroom and approached Bonnie in the kitchen. "I'm sorry I acted out."

She turned to me with soapy hands. "Anything I need to worry about?"

"I'm just irritable."

"Why?" Soap dripped to the tile.

I handed her a dishrag. "I talked to Margie today. She had Braxton Hicks contractions. She's upset because she's experiencing all of these pregnancy things without my knowing. I haven't been around much."

Bonnie wiped her hands. "If you want to go spend time with her, don't let me stop you."

"I should visit her."

"Then make plans with her." She tossed the dishrag on the counter and continued washing dishes.

"Are you okay if I slip out for a few hours tonight to see her?"

She spun around again. "Kelly, you said you were coming with me and Cliff. He's looking forward to seeing you. He wants to play us a new song he learned."

We visited Cliff two nights a week. "We just saw him on Sunday."

"Can't you just go out with her tomorrow night?"

"She's whiney and needs me to help her decide on carpet colors for her living room." She didn't need to know I already saw Margie that day. "She called me up at lunch today to invite us over tonight."

She shut off the water and placed the sponge back in its rack. "You know what? You should just go. Cliff and I will be fine. I'll tell him you had to work."

I hated that she babied her twenty-year-old brother. "Why don't you just tell him the truth?"

"Kelly, you know better than to suggest that. He's super sensitive."

She needed to stop protecting him from reality. No wonder the poor guy still couldn't pick out his own clothes. He was autistic, not stupid.

"Fine. Tell him I had to work." I kissed her cheek. "I'm going to get dressed." I scooted out of the kitchen, trying to outrun my guilt for lying and to gain some strength for what I was about to do.

Chapter Two

Within half an hour, I stood in the back of McFadden's Pub, acting every bit the part of a stalker. I huddled behind a potted plant that Becca purchased for the pub a few years back. It had grown to a mighty miniature tree, providing me with a clear view of the scene while still offering privacy.

Two guys performed a James Taylor song. The singer strained his face, singing about Carolina being on his mind, and the other guy played guitar, sealing his eyes shut as if making love to the song. A waitress I'd never met asked me if I wanted a drink. I waved her off, not wanting to draw attention to myself.

I planned to wait until after her performance to talk with her. I would walk right up to her, thank her for the flowers and treats, and walk away. That would prove I walked the high road in my life, and I didn't spend my days wiping up tears because we lost each other along the way. I needed her to know that so I could move forward and put her behind me.

When the two guys finished, the crowd peppered a few claps.

Joe took the stage. "Ladies and gentlemen, we've got a special talent with us here tonight. I'm sure a few of you will recognize her." He chuckled. "Everyone, please help me welcome Becca James to the stage."

Everyone stood and clapped, including the woman at the table in front of me who clung to her crutches. They applauded as she climbed the stage with

11

her beloved guitar, Tangerine Twist. Joe wrapped her up into his big arms, kissing her cheek, patting her shoulders, and beaming like a proud father.

She cried in his embrace, and he wiped her tears with the back of his hand.

I fought to maintain my resolve. I came to prove I had control over my emotions, and yet there I stood, huddled behind a plant, fending off chills and a moan from the pressure of pride pushing against the back of my throat.

Becca stood before us, rosy-cheeked and looking every bit like she wanted to dash away. I could see the creases on her forehead spread, as if the nervous wheels of self-doubt that she'd long ago buried, resurfaced and started cranking again. She never performed solo. She always had Kara up there with her, supporting her, acting as her safety net should she mess up. That wheel cranked, surely blinding her and spinning her off her feet.

Becca's stage fright caught up to her even after all the time she'd spent in front of crowds.

I looked around to see if anyone else noticed the eminent breakdown. People stood mid clap, watching as she bowed, nodded, and sat down on a large exhale.

Even from the back of the room, I couldn't miss her trembling hands as they gripped the stand and adjusted the mic.

Becca sat before us, afraid and weak.

I felt sorry for her.

Her pain traveled across the dead space, along the ceiling beams, across the wooden planked flooring, and straight into my heart. I could taste the salty tears forming in her eyes. I could hear the low grumble of her tummy roll in angst. I could hear her private rants cursing herself for her fears, and regretting each day that had led up to that exact moment—the moment her career would end on a thud in the middle of McFadden's Pub.

She began to strum and cleared her throat with too much force. As if projected on a movie screen, I saw her anxiety take stabs at her, riddling her, telling her she would never survive the stage without Kara by her side. Her eyes swept from one end of the stage to the other. She had no Kara to save her. No one could save her but herself.

I clung to the counter and sunk lower behind the plant, trying to figure out a way to leave without being noticed. I couldn't bear witness to the unfolding disaster. I'd seen enough. Her unraveling would haunt me in the middle of the night, stealing the place of resentment and replacing it with pity.

I wanted to resent her, not pity her.

Pity planked down on the heart, and stole precious sleep, good memories, and an ability to move on in life to pursue greater things. I didn't want pity emblazing itself on me.

I didn't want her to fail.

I wanted her to grasp the mic and sing like she'd done countless times with Kara. I wanted her to show off her skills and talent to the room full of people who now fidgeted in their seats, looking every bit as uncomfortable as one would look in the face of a celebrity falling flat on her face.

She picked at the strings, and I summoned for her to find that confident part of herself that fame had created. Her cocky ego could set her free, help her fly high, and lift her up so she could, at the very least, walk off the stage untarnished and in-check.

She needed her ego.

She needed to inflate her presence.

She needed to stand taller than everyone in the room.

She couldn't shrink herself down to fit the mold of a normal person because to do that would extinguish her light, the very light that her fans needed.

13

She was a musician with a gift.

She needed to share it.

She needed to be the Becca James that hurt me; the star, the artist, the girl of everyone's heart.

My blood pressure spiked with each pass of her tongue over her lips, each cock of her head, and each failed attempt to break into her song.

The room shrank, and I had to cling tighter to the counter to keep balance.

My heart hurt for her.

I wanted someone to rescue her. I looked around for the two guys, hoping they might take the clue from Joe who stood frozen by the stage with a look of horror etched on his face. Unfortunately, the two guys were nowhere to be seen.

She stopped mid strum, and hung her head as if struggling to find her place on that small stage. No one spoke. People glanced around at each other, raising their eyebrows, twisting their mouths, and sinking into their chairs to wait out the awkward silence.

I stopped breathing while waiting for her to recover.

I wished I was with Bonnie, listening to Cliff play us a song on the piano in the safety of a quiet living room. I didn't want to witness the train wreck.

Finally, she looked up at the audience, and sighed. "You know," she said, pulling the mic off its holder. "This stage still scares me." She paused and reflected on Margie and Marc who tilted their heads in unison to the right, offering her a thumbs up. From my angle, I could see the pride swell on their faces. Margie rested her free hand on her pregnant belly and smiled.

"Sitting up here all alone reminds me how vulnerable I am to the human experience. When my grandfather died many years ago, I promised him I'd play at his funeral. When I got up and tried to sing, I lost my voice. Fear came in and swiped it away from me. I couldn't remember the lyrics to a song I

14

used to sing over and over again with him. That moment burned itself onto me, and it tortured me for years. It stole my dream. The shame that fell on me that day, and for the years that followed, just landed right up here with me again tonight. It helps for me to talk this out." She spoke to Margie. Margie nodded her head up and down.

"I relied on my duo partner, Kara, too much," she said. "Obviously." She laughed at herself.

We laughed along with her.

Her forehead relaxed and her skin smoothed.

"See here's the thing about fear. The more I allow it in, the stronger it becomes. It takes on its own power and becomes my leader. I'm not okay with following that. I'm not okay with bowing my head to it in reverence, as if it were a mightier force than me and had any rights to my freedom."

Even the wait staff stopped walking and serving to take in the intimate moment.

"Every time I cave in to my fears, I surrender my freedom to it. It gains strength in the face of my weakness. And I'm tired of it. I won't stand for it."

She paused, taking us all in. "So, here I am, sitting up on this stage, fending off nervous jitters in my stomach, and struggling to suck in a full helping of air so I can sing without cracking. Fear is staring me in the eye and willing me to surrender myself to it."

She looked up to the beams, pulled in her bottom lip, and broke out into a laugh. Like a mist from a waterfall on a hot summer day, her laughter refreshed and cooled the anxiety.

We relaxed under her authority over fear, giggling along with her. Our laughter glided through the air like a paper airplane, unstable and wavering, yet brave and undeterred.

15

She strummed her guitar with a heavy flick of her wrist, creating dramatic tension.

Becca's whole face lit up with a new beauty. As if a switch had just been lifted into its upright position, her entire being sprang to life. Her fingers brushed the strings, whispering a soft melody. "Many of you may be wondering how I could suffer from fear after all the time I spent performing with Kara Travers on a different stage most every night of the week."

She arched her eyebrow.

"The answer is, I don't know why." She reflected on her guitar pick, bowing her head. "Tonight, I sit before you as a humble person plagued by stage fright, willing to fall flat on my ass and get back up as many times as needed to stand up and tell this fear to get the hell out of my life."

Chills soared through me. The hairs on my arms stood tall. I was proud and inspired by the power Becca harnessed.

"So what do you say? Are you with me?" she asked us.

I joined in with everyone else, cheering as if the Ravens just scored the winning touchdown for the Super Bowl.

Becca played to us. She cradled her guitar and reached for notes that hung up where few would ever reach. She played her guitar and sang for me countless times in her condo, and her music never sounded as good, as precise, or as angelic. Becca James had transformed from a backup performer to a front-runner capable of mesmerizing a pub full of patrons to the point of silence. In the spaces between her notes, I could hear my tummy gurgle. She carried us in the palm of her hand, bringing us along on her breezy ride.

I came hoping to knock her down a few notches so I could raise myself up higher, only to realize Becca could never be knocked down. She was a force who hadn't yet even begun to tap into her power.

16

She had a real gift, and people clung to it like they would cling to the side of a vessel in raging water. She offered them respite. Surely her ego would grow even bigger now that she could manage the crowd on her own accord. That had to happen.

Like a jolt from an electrical socket, Becca's ingenuity woke me from a stupor. She was no ordinary person. She was somebody special. She was an artist of music, and such an artist would choke to death if tethered to a life without a stage, guitar, eager fans, and an extraordinary mentality.

She rose to the occasion. She pushed herself and she thrived. She deserved her moment. She earned that moment. She belonged in that moment.

She didn't just get lucky when Kara offered her the chance at stardom. God had waved his powerful gift in front of her, and she reached out and embraced it. A pride welled up in me for her. Tears stung my eyes. I wanted to shout out to her and tell her to latch onto that gift and run with it. Let it take her as far as it could take her.

I wanted her to succeed.

I wanted her to stand up, bow, and then raise up her head in confidence.

Suddenly, I sprang into cheerleader mode, whistling like the rest of the pub when she hit a high note. The hairs on my arms stood up, drinking up the energy.

I fixated on her fingers as they plucked the melody to a song I'd never heard, mesmerized by their fluidity and charm. I snapped away from them and stole a glance at Joe who was standing behind the bar with pure love and admiration etched all over his face.

She ended on a soft note, bowing her head in a reverent moment of silence before lifting to face the awe-stricken crowd. My eyes locked onto a new side of Becca, a person emerging from the depths of ordinary.

17

Her moment arrived, the moment when she finally found herself, and inextricably, the moment when I lost myself all over again.

I started the first clap. Then, the audience joined in.

She climbed off the stool and waved to the crowd. Not as a diva, but as a true celebrity in her own right. The audience stood up in an ovation, and she bowed several times, waving off their accolades in a humbling sweep. That just fueled more applause.

Joe whistled and turned red. Margie and Marc stood tall, applauding and raising their arms up in harmony. Becca bowed over and over again, tensing her jaw and blinking away tears. She spanned the crowd, acknowledged everyone with a nod, and then walked off the stage, cradling her beloved Tangerine Twist.

The stage hollowed without her.

That stage had created a superstar.

I choked on a joy too big to hide.

She did it.

She let go of all that corralled her and ran through that wild field with her arms spread wide, embracing her gift.

She walked off in the opposite direction. My rational mind warned me to stay put and let her go. But, my heart won out. I chased after her.

She turned around when I shouted her name, a mere foot away from her freedom into the backroom. Her eyes widened and her cheeks flushed. I never remembered seeing her hair so shiny and rich or her lips more rosy.

"I'm so glad you came," she said, a small cry twisting on the edge of her voice.

"Me, too."

Her eyes twinkled in the dim light. "What did you think?"

Her question poked a part of my brain never before touched with such sincerity. "You took me on one hell of a ride."

A tease tugged at her lips. "Really?"

I mirrored her smile. "The Becca I saw tonight was different than the one from your duo. This Becca is one who's going to heal broken hearts and inspire people to climb out of bed in the morning to do something incredible with their days."

She arched her eyebrow, waiting on more of my words.

"You created more than just music. You just created art up on that stage, Becca."

She brushed away my compliment. "Aw, come on, Kelly. You're just being nice."

I moved in closer, drawn to the vulnerability surfacing on her face. "I think you know me better than that."

Her hand brushed my cheek. "At first, I was freaked out tonight. I don't know what happened to me. I just sat up there, stared out at everyone, and blanked. All the fear from years ago rushed back at me. Then, I found Margie and then Joe, and my heart slowed down enough for me to catch up with it. When I began to play, my grandpa's spirit settled into me. That's when the music took over. I connected to it in a way that usually only happens when I'm alone."

I nodded, willing her to stay with me in that moment when our guards disappeared and blame didn't sit idle on our hearts.

"My fingers lightened up and I could taste the harmony as if it was right in front of me. The notes opened and allowed me to become an intimate part of the music."

I latched onto her hand still on my cheek and pressed it. "I believe that's what they call the zone."

19

She blinked. "I finally get it."

The room blurred into the background. An extraterrestrial energy passed between us, one that riveted and grounded me simultaneously. The resentment from hours before vanished. Involuntarily, I leaned in and kissed her. Her lips, soft and plump against mine, heated me to the core. Emotions piled up in the back of my throat and resulted in a soft release of tears and moans. She cupped my face in her hands and inched backwards.

"I'm so sorry I canceled on the dinner invite. You understand why, right?"

I could only shrug.

"She makes you happy, and that makes me happy."

Desperate, I clung to her shirt. I wanted to tell her how I could never love Bonnie the way I loved her. I wanted to tell her that there were things I didn't enjoy, like how Bonnie didn't like Margie and how she enjoyed lazy afternoons a bit too much for my taste.

The twinkle in her eye reminded me of the superstar she had become and of all the pain, jealousy, and insecurity that comes along with loving someone who so many others loved too. A sadness crawled against the back of my neck, knowing I belonged nowhere near that kind of life. "She's a good person."

"I can tell." Becca dropped her hands. "I'm so sorry, but I have to go."

"Okay," I said, raising my chin.

"Take care of yourself, okay?" She lifted her hand back up to my cheek. "I hope you two have a happy life together." Her hand warmed against my skin, but her words sliced through me like cold steel. "You deserve it."

I gulped back the finality of her words. "Thanks." My voice weakened under her serious gaze.

"Until we meet again."

"Hmm," I said, numb and hurt by her lack of fight for me.

20

She dropped her hands. "Tell Bonnie I said hi." Her relaxed sigh hurt more than her words.

I chuckled as if it didn't bother me in the slightest. "I sure will. You take care." I turned and shuffled away, leaving the pub without saying hello to Margie, Marc or Joe. I just ran straight for my car and drove as fast as I could to the edge of the parking lot so I could try to find myself in my sobs before heading home to paint red walls with my fiancée.

# #

When I returned home from seeing Becca perform at the pub, I couldn't face Bonnie right away. I needed to internalize everything from the past few hours. So, as soon as I entered our place, I ran past her lounging on the couch. "I have to use the bathroom."

Zoey, my trusted confidant, followed me down the hall and into the bathroom. I closed the door behind us and sat on the covered toilet seat while Zoey put her head on my legs. She stared up at me with her dark, soulful eyes.

"She wasn't supposed to look so beautiful on that stage."

She nudged her head against my legs.

I scratched the space between her eyes. "I need to tell your mommy the truth."

She didn't budge.

"I know I shouldn't have gone." I circled her eyes, and she blinked.

"Don't worry. Momma Kelly isn't going anywhere."

Her eyes grew larger and she bowed her head.

"I love you, sweet girl."

She raised her paw and I tapped it.

"So should I keep this our secret?"

She backed up and wagged her tail.

21

"Maybe you're right. Why bring it up? What would be the point? Worry her? For what?"

I stood up, and Zoey circled my legs. She barked.

I waved her along with me, and we headed out to the living room to enjoy some quality down time.

Bonnie was sprawled out on the couch, watching a recorded episode of *Castle*. I plopped down next to her.

She took my hand. "How did it go?" Her eyes still glued to the television.

I fixated on a dog figurine that resembled Zoey on the television console. "Fine," I said.

"So, what color did you go with?" She locked onto that television screen like a fighter pilot would her target.

Zoey jumped up and sat between us. She looked at me as if warning me to keep my big mouth shut. I petted her before sinking my face into her fur. "We couldn't decide," I mumbled.

"Kelly, you've been gone for three hours."

I raised my head. "She needed to vent, I told you." My skin prickled.

"What's bugging her now?"

"Just the usual venting." I couldn't master a lie any more than I could perform brain surgery. "It's over now. Let's just enjoy the rest of our night together."

Bonnie squinted and her eyes circled my face. "You seem off."

My defenses flared. "Would you stop with the digging? Let's just enjoy the show."

Her eyes flew open wide. She flicked off the television. "Come on, babe. Tell me what's going on."

I couldn't lie to her. I couldn't do it. I nudged Zoey off the couch and scooted up closer to her. "I didn't go to Margie's tonight."

22

She dropped her eyes and rolled her tongue around the inside of her cheek the way she did whenever she got upset. "Where did you go?"

I placed my hand on her cheek, and she looked back up at me. "I went to McFadden's to see Becca perform."

She backed away from me. Her lips parted and her face turned white. She stood up and began pacing the room.

"Say something."

She continued pacing. "So, you represented both of us with your thank you?"

I protected my new memory by locking it up with my other endearing memories of Becca. "Yes."

She nodded and walked towards the kitchen. "I'm going to get some water. Would you like some?"

"No, thanks." My voice crawled out as if buried deep within the carpet fibers.

I watched her disappear behind the kitchen wall, and a strange new silence took over the room.

# #

Bonnie and I strained to find safe ground after my visit to the pub. Instead of my honesty bringing us closer, it drove us apart and caused her pain. The things that normally brought us pleasure, like thumbing through coupons and walking Zoey, felt forced now. Justifiably, she looked at me through suspicious eyes, even while I brushed my teeth, washed my face, or read a book in bed.

I wanted her to know that I was happy in our life together.

I wanted us to move forward in life, and not get stuck in a place of uncertainty. So, one Sunday morning while we sat down to eat some eggs and toast, I asked, "What do you say we take a hike in Oregon Ridge Park?"

"Kelly, do you love me?" she asked, sidestepping my question altogether.

I pulled my fork away from my mouth. "Of course."

"Because if you don't, you can tell me the truth." She clenched her jaw, as if bracing for impact.

"I do. I love you. Please don't question this."

"I love you so much, and the thought of losing you hurts. It would hurt me more, though, ten years down the road. I would never want to make you feel boxed into what we have here. I just want you to be happy and comfortable."

I adored her selflessness. "I am happy and comfortable."

"I want you to be sure. If walking away would make you happier, then I'm willing to take the pain. Your happiness means more to me than my own."

I dropped my fork and reached out for her wrist. "Why are you talking like this?"

"I'm still having a hard time processing why you needed to go to the pub without me that night."

I pushed my plate aside. "I only went to thank her for thinking of us with the flowers and treats." In the silent wake of my words, I realized how ridiculous that sounded.

"Why did you lie to me?"

I shifted up in my seat. "I didn't want to make you worry for no reason."

She scooped up a pile of scrambled eggs and shoved them into her mouth. She chewed them while glancing out the window at the large Japanese Maple tree. "If there is a reason, I want you to feel safe in telling me."

I reached out for her. "I've never given you a reason to doubt my trust. Have I?"

She looked back at me. Worry stretched across her face. "No, you haven't."

"Aside from this incident, I've always been honest with you. I always will be. You never have to guess what's going on if it affects you."

"I will never be Becca James. I could never be Becca James." She swallowed hard. "I don't ever want to be Becca James. Are you okay with that?"

Her words sat heavy on my heart. I wanted to wrap her in my arms and comfort her the way she always comforted me. "If I wanted to be with Becca, I'd be with her. I'm not with her. There's no reason for you to question this."

Her shoulders relaxed, a clear sign that I had just gifted her with a huge relief. "I love you so much."

"I love you, too."

We finished our breakfast in peace. The air between us opened up and felt like a spring breeze, blowing away all that wasn't fresh and lively.

As we relaxed over our coffee, she took my hand. "What do you see in our future?"

"Well, I see us traveling the world with our cameras, snapping exotic photos and submitting them to *National Geographic Magazine*." I propped my knees under me, excited to focus on something other than Becca. "What about you?"

"I want to have kids. Lots of them."

My throat tightened. I slid my knees back out from under me. "How many kids?"

Her eyes relaxed, dreamlike. "Four, maybe five."

"I thought you were a dog person."

Her smile faded. "You don't want kids?"

I pulled my hand back. "I didn't say that." I perused her sullen cheeks. "I think we should travel first, though. Get that out of our system."

She gathered our mugs and then took them to the sink.

Dread dug its claws into the root of my stomach, destroying the peaceful vibe from moments ago.

She turned on the faucet and began rinsing the plates. "How long do you think we should wait?"

"A few years at least. Don't you think?"

She scrubbed the cup. "I'm already thirty-two years old. If we waste years traveling, we're going to lose out on valuable time."

I giggled. "You're thirty-two, not fifty."

She turned around and offered me an uneasy smile. The water still ran. "I'm afraid we're going to get so caught up in chasing our dreams that we'll never accomplish the one thing that's most important."

"Having kids isn't a task on a to-do list."

"I know. It's just growing our family is something I dream about." Love wrapped itself around her like a halo. "I can't wait to adopt babies with you. You want this too, right?"

The room grew smaller. "I'm not ready for a baby right this second."

She took a few steps closer to me. Her eyes softened. "I'm not saying right now, babe. I'm just letting you know how much I love *us*, and can't wait to grow that even more."

Her soft glance caressed me. "That's really sweet."

"I just want to have a good life together; free of stress, free of drama, and full of love."

I stood up and walked into her arms. "That's all I want too."

26

Chapter Three

KELLY AND BECCA, *Fall 2007*

I swept my hair up into a messy ponytail and applied just a little bit of mascara so my face didn't swallow up my eyes. Then I drove over to Lake Elkhorn to meet up with Becca for our third date.

The smell of pine and earth swam together under the soft light of the setting sun. I wore my green running shirt, the one that sucked in my waist. Becca hopped out of her car and ran over to me. She wore her hair down, and it bounced on her shoulders.

"Beautiful night for a run," she said.

I hadn't run since middle school. "Let's see if you can keep up." I dashed off down the path, and she followed, giggling. I barely survived my jog to the dumpsters by the lake, a mere quarter of a mile away from our starting point, before I slowed to a crawl and bent over at my waist, gasping for air. "Phew, is it me or is this a difficult night to run?"

Becca panted. "The last time I ran, I was a chunky kid chasing an ice-cream truck." She fished for air, squinting and looking very much like she would vomit if she so much as leaned too far to one side.

I couldn't help but laugh at us. "Oh, thank God."

She straightened up and landed by my side. A slight wheeze accompanied each of her exhales. "What do you say we just stroll?" she asked.

I clasped her hand in mine. "Stroll it is."

We followed the curvy path around Lake Elkhorn, taking in the early fall night. The song of tree frogs served as backup music to our lively conversation about how she loved playing guitar and how I loved creating photo albums full of captions.

By the time we arrived back at our cars, the night sky had lit up into a carnival of lights for us to enjoy. We sat on the roof of her car and enjoyed creating shapes out of the stars. At one point, she leaned in close to me and laced her fingers in mine. She brought our entwined hands up to her lips and kissed them as we gazed at each other. The golden lights from the parking lot danced in her dark eyes.

Beauty and grace had never connected to me with such love. The cool autumn air swirled around us, as if teasing the intensity of that moment, the moment my lips met up with hers. She kissed me with a desire that teased a hidden reserve of sensual energy. That energy circled around us, leading us to that place where our breaths melded together and embraced the most beautiful first kiss I'd yet to experience.

# #

After that first kiss, our love blossomed into something beautiful and timeless.

We spent almost every night together, dreaming up our future. We talked about careers, houses, and vacations. It wasn't until about a year after our first kiss that we talked about having children one day.

I belly flopped onto the bed, ice cream pint in one hand, spoons for Becca and me in the other. I lifted one up to her. "Ice cream?"

She clasped her spoon and brought it up to her tongue, teasing me with a sultry gaze.

I scooted up closer, brushing my legs against her. "That looks an awful lot like a flirt on your face right now."

She tapped the tip of my nose with the spoon. "If it was?"

I reached for the spoon and she pulled it up and away from me so I had to rise up on my knees to come within its reach again. "Am I going to have to wrestle you for it?"

"Depends on how badly you want it." She rolled over and off the bed.

I spread my arms and legs, arching my back like a feline, and crawled to the edge of the mattress. Becca placed her hand on my shoulder and moved in closer. Her eyes feathered me in long, bold strokes, sending tingles through me.

Her scent was bed ruffled and sweet. As she massaged my scalp, I closed my eyes, relaxing into her touch. Then her warm breath landed on my cheek and her lips brushed it. I turned inward to her soft skin, towards the curve in her neck, and planted soft, feathery kisses on her. She climbed back on the bed and knelt before me, opening me up to more of her beautiful skin. I tickled her with my tongue, and she responded with a gentle moan that sent me floating.

Becca reached up to my cheek and circled her fingers, continuing to caress my senses with her moans. Hungry for her, I cupped her jaw in my hands and sought out her soft lips.

She teased me by pulling away then going back in for more, trailing that with a murmur so seductive, sexy, and powerful. I responded with a ravenous kiss, going in deep to enjoy her hot breath, her addictive tongue, and her fiery spirit. That spirit ignited a passion and increased the tempo of our thrilling dance several notches above what I ever considered humanly possible.

31

Our passion heated up, sweltering under the hungry flames of a fire too out of control to stop. My breasts tingled as she traced her fingers along their delicate curves, teasing me as she circled the epicenter of my pleasure, taunting me, setting me further ablaze. When her fingers reached my nipples, a moan escaped, one that erupted from deep inside my burning, bottomless well of desire for everything Becca.

With each stroke, each pull, each nibble, my self-control evaporated. I sought out her wetness, and she quivered under my touch, sending my heart further along a ride that bucked, sped up, and climbed higher towards that bright spot that up until then, only Becca could take me to.

She sought out my wet folds. Staring into each other's eyes, we teased each other. We tested our pleasure limits until finally the flames lapped at our souls and set us both on fire, sending us off into one hell of an orgasmic thrust. We clung to each other, panting, trembling, until we collapsed in a spent heap.

We spent the night curled up under the blankets, our bodies tangled together.

When we woke up, she brushed her lips across my cheek. "Bumbles, you are amazing."

I closed my eyes to seal in her love. "I could be here with you like this every day for the rest of my life and never tire of it."

She breezed up by my ear. "Why is that exactly?"

"Because when I'm with you, I feel euphoric," I whispered.

"Then it's settled." She nuzzled up against my neck. "You must always stay with me."

I propped up on my elbow, and her head fell back against the mattress. I ran my fingers through her hair. "You know what I dream about?"

She cupped her hand around mine. "Spending our lives indulging in Ben and Jerry's Cherry Garcia and never gaining a pound?"

32

I tickled her tummy, and she squirmed below me.

"I see you and me, ten years in the future, sitting on the front porch of one of those large Victorian type houses. We are leaning back against pink Adirondack chairs, sipping on cold lemonade, and laughing as we watch our kids chase our dog in the front yard."

She exhaled slowly. "Ah, that sounds so nice." She massaged my hair with our enclosed hands. "I want a bunch of kids with you."

A warm feeling of love trickled through me. "You do?"

"I do."

"How many exactly?" I asked, dreaming of swaddling our new baby in a pink blanket covered in cute hearts.

"I don't know. How about three? Or maybe four, this way no one is the third wheel."

"You can carry two, and I can carry two," I said.

"They have to go to regular school. No private academy. I hated private school."

"I can live with that."

"I want to name our girls Amanda and Catherine," she said.

"Okay, but if we have a third girl, can we name her Prism?"

"Prism?" Becca sat up.

I straddled her, taking her face in the palms of my hands, and kissing her; a deep hungry kiss. "Got a problem with that?" I whispered.

As if drugged by my kiss, she whispered back, "Prism it is."

# #

Becca and I were inseparable.

I adored her. Her soft brown hair, her gentle eyes, and her pink petal lips floated beside me as a constant companion, like wispy clouds on a bright, crisp fall day.

We spent many days sprawled out under the big maple trees at Lake Elkhorn. I would sit on the ground, and without hesitation, she'd sit beside me on the damp leaves and finger her guitar strings, creating lyrics from words I'd toss out. Some of her best lyrics came from those moments when the sweet smell of fall leaves surrounded us and our dreams of life on a road to infinite joy stretched out before us. We'd walk away, high on life, and I'd always giggle at how she strolled off with her guitar in hand, mindless of the twigs and grass clinging to her butt.

After a while, Becca never went anywhere without a notepad and pen. She filled up pages with musical stances, lyrics, and smiley faces. The skies of possibility opened up, splashing lyrics on her, wetting her with nourishing insights and inspiring words. Those lively episodes would break out at random moments. They sprinkled down on her as she drove her car, took a shower, or engaged in important conversations. She would pull out her recorder and record the words as they flowed from some mysterious, invisible place. "I see words to songs on the tips of leaves, on a dog's face, on a steamy stretch of open highway. The ideas are everywhere," she once said to me. "Hell, I can see them in the spokes of your eyes. If I don't get them out of my head and recorded, they plague me. They sit there on the edge of my brain and allow nothing else to enter until I release them safely and securely."

# #

I loved photography, and Becca saw to it that I enjoyed it and developed my skills. As our love continued to bloom, so, too, did my career aspirations.

Since I was eleven years old, I knew I wanted to be a photographer when I grew up. My parents had given me a camera for Christmas. It had a panoramic lens, and despite the below freezing temperatures that Christmas

Day, they took me out to the waterfront in Annapolis so I could shoot some pictures. My fingers nearly fell off that day, but I didn't care. I took pictures that spanned the entire harbor, all in one frame! After that, I became the neighborhood photographer. I photographed birthday and anniversary parties, summer picnics, and any other occasion where cake and potato chips were the mainstay on the food table.

When I entered high school, I became the yearbook photographer. That allowed me special entrance into things like committee meetings for prom, student council votes, football and cheerleader rallies, and behind the scene sneak peeks at the talent show. People wanted me to point that camera lens at them and take their picture.

My camera became an extension of me. Without it, I was just an ordinary girl with no purpose. With it, I turned into someone more exciting than I could ever be on my own.

I majored in fine arts and dreamed of graduating college then landing a job as a traveling correspondent for *National Geographic*.

My dreams ballooned far and wide.

Becca and I would sit on a log at the lake. She'd play her guitar while I snapped photos of the turtles basking in the sun on driftwood, and we'd talk about our dreams.

"Promise me that if you ever become a star in the music world, you'll let me be your photographer," I asked.

Becca's sweet breath washed over my face. "If?"

I laughed. "I mean when."

She blanketed me in soft kisses. "That's more like it."

"Promise?"

"I promise," she whispered.

She encouraged me to dream big.

In the early spring, I saw an ad for a job at a publishing company. We were hanging out on her couch reading the newspaper. I glanced through the help wanted section as I always did, innocently hoping I'd see a headline that said 'Photographer Needed.' The ad was for an Administrative Assistant in the Creative Department of Patapsco Publishing Company. They were looking for someone creative, an out-of-box thinker, and a team player. I rocked all three. I applied to it that very night, and within two days, I received a call for an interview.

Becca spoiled me and took me shopping.

We stood in front of a mannequin outside of Nordstrom's and stared at an adorable business suit. "That is so perfect for you." Becca rested her arm around my waist.

"It's just an assistant position."

She spun me around to face her. "You have to start somewhere. This is your foot in the door. This is your chance to show them the talent within you. This isn't just an assistantship. You have to walk in that room and claim it. Prove to them you're serious about your future, and you're going to take their company to the next level with your expertise."

Her confidence in my future both touched and intimidated me.

She believed in me, and I didn't want to let her down. She looked at me with such awe, as if she were looking straight into the eyes of a true artist, an accomplished professional, the next award-winning photographer whose work graced the covers of every leading magazine in America.

"Let's buy it then," I said.

She smiled. "You're going to look so beautiful." Then, she took my hand and led me into one of the most expensive stores in the mall to buy an outfit I still didn't believe I had the right to wear.

#

A few weeks into my new job at the publishing company, Becca and I pulled into the parking lot at Lake Elkhorn. Honeysuckle fragranced the air and danced alongside my light heart. I stepped out of my car and inhaled the beauty. A butterfly danced on the aromatic breeze, circling around a family of daisies along the edge of the parking lot. I grabbed my camera and snuck towards it, not caring that I'd just left my driver's side door open. I didn't want to miss the chance to capture the yellow spotted work of art as it enjoyed a day of sunshine and admired what most of us walk right past.

I knelt on the ground and snapped a series of it flapping its wings, fluttering up and down, and then landing on the face of a yellow daisy.

Becca snuck up behind me. "This is going to turn our walls into a masterpiece," she whispered, tickling my ear.

"Indeed," I said, filling up on her love.

I looked over my shoulder at her and she just stared at me as if mesmerized. I don't ever remember her looking as beautiful and at peace as she did in that moment.

"I once read that butterflies spend seventy-five percent of their lives as an egg, caterpillar, and pupa, and only thrive in the last twenty-five percent as flying adults," I said, staring into her eyes.

She traced her finger along my jaw. "You don't say."

I basked under her caress, watching the butterfly dance on the breeze again, enjoying its moment of freedom in the sun. "Butterflies can teach us great lessons."

Her fingers tickled my skin, causing me to nuzzle up against them.

"Like what?" she whispered.

"They do as they want. They claim what's rightfully theirs. If they want nectar, they drink nectar. If they'd rather land on that flower across the way, they fly to it and land on it. They come equipped with opportunistic instincts most of us humans ignore when comfort calls."

"Spoken like a true artist." Becca kissed my neck. "I need to keep you around to remind me to keep flapping my wings."

Her warm breath sent tingles up and down my spine. I placed my camera on the ground and turned to face her. We knelt on the sweet smelling grass, facing each other. I leaned in and kissed her, unable to resist her delicious lips.

"Promise you'll remember me when you get all rich and famous," she said.

"The only way such a life would matter is if you were there with me to enjoy it all," I said.

"Well, then, we must never separate."

"Never," I said.

"Mark my words, these are the photos that will one day be the ticket to your dreams."

I kissed her harder, urging her backwards. I pressed her against the grass, pouring all my gratitude into her.

That night, Becca took out her guitar and started writing a song just for me. I sat on the couch, sipping tea and watching her. I grazed her bare leg with my toe, teasing her as she dug into a vulnerable place that only I was privy to witnessing.

Chapter Four

Another two years of our relationship passed by. As I attempted to work my way out of my assistant position and into a full-fledged photographer role at the publishing company, Becca worked hard at McFadden's Pub as a waitress. She dreamed of a music career, and waited patiently for her big break.

Then one day, she showed up at my work, wearing a smile two sizes too big for her face, on one of the worst days of my life. I had just learned that the photographer position I applied to was given to someone else. "Take a walk with me," she begged, taking my lunch tote from my arm. "Let's put these in your car."

I followed her, and then I dumped my belongings in the trunk.

We walked for a few hundred yards before I finally asked, "Why haven't you returned any of my calls?"

"I sent you text messages," she said, kicking pebbles with her sneaker. "You didn't get them?"

Dismay toyed with my balance. "Nope. I checked and never got any."

Just then, a truck sped by and kicked up dust and rocks. I shielded myself from the grit by turning away from Becca and her guilty face. She pulled me back, lifted my chin, and told me, "You're beautiful, you know."

Beautiful. Beautiful was a word a woman would use to describe how her

39

lover lifted her to higher ground when the rest of the world turned their back on her. Beautiful was not a word you used to describe someone who disappointed you because she wasn't prettier, more talented, or set up for a life of opportunity.

I turned on my heel and kept walking.

She reached for me again. "What's wrong?"

"A new person started today," I said. "She's the new photographer."

"The new photographer? Wasn't that job supposed to be yours?"

"Matt told me I needed more experience. He suggested I take some classes, and then he'll consider me for future openings."

"Well, that's encouraging. Isn't it?"

"It'll take ten years for the next opening."

"Keep plugging away."

I tied my hair in a ponytail to avoid throwing a tantrum over her happy-go-lucky approach. "Let's change the subject. Tell me why you're so happy."

She took my hand in hers and continued to lead me forward in a brisk gait. "I've got a gig Friday night."

I stopped walking and tugged at her. She'd been waiting since the day her grandfather first taught her the bass to get such news. Her skin glowed under the persistent rays of the setting sun. I'd never seen her look more at peace and sure of herself. A gig. A real live gig. Her dream. The thing she craved more than food, more than water, and more than me.

"You have a gig?"

"Yes, I do," she said, restraining her joy.

I embraced her good news with wide eyes, ignoring the pull of my disappointment. "Wow. A gig. This could really lead to some great things for you."

"I hope so." She squeezed my hands, and we swung our arms back and forth awkwardly.

Under the glare of the golden sun, poking through the branches of the Poplar trees, my heart ached, conflicted over feelings of joy and jealousy.

I shook off that selfish feeling by pulling her into my arms. "I'm so happy for you."

# #

Six months into Becca's music career, she climbed out of her initial insecurities and into the spotlight.

Becca took life by the hand and lived it with great purpose. She focused in on her new purpose like a sharp shooter focused on her target. Nothing could sway her attention unless it had to do with notes, octaves, guitar strings or Kara Travers.

I walked into her first professional gig, gripping my heart. I took one look at her duo partner, Kara, and wanted to cry. She was beyond gorgeous. Her curves went on forever. Her hair shimmered and her eyes sparkled, and she was so damn sweet and welcoming, inviting me to taste test all the delicious food she had spread out. No wonder Becca stopped paying attention to me. How could anyone look desirable next to someone with such perky boobs, plump cheeks, and a set of lips that defined sexy?

My spirit faded the moment she and Becca took off to a quiet corner and warmed up before they took the stage. Kara flirted, and Becca drank it up like a thirsty desert dweller seeking her oasis. I guzzled merlot with Margie in the corner. I would never compare. I would never be enough again. As quickly as the horizon swallowed up the sun each day, Kara swallowed up Becca's innocence and turned her from an insignificant blip in the night sky to a bright, shining star that would only continue to burn if stoked by the energy of someone as dynamic as Kara.

# #

A few days later, as I was scanning through old copies of our magazines at work, a new assistant arrived in the marketing department. She was wearing a buttoned down shirt under a brown sweater and a pair of khakis. Her hair sprung with curls, and with every step she took, they bounced as if giggling and enjoying the rush of their first day on the job. She followed my team leader, Sara, down the cubicle aisles, looking very serious despite those bouncy curls. She tensed behind her boxy brown eyeglasses and glossed lips. She shook every one's hand, and when Sara introduced us, I stood up, unlike everyone else, and welcomed her with a warm shake and an extra pat on her upper arm.

"Welcome," I said. "I'm Kelly. I think we're going to be cube mates."

Her shoulders relaxed and relief spilled over onto her face. "Hi, Kelly. I'm Bonnie. Excellent to meet you." She glanced down at my container of grapes. "Those go great with Greek yogurt."

"I love Greek yogurt."

She smiled broadly.

I just knew we'd end up good friends by month's end.

Sure enough, we worked in the same double cubicle and shared yogurts and grapes, and the occasional pound cake. We giggled about quirky coworkers and funny jokes we found on the Internet. We walked together at lunchtime, sharing our secret likes and dislikes. On those walks, I discovered she preferred bookstore cafes over club scenes. After that admission, I began to see an internal sweet spot that calmed me, lifted me, and eventually pulled me in. Then, I accepted an offer to attend her Pampered Chef party. I arrived at the hour she said, and she greeted me with a corkscrew and a bottle of Riesling.

A young man with disheveled brown hair, not more than twenty years old, sat at a piano in the living room, playing a classical song. Wrapped up in his music, his fingers danced across the keys like they had tiny engines powering them. He sounded like Beethoven himself. At one point, he closed his eyes and swept his head back and forth in rhythm with the melody. When he finished the song, Bonnie hugged him.

"Did you like it?" he asked her in a rushed, childlike tone. "I liked it. Did she like it?" He pointed to me, but failed to look me in the eye. He rocked back and forth, bouncing his shoulders up and down, unable to still himself.

"Cliff, why don't you go see if Mom is ready to take you out for your bowling outing?" She nudged him towards a long hallway.

He skipped away, and the back of his plaid shirt waved behind him.

She turned to me. "He's my younger brother. He's some musician, isn't he?"

"I'd say."

"Music is his life." She adjusted her leather belt, circling her eyes around the room as if she lost something.

"He seems sweet."

She cleared her throat and finally settled her eyes on me. "Before my parents bought him the piano, he barely spoke two words. Now, he's come around and is able to carry on a conversation."

A moment later, Bonnie's mother, a pretty woman who looked to be in her mid-fifties, entered the living room wearing a pair of jeans, heeled boots, and a fitted turtleneck sweater. Cliff followed after her, hugging a hooded sweatshirt and repeating how he wanted to go bowling.

43

"You must be Kelly," she said, extending her hand. "There's plenty of food in the kitchen, so help yourself."

"Absolutely. Thank you." I shook her hand firmly.

"Well, we're off." She kissed Bonnie's cheek. "Have fun."

When they left, Bonnie closed the door and rolled her eyes. "Moving back to my parents' house last month has been painful. I need a place of my own again, and fast."

"Where were you living before this?"

"I lived with my ex-girlfriend. She liked cats. I'm more of a dog person." She winked and headed into the kitchen. "What about you?" she asked over her shoulder.

Ex-girlfriend? I swallowed a smile and followed her past a bookcase of classical, leather-bound books and eccentric wire-framed art of dogs, bicycles, and pianos. "Dog person. Definitely a dog person."

"She liked to party, and I prefer quiet nights of reading or watching television."

A stable person; how refreshing.

"So where is everyone?" I asked.

"I opted for a catalog party instead." A sparkle sneaked into her dark eyes.

"I see." I plucked up a catalog from the counter and escaped into it.

"Wine?"

"Please. Yes."

She poured us a generous amount of wine, and then she guzzled it as if it was water.

She wiped her mouth on the sleeve of her sweater. "You need to catch up."

I sipped mine.

"No." She poured herself another helping. "Like this." She guzzled more.

44

"I don't drink much. I don't even like the taste of alcohol."

"Just for tonight." She held the wine glass up to my lips, and I tilted my head backwards and guzzled the sweet, fruity wine.

By the time we finished the oversized bottle of wine, I decided on purchasing a corkscrew. I handed her my order form, and lingered on her gaze.

"Kelly, you are incredibly beautiful," she whispered.

I needed the attention the way a patient needed drugs. With great hunger, I devoured her sultry gaze and quivered from the soft touch of her fingers tracing my face. She leaned in closer, zeroing in on my lips. Her strawberry scent swirled in front of me, daring me to cross that line between right and wrong. I pulled away just as her lips brushed mine. "I can't," I said.

"Becca?"

"I'm not a cheater."

She smoothed my hair behind my ear. "I'm glad to hear you say that. It's refreshing."

# #

In the months that followed that romantic night spent guzzling wine under the golden lights of her parents' kitchen, she wrapped her friendly love around me like a fluffy blanket. She raised me up from the depths of shadows and into my own light, where I didn't have to compete with anyone but myself.

Chapter Five

Becca met with Kara almost every night to rehearse. She was changing faster than I could keep up with. Becca would open up her door, on those few nights she reserved for us, exploding with news about her surreal experiences. She talked about the thunderous applause she received and the autographs fan requested.

Her ego overtook the room. A rush of fans grew overnight and fed her inflated ego until it ballooned out of control. Instead of taking quiet walks or enjoying peaceful dinners together, she bragged about how fans emailed her, professing their love, asking her on dates, or telling her how beautiful she was. She'd laugh about it, and then dig back into our moment. Then, two seconds later, she'd read another positive review and off she'd go on another ride to the top of her glorious peak.

I studied her ascent to greatness. The praise and instant fame saturated and bloated her until it reached its breaking point and overflowed, drowning her soul, destroying the lively ground she would eventually need to flourish back once the fame reengineered her landscape.

Becca even began to drink. She'd laugh about how drunk she and Kara would get before practice and how that helped them create new songs.

One night, about five months into her newfound fame, I agreed to go see another one of her shows.

We were backstage, and I was helping her get ready.

"You've got a loose string," I said to her. "Sit tight. Let me cut it off for you before it unravels." She bounced her leg up and down. I was mid cut when her manager, Kara's sister, Gabby, ran into the room. She balanced a radio in her arms. Their new song, "I Can Presume" was playing. "It's official. There's no turning back from here."

The scene turned chaotic in a flash.

Gabby jumped up and down like a teenager, completely out of character.

Kara ran over to Becca, pulled her up and started spinning her in wide circles. The two of them screamed and knocked everything down in their path. Water bottles, lipstick, hairbrushes, and guitar picks flew everywhere.

Kara twirled and dipped her, and all the while I just stood back and watched the surreal scene unfold in front of me.

I didn't belong there.

That scene belonged to them, not me.

Her dream had come true, not mine. Music and fame thrilled her, not me.

Fans would never leave her alone now that she had a song on the radio. What would my life become? I'd be no more significant than the bottle of water rolling around on the ground at our feet. I'd get stomped on, squashed, and kicked out of the way so Becca could continue climbing the charts, climbing the ladder of success, and forgetting about all the people who helped her get there.

That night, I called Bonnie. She talked me down from my anguish. "It's just going to get worse, Kelly," she said. "The more famous she becomes, the more out of control she's going to get."

"I can't take this new Becca. She's egotistical. She acts like a diva. She's all flirty to strangers, and all she talks about is Kara. Kara this and Kara that. I can't take it anymore. I need a life of my own."

"Fame turns people into monsters," Bonnie said.

"I guess it's not all it's cracked up to be."

"I prefer the simple life where I can walk through a mall and not be looked at twice," she said. "And where it's still cool to hang at home, watching television, and getting cozy by a fire."

All of that sounded so perfect. "I could sure use a friendly game night or something. Are you free tomorrow?"

"I'm free whenever you want," she said.

"I also wanted to shoot an idea by you."

"Tell me now. I can't wait."

"I took some photos from the Pet Walk we all did from work. Of course, Matt wasn't interested in them, so I thought about submitting them to *The Post*. I wanted to get your opinion on them. Can I bring them to you at work tomorrow?"

"Bring anything you'd like, babe."

I softened at the use of the pet name. "See you then."

# #

Bonnie and I enjoyed chatting in our cubicles at work, playing online scrabble, and eating lunch together. I told her all about how Becca started to drink, ruining her life as she ate up her newfound fame.

Becca's ego outgrew her. She lost her charm. I no longer even liked her. I couldn't even stand to be in the same room as her. The Becca I had fallen in love with disappeared and was replaced by a shell of who she used to be.

I babbled on with Bonnie about how I hated that new side of her, and Bonnie nodded in agreement, urging me to talk it out. I vented to her almost every day, crying, complaining, and pointing my finger at all of Becca's weaknesses.

49

I didn't leave out any detail when I'd go off on those vents. I even embellished them to gain more leverage and support for my emotions. Bonnie reached out her hands, and I placed my burdens in them. I sat in the comfort of her embrace as the wounded one, the displaced one, the wronged one. I left no room for second chances and rebuilding Becca's reputation. Without having met her at that point, Bonnie could only envision Becca James as a disgraceful, obnoxious star who deserved none of me.

Bonnie stood by my side, hand on my back, pointing the way to bluer skies and straight, uncluttered passageways.

She offered me courage with her soft, yet powerful, direction.

She counseled me on how best to break it off with Becca. "Just be honest with her. Tell her how much she's hurting herself. Let her know people care. Let her know you need to walk away though."

A few hours later, I stood before Becca and dismantled her ego. I managed to unload every bad habit of hers that irritated me and every hurtful word she'd said to me, accusing her of being a monster who deserved only the cold echo of my love.

No one has ever stared right through me with hate the way Becca did. When I walked away from her, she reminded me of a broken teenager who hadn't yet learned to take blame for her mistakes. Abandoning her broke my heart.

Bonnie helped me calm down with a drive to the Eastern Shore. We arrived in time to see the sunrise. I stood at the shoreline, craving to be swept up in renewal, strength, and power. But the water just passed me by without notice.

Becca needed me to bring her out of the jungle of her life, and I abandoned her. A chill snuck in, the kind an icy storm created, and settled into the deepest parts of my bones.

# #

Bonnie and I spent a great deal of time together after Becca and I broke up. We especially loved going to eat at a quaint Chinese restaurant near my parents' house. The owners always came out and greeted their guests at the end of a meal with bows and fortune cookies.

On our first date there, Bonnie handed me her fortune cookie, and I handed her mine. It became our tradition. So, that night, she handed me one and the fortune read: It is a rough road that leads to the heights of greatness.

Later on, when she pulled up in my parents' driveway, I asked her, "So, any deep insights on the fortune?"

She stretched her gaze out in front of us, as if studying my father's overzealous hydrangeas. "Yeah, it assumes everyone wants a life of greatness."

"Well, don't you?"

"Do you want to know what I believe, Kelly?"

I inched up taller. "Tell me."

"The pursuit of greatness just leads to trouble. Bigger isn't always greater, especially when it comes to living life right here and now." She shifted her gaze back to me. "What's wrong with simple?"

I wanted simple. My whole life I chased greatness, only to discover it was full of trickery and pain. I could slip into a simple life as easily as I could a bed dressed in four hundred count Egyptian cotton. I wanted to ease my tired body and beaten heart into the comfort and softness of such a life. "I'm so glad you said that," I whispered.

Bonnie moved in closer to me, maneuvering around the gearshift. "Marry me?"

"Marry you?"

She gripped my hands in hers. "One day, when it becomes legal here, I want you to marry me."

"That could be a long time," I said.

"Then so be it." She pressed her lips against mine. She tasted like soy sauce and garlic.

I didn't say yes. But then again, I didn't say no.

A few days later, she placed an engagement ring on my finger. I let her slide it right over my knuckle, swallowing a gasp that fought a mighty fight to free itself from the dungeon of my fearful soul.

For the days that followed, my head circled without a break, dizzying me and causing great headaches. I contemplated the quick jump from Becca to Bonnie, but decided after a few days that Bonnie was good for me.

I loved how she calmed me down. Instead of racing down the freeway to fame and fortune, Bonnie strolled along a straight and predictable path, decorated with fresh sprigs of green, colorful wildflowers, soothing daisies, and adorable bumblebees. She took in the beauty instead of speeding by it on a wild pursuit of something better, brighter, and more colorful. She appreciated the here and now.

I could stand beside her in a field of grass and she'd never tire from the scenery. She'd never yearn to see the life growing on the other side of the field. I'd never have to worry that she might look on the other side of that field and like it better than what she had with me right where we stood.

I needed that safety net after Becca. I didn't want to compete. I didn't want to chase and worry. I just wanted to sit for a while, take in the gentle breeze, and rejuvenate the part of my soul that bled from too much travel over ground that was much too rocky for anyone's good.

Bonnie was my gentle breeze. She wrapped me up and cuddled me as I healed. She was the quiet that followed the turbulent waves of jealousy and hurt.

She was marriage material.

She could satisfy me.

She could furnish me with a life of stability and security.

She could protect me from hurt and pain.

I wanted predictable. I wanted protection. I wanted happiness.

Bonnie was a great woman for me. She accepted me as is. Freckle-faced, birthmark spread across my upper right thigh, thin-lipped and all. I didn't have to wear makeup or dress provocatively to keep her attention. She fit right into my family like she had been there from the very start of life. She could cook a delicious meal with the basics, and whenever I got sick with a cold, she nurtured me with soups, full control of the remote, and all the popsicles a sugar-loving girl could ask for.

She was perfect in every sense.

Picture perfect.

Everyone loved Bonnie like they loved a good, loyal, friendly dog. She livened up the magazine headquarters with her American sweetheart aura, exuberant greetings, and counseling sessions to those in need of a pat on the back or a venting session. Bonnie mediated arguments, resolved conflicts, and became the company go-to person for cook-offs and parties.

Management loved her. When a project needed doing, they called on her. She'd come to me all pink and glowing, and tell me how management honored her by asking for her help with drafting plans for this event or that. She'd survive for days on those good fuels, and then eventually fall into my arms and beg me to help her. Bonnie procrastinated about everything. Even taking out the trash can from under her desk so the maintenance man could empty it on schedule.

At first, I adored her lazy side. She'd reward me with lavish praise in the form of chocolates and flowers and compliments when I stepped in and helped her out. She viewed me as invaluable, and that motivated me to help her even more. Well, one project turned into fifty, and before long, I'd fall asleep at the end of the day, exhausted because I enabled a procrastinating little monster.

That side of her didn't present itself fully until after we got a condo together and adopted our dog, Zoey. I learned rather quickly that Bonnie enjoyed lounging in her pajamas on the weekends until the late afternoon, which meant I ended up walking Zoey, cooking breakfast, and washing the dishes.

My Bonnie was lazy.

My Bonnie was not a dream catcher. She had no desire to sprint ahead past the masses to achieve a success.

My Bonnie was perfectly satisfied with the status quo.

And me? I wanted to jump out of my skin.

I tried to get her excited about things other than marathon episodes of *Law and Order*. She didn't crack easily. I'd beg her to come out for a walk in the park with me to snap photos, and she'd pull me down to the couch, tickle my belly and say, "Oh, come on. Don't be upset. Let's just pop some popcorn and relax with Zoey."

Her soft eyes melted away the disappointment most times, and I eased into the comfort of her arms. She embraced downtime. She kicked up her feet and reclined into it the way one would embrace the comfort of a well-deserved vacation. I'd remind myself that I needed downtime too, and I shouldn't have been spending too much time chasing task after task. I deserved to enjoy those guilt-free moments with her and Zoey. I definitely should've been sitting down and enjoying the taste of popcorn on my tongue.

I'd remind myself that when I dated Becca, I had to rush through my life to get somewhere. If I didn't, I would eat her dust.

I enjoyed popcorn a hell of a lot more than dust.

Chapter Six

Several Months Later

I learned that the pressure of fame caught up with Becca eventually. Of course, pairing up with a partner like Kara didn't help. Kara was like a lit firecracker in a hayfield. She burned the very sustenance that gave their duo life with her pornographic dance moves and ridiculous new drug and drinking binges.

Margie called me up and told me Becca broke down in tears, claiming she would be quitting the duo. She begged Margie to help straighten her back into the person she used to be before all that crazy stuff blazed into her life. Apparently, the night before that break down, she had crossed over the line with Kara and some other skanky chick. The three of them took drugs and woke up in a heap on the floor of some nightclub's backroom, all tangled up.

I predicted that would happen.

After she confessed that to Margie, she took off on a journey across the country to find herself. When she returned, she called me.

"Please meet with me." Her voice begged for reprieve.

She needed a friend, and I felt sorry for her. "I'll be going for a run tomorrow at the lake. Would you like to join me?"

"You bet."

That next day, when I kissed Bonnie before heading out for my rendezvous, I never mentioned that I'd be seeing Becca. Some things were just better left unsaid.

I arrived first and stretched by the pathway's entrance. Right on time, Becca pulled up and climbed out of her car. She appeared fresh and lively like she'd just filled her lungs with healing, soothing energy.

She greeted me with a hug and compliments on the twenty pounds I'd lost since our breakup. We exchanged pleasantries and began our stroll down the path. Our words jumbled in front of us, along with the crunch of fallen leaves. I struggled to find the comfortable footing we used to enjoy back in the early days when running around that lake filled us with euphoria instead of anxiety.

We talked about petty things as we broke into our light jog.

Soon, Becca ran out of stamina. So, we walked.

The sunshine poked through the tree canopy and drizzled golden specks on the ground cover. The air smelled like moss and harvest vegetables. By the time we walked half way around the lake, we relaxed in each other's company, and I prematurely assumed Becca and I might just succeed in turning off our hurt and embracing a new friendship.

We began to talk about the past, digging up her fall down the hill of fame.

"I did some pretty stupid things," she said. "But that's all behind me now." She stopped and placed her hands on my shoulders. "I'm so sorry that I was such a selfish person to you."

"You did act pretty selfishly. I didn't even recognize you. It was sad. It was like you died."

"But here I am again. I want to make it all up to you."

"That's not necessary. I understand you were going through some sort of growing period. I kept you grounded. It was hard for me to let go of you. What choice did I have, right?"

"I'm so sorry." She rubbed my cheek with the back of her hand as if trying to soothe away some of the hurt she had caused.

"We both needed that little push," I said. "I was falling apart before we broke up. I was pitiful. All I did was mope around all day and nag you instead of getting on with my own dreams."

"I'm sure I was no help," she said. "I wish I could make things right again." She cupped my face in her hands like a chalice and stared into my eyes, penetrating straight to my soul. In her eyes, I saw the old Becca, the Becca I first fell in love with and couldn't imagine living without.

A leftover breeze shook the maple leaves above us, sending raindrops down onto our heads.

She leaned in and kissed me. Her lips delivered a passion and a love she hadn't offered me in a long time. "I love you so much," she said into my mouth.

I started to cry, and she wiped away my tears as they rolled down my cheeks.

"Why are you crying?" she asked, smoothing my hair.

"Because what you are doing to me is so unfair."

"Unfair? How?" Becca held me in her arms, swaying me side to side.

"Because I'm not free to love you anymore." I pulled out of her arms and walked away, back up the path we'd just walked on together.

"Why not?" Becca yelled out.

I swung around, spraying tears onto the dead leaves below. "Because while you were out fucking Kara Travers and ignoring me, I fell in love with someone else. She is someone who respects me and loves me back the way I deserve."

"Bonnie?" she whispered.

"Yes," I said, breaking into heaving sobs. "Yes, Bonnie."

"Break up with her," she said, approaching me.

"You're too late, Becca. I moved in with her. My family comes to dinner at our house every Sunday. My mother helped her pick out my engagement ring."

She blinked rapidly. "Why does she get to be part of your family?"

"Because, she wants this life with me, and she didn't let my silly fears get in the way of that."

She cringed. "So that's it then? There are no more chances for us?"

Tears leaked from my eyes. I shook my head no.

# #

A few hours later, I sat with Margie in the shallow end of her indoor pool. She looked away at a potted plant. Somewhere between 'pass me my bottle of water' and 'I ended it with Becca for good,' Margie succumbed to regard me with little more than a tilt of her head to a dead plant.

My head pounded. "She says she's done partying and wants to get back to her roots of just playing music for the sheer joy of it. Can someone just shift back from the limelight like that and be okay with a normal life? I don't see how that would be possible."

She staved off my argument with a flash of her hand. She hated arguing perhaps as much as she hated smokers and anything to do with generic hair products. "I agree. She's never going to live a normal life again."

I thought about the women tossing themselves at her and the constant flood of threats to my heart as a result. "I could never be happy living that kind of lifestyle. Every day would turn into one-upping each other. Love would turn into a competition."

"Love isn't a competition."

"With her it is. That's the problem with her. Becca's on top of a mountain

60

and, in her eyes, everyone else is below her, trying to reach that same peak. How can someone with such an ego be attracted to anyone not experiencing that same powerful current of fame?"

She didn't say anything for a long moment. "You sound like you're the one standing at the foot of that mountain and staring up at it with envy."

"Give me a break!" I hated when Margie psychoanalyzed me. Everything had to be by the psychological book with her. Her arched eye, her pouty lip, and her subdued vibe pissed me off, pushing me to the edge of control. "There's no envy here. I have no desire to be a famous musician or live in the shadows of one. Give me my normal life any day."

She settled back against the pool's wall. Her face folded up into a satisfied grin. "You're in a healthy place. Good."

"I am. We're on totally different levels these days. I'd never want to be where she is. She lives in the upper atmosphere where the air is too light. I much prefer the view from the valley right now. It's green, alive and full of beauty she'll never find at the top. The two levels can't compete with each other."

"I hardly think Becca is looking for a rival in her lover."

"I don't disagree. Take you and Mark, for instance. You work because you're on the same playing field." They were both gorgeous with their towering, athletic bodies, radiant skin, and tailored clothes. "If he worked a regular nine-to-five job and had nothing in common with your business, you would be bored after the first round of orgasms and call it a day. Admit it."

She opened her mouth and closed it a moment later. She looked around as if searching for the right answer in the water. "I see what you're saying. But sometimes a little variety would be nice because then we'd have something to talk about other than products and new hair trends."

"He'd still need to be a president of a company or out gathering up excitement for some venture for you to remain interested in him. It would not work if he were a mail carrier working for the government, worrying about a pension and health plan. You're a risk taker. He is too. That's almost a requirement in your situation, don't you think?"

"I suppose. So you don't think you and Becca are equals?"

I looked down at my clasped hands. "Becca's too out of control. Bonnie and I are equals. That's what matters to me. We enjoy the comfort of home, our weekly paychecks, and our weekends spent under a blanket on our sofa."

"What about your dreams?"

"I'm tired of chasing them right now. I just want to sit and be still for a while. Bonnie helps me do that."

"So you love Bonnie, huh?"

"Yes. I love her."

"And, you're completely over Becca?"

"Yes. Completely. I enjoy never having to worry about whether my girlfriend is going to stop looking at me one day and start craving someone younger, prettier, and more in tune with life on the road. I can't be bothered with that kind of trivial crap."

"You would need to step up your game and take some risks to be in Becca's field," she said matter-of-factly. "I get what you're saying now."

She didn't get what I was saying at all. "I would never want to take those kind of risks or be on her field. Kara can have her and that crazy lifestyle, for all I care."

"Becca's not looking for someone that shallow." Margie slid down under the water. I watched her hair wave around. It reminded me of seaweed. She resurfaced. "She wants someone she can look at and call home now. Kara's more of a Vegas vacation. She's good for some fun, adventure and intense orgasms, but she comes up short in the trust and 'hey, I've got your back' category."

"Becca doesn't want someone settled any more than I want a wild life."

Margie shrugged. We remained silent amongst the soothing ripples.

Chapter Seven

Bonnie and I enjoyed the cold winter nights, curled up under blankets, watching endless hours of *Jeopardy*, *American Idol*, and reruns of *The L-Word*. If we weren't at home, we were at her parents' house admiring Cliff's piano music while drinking beer and eating cheese curls. Those cheese curls tasted so good that over a few month's span, we put on a few pounds together. We'd laugh about that and talk about how the following Monday we'd start an exercise program, and bring carrots sticks instead of junk food whenever we visited Cliff.

Well, that Monday-carrot-stick thing sat out there in front of us like an insurmountable mountain. We saw it. We set out to conquer it. Yet, we kept circling around the base, waiting for the snow to clear, or the air to warm, or for more energy to arrive.

I slid into that pocket of comfort with Bonnie and found it difficult to crawl back out. She made relaxing a cool thing, the way women in the sixties made smoking a cool thing. I figured eventually we'd get on a more ambitious road together, and until we did, we could just indulge in the calm that preceded the effort.

Why rush a dream? The journey towards it should be savored like fine wine, like delicious sushi, or like a giant Hershey bar. At least that's how Bonnie always put it. I couldn't have agreed more.

I learned to embrace that lazy lifestyle the longer we stayed in it. I discovered the joy of soft pajamas, the beauty of make-up free days, and the peace of not worrying about impressing others.

Then, early one morning, several months after seeing Becca perform at the pub, I was taking a bath and flipping through *Hip Magazine* when I saw a picture of her. Right there, in the top right corner of page thirty-three, was Becca. She was holding hands with a tall woman with short, spikey blonde hair. The woman was laughing and resting her head against Becca. Becca gazed at her the way one would revere a priceless heirloom, the kind of look she used to shower me with back in our early days of dating.

Becca was fit, healthy, and glowing. She wore a beautiful pair of jeans and a colorful orange and blue top that showed off her toned waist.

I looked away from the magazine and down at the naked body I'd fed one too many cheese curls.

I sighed.

I'd become lazy and chubby, while Becca became more successful and sexier.

I looked back at the magazine. The headline read, *Tour de Hollywood*. Becca's hair bounced in big, loose waves at her shoulders. Her body leaned into the woman's as the two shared a private moment under the glare of a camera lens.

A jealously, renewed by her success and my lack thereof, raged in me. My stomach lurched. My throat numbed. Tears burned the back of my eyes.

Becca had reclaimed her stardom in the months since I'd seen her, and what had I done? I'd become an expert in how to fluff my pillow so my back didn't hurt when I watched television characters come to life. I'd placed my camera on my closet shelf and allowed it to act as a dust collector. I'd stopped reading photography magazines and websites for tips. I'd stopped learning, stopped dreaming, and stopped living a life in pursuit of purpose.

I sat in a tub of bubbles, waterlogged and suddenly very aware of my oversimplified life.

I closed the magazine and threw it at the sink. Water from the faucet dripped on it, creating an annoying tap-tap-tap sound.

For several long minutes, I stared over at the wet magazine, uncomfortable with the truths it held. Becca lived the high life without me, and honestly, that killed me.

I sunk into my water and surfaced a moment later. I shook the water from my face, and then I picked up a handful of suds and piled them on top of one of my nipples. They quickly dripped back down to the water where they belonged with others of their kind. Together, they formed a massive pile of suds. I scooped some up and examined their silky crevices. I blew gentle puffs on them, whittling away their landscape. My puffs reshaped it, carving out new crevices, new ledges, and new peaks. Before long, I stared at a completely different object, one that withstood the tests of adversity.

Everything could be reshaped.

I climbed out of the tub and dried off before sitting on the covered toilet. I plucked up the soggy magazine again and flipped to Becca. She had chosen her path. She set goals and reached them. Luck had kissed her. Yet, she prepped for that moment. When the opportunity presented itself, she harnessed all of her hard work and lifted herself.

What had I done recently to set that kind of course for my life?

Nada.

Zilch.

Zero.

I emerged from the bathroom, dressed in a bathrobe. Bonnie was still asleep on our bed. Her snore filled the chilly bedroom. I looked around the room. Clothes that we planned to fold were still lying in a heap. Dust clung to the dresser. Four glasses of water remained on our dresser. My laptop case sat open-faced with paperwork spilling out of it on the floor near our door.

I sat down beside her, suddenly annoyed with our carelessness. I nudged her, and she opened her eyes a slit. "Come on under here with me, Kelly." She opened up the blankets. "Come on. It's nice and warm in here."

I didn't want that. I didn't want to hide under blankets in a dark bedroom at the start of a beautiful day. I didn't want to be chubby. I didn't want to be okay with settling for an assistant position in a creative department. I didn't want to just exist. I wanted my life to mean something more than taking up space in a condo I could barely afford.

I wanted to thrive.

I wanted my life to have purpose.

I wanted to reignite that spark I used to have.

A new energy surged in me. Desire burned through the residue of comfort and resurfaced like a blowtorch, ready and armed to ignite a new, determined path towards something purposeful, something greater than myself, and something I hoped Bonnie would be compelled to latch onto and follow.

Before I met Bonnie, I had a hungry fire burning in me. I had long since extinguished that fire by tossing dirt on it. Well, in the time it took me to take a bath, a spark escaped the rubble of my laziness, and that spark ate the air and began engulfing the scene.

We couldn't afford to sit idle and become victims to complacency for one more minute. A current pushed through my veins, forcing out the stale energy and rejuvenating it with fresh fluid.

I could no longer eat cheese curls. I could no longer sit like a log covered in moss in front of a television screen. I wanted more for us.

We needed to move with the new current. It grew stronger as I sat there on the bed, staring at my adorable, comfortable fiancée. The current pushed me along and caused me to fidget. Those fidgets suddenly created massive pools of energy that I would never be able to handle with a remote control. Sitting there pained me by the second. I felt like a runner trapped in ice, needing to spread her stride and break free into an all-out sprint to the base of the mountain I needed to climb despite the warning signals of it being insurmountable.

I flung the covers up. "Let's get out of the house today. We'll go for a walk."

She wrapped her hand around my wrist and guided me under the blankets with her. "Just relax with me. It's such a perfect morning to snuggle."

I yanked my arm away and stood up. "No. I mean it. Let's get up and do something. It's a gorgeous day. I don't want to hide away in bed until two o'clock in the afternoon."

She moaned and covered her head. "I'll be up in a few minutes."

I sighed, staring at her unaffected body under the blankets. "Fine." I turned and marched out of the bedroom.

I entered the kitchen, intent on cooking something nutritious before taking off on our walk. I opened the fridge and pulled out a carton of eggs, some wilted scallions, and a gallon of milk.

We needed to get out of our comfort zone. We could brainstorm how on our walk. Renewed energy tingled through me.

I opened the cupboard to get a bowl and a pile of plastic containers tumbled down on me. Organizing would have to be on the top of the priority list.

69

I turned on the iPod and began singing along with Billy Joel.

Within a minute, Bonnie emerged, wrapped in the blanket, wearing a face of bed wrinkles. Her hair sprouted up in all different directions. "Someone woke up with a ton of energy."

"Yup. It feels great, too," I said, pulling her into my happy vibe.

She shuffled her feet against the tile like a teenager, inching up to me. "How can I help?"

I cracked an egg into the bowl. "How about if you start with cleaning up the bedroom? We've got clothes to fold, dust to clear, and dirty water glasses all over the dresser."

She moved in close and rested her chin on my shoulder, pressing her chest against my back. "What's wrong?"

"Nothing's wrong. I'm just eager to get the day started."

"It feels a little like I woke up in my parents' house, only my mother used to toss water at me if I didn't wake up when she asked." She nuzzled her face against my neck.

Annoyed, I walked out of her embrace, sliding the bowl over to my new spot.

"Something is bugging you."

"Well, yes, now something is." I stopped mid crack. The egg dripped onto my fingers and down into the bowl. "I'm trying to get us to do something together today, and you're fighting me on it."

"Fine, I'll clean the bedroom."

"Thank you," I said, with too much sarcasm.

Bonnie's eyes opened wide. She backed away without saying anything else and walked down the hallway, still wrapped up in her blanket, hobbling like a homeless person.

70

I beat those eggs with a fork before tossing them into the skillet. I was pulling the toaster from the chef's cart when Bonnie returned, cradling the four glasses. She put them on the counter, opened the dishwasher, and tossed them every which way.

"They're going to break like that," I said to her. "You need to secure them better."

She rearranged them, clanking them up against each other. I would have to reorganize them on my own. She had no clue how to load a dishwasher.

She sat down at the table and watched me as I finished prepping our meal. I slammed drawers, cupboards and the dishwasher door as I proceeded to correct the glass positions and stick the pan and utensils in with them.

"Please tell me what's happening here," she said.

"We need to take better care of ourselves and get our lives back in order."

"I didn't realize our lives had gotten out of order."

"Look at this place." I waved my hand around the kitchen. "It's a mess. We have grime all over the cupboards and behind our appliances. Crumbs are lining the edge of the floor. I nearly got a concussion when I opened the cupboard to get a bowl. I can't take it anymore. We need to get rid of the clutter and get our acts together."

"There is nothing wrong with our act. And who cares about the clutter?"

"Me. I care. We're stuck because of it."

"Stuck?"

"Yes. I feel like we're floating in the middle of a lake and we're never going to get to shore. We're just sitting here in our flannels and getting fat, while everyone else is paddling away from us."

She flinched. "I thought you were happy."

"I am. It's just that we want these things to happen, but we're not doing anything to make them happen."

71

"Like?"

"You say you want to have a big family together. We can't even clean our house correctly. How will we ever manage to raise a kid properly?"

She loosened her grip on the blanket. "We're going to make great parents."

"All we do is nap," I screamed. "A kid needs more stimulation than that."

"You think all we do is nap?" Her voice landed at the edge of hysteria.

My heart beat way too fast. I couldn't get the right air in my lungs. "Are you really arguing that point?"

We stared at each other. The room inhaled the empty space, chewing it up and swallowing it, leaving nothing left to sustain us.

Finally, Bonnie dropped the blanket. "I don't want to fight with you."

The fire in me still blazed. I couldn't stop it. "We need to do more with our lives than take naps."

"We do a lot more than sleep."

"True," I said. "We go to work as assistants."

"We've got great jobs."

We had turned into a couple of complacent women. "We need to get out of our comfort zones."

"Why are you rocking the boat all of a sudden?" she asked.

Because our boat offered no new challenges or opportunities to showcase our creative sides. Because we were getting paid shit in our boat, and we could do a lot better. Because other people, like Becca, were out there rocking their boats and being rewarded. "Because, we need to do more with our lives."

"You're not happy with where our life is?"

I suddenly woke from a long winter of hibernating in a cave without light, heat, or spark. I stood and faced a wall of dead, dried up land that used to be full of vibrant, fresh life.

"We're artists. We should be out there creating art. I can't watch any more television. I can't lounge in bed until noon. I can't stand to put another fried piece of food in my mouth. I can't stand living paycheck to paycheck. I hate driving that beat up car that smokes every time I press the gas pedal too fast." I looked around the kitchen at the crumbs lined up on the counter and the grime lining the dishwasher. "I can't stand to live like slobs another second!"

Bonnie rose. "Babe, relax."

"I hate that the rest of the world is speeding by us, and we're stuck on the hiccup of a stroll. We should want more from each other."

She tilted her head, taking in my full view. "I'm happy the way we are. How could I ever want more from you? You're beautiful as is."

"I want you to push me and yourself. I need that from you."

"I don't want to push you, though."

We stood like two wilted flowers, tired from the rigors of overnight frost weighing us down. She loved me as is. That shouldn't have bothered me. But, it did.

"Fair enough."

We both exhaled.

I continued to prepare the eggs as she gathered plates for us.

When I finished cooking, I plopped them onto plates and just stared at the steam rising up.

She picked up a plate and handed it to me. "Eat before it gets cold."

I put the plate back down. "I still don't feel settled with this."

She squinted, as if a provocative question dug at her. "Kelly, all you need to know is I'm here for you. If you want to chase artistic photo opportunities, then by all means, chase them."

"I want you to chase them with me."

"All that chasing sounds like a lot of work," she laughed.

I didn't think it was funny. "I'm going for a walk. Do you want to come with me or not?"

She forked at her eggs. "I think I'll just stay back and give you some space to get started on your artistic journey."

I emptied my eggs into the trashcan, unable to eat. "I'm going to get dressed. After my walk, I'm going to assist Matt in photographing the mayor."

# #

A few hours later, I stood with Matt in the front row and watched as he snapped a photo of the mayor shaking hands with the president of the community college at the groundbreaking site of the new humanities building. That was my job, to help Matt capture moments and build excitement. How excited could one get about two silver-headed men shaking hands in front of a pile of dirt?

I needed more out of my life than adjusting lights while my boss photographed old men shaking hands.

# #

In an attempt to avoid scrunching up in front of the television after I returned from the mayor's photo shoot, I decided to clean out my closet. I took out all my clothes and sorted through them, creating piles for Goodwill, piles for clothes I'd fit into again one day, and piles that I fit in just fine. I tackled my shoes next, tossing five pairs of old, beat up sneakers into a trash pile.

Next came the shelves where I had placed old photo albums from my childhood and stacks of boxes containing thousands of photographs I'd snapped through the years. When I came across the box containing the butterfly pictures I'd taken with Becca, I pulled them down and sat on my bed. I stared at the floral lid, afraid to open it and spill out the memories.

Curiosity won.

I eased up the lid and peeked inside. I had edited them with care, printed them, and matted them for Becca. I pulled them out one by one and examined them. My heart tightened. Those were good times when the world shined like a prism for us as a couple.

I sent those photos to so many publishing houses, hoping someone would offer me that ticket to my future, only to be rejected over and over again. It seemed with each new rejection came a second blow in the form of golden opportunities, polished up and delivered straight to Becca. Each time someone sent me a form letter that wished me luck with my future endeavors, new stones appeared for Becca to step on and bring her further away from 'us.' My unlucky rejections brought on her lucky breaks. That was how I felt back then, always sinking into a murky pond of embarrassing self-pity.

I inspected the photos that once hung on Becca's wall. Back then, I thought Becca was just massaging my ego when she told me they were brilliant. I traced my finger across the wing of the butterfly. I had forgotten how much I loved those butterfly pictures.

I brought the photos out to Bonnie. Once again, she lounged in front of the television. I sat down with them, supporting them as if they were a newborn baby to introduce.

"I found these in my closet." I handed them to her.

She glanced at them. "Nice work, Kelly."

I wanted her to gush. "Do you think so?"

She glanced at each photo the way one would roll over a banner ad on a website. "They're beautiful."

I didn't trust her compliment. She praised me with the word beautiful with everything I did, even the way I brewed coffee, folded a towel, and arranged the cereal in the cupboard.

"I'm thinking of submitting them at work. So, I need to hear the truth."

"I told you that they're beautiful." She reassured me with a smile, and then she looked back at the television.

She would never criticize me. Bonnie was too sweet to do that. "Thanks, sweetheart."

I walked away, and when I looked back over my shoulder, she was laughing at some idiot on television jumping on a trampoline. Oh how I hated that show and everything it suddenly represented in my life.

I couldn't stand to be the complacent Kelly anymore, that girl who sat idle while everyone else in the world got on with their lives and did amazing things. I feared of growing stagnant in that condo, instead of taking flight and enjoying the aromatic breezes that surrounded the world outside those artless walls.

I headed to my usual break room, the bathroom. I turned on the faucet and splashed my face with cold water. I wanted Bonnie to challenge me. I wanted her to have ambition. I wanted her to set goals and take action on them every day. I wanted her to reach for her dreams and encourage me to do the same.

I wanted her to be someone she was not.

# #

I, Kelly Copeland, was a photographer who understood how to adjust her lens in most any situation. If only I could've adjusted my life with the same ease. Bonnie was not a photograph I could open in Photoshop and transform. I couldn't place a blur tool over her and blend her into the background as I put on my backpack and climbed the great mountain of life alone. She was a layer who needed grouping.

I sat perched in front of the panoramic view of my life and questioned how we had spent the past year building a life together, only to discover we'd been following a different set of blueprints.

A few days later, Bonnie surprised me with a gift. She sat next to me, watching me open it with a huge smile. I opened the package, and my mouth flew open. She had picked out the same camera case I pointed out to her a few months back while we window-shopped. "You remembered?"

"I never forget anything."

After that, we were back to giggling over funny sitcoms. She might not have been a go-getter in the career sense, but she was a comfortable companion with a contagious laughter. That was why I loved her. She brought joy and comfort to my life. What more could a woman want?

A few weeks later, I sat on the couch with her and scanned Facebook. My heart stopped when I saw that Margie had posted a picture of Becca performing at the pub. In one quick tug, my heart zoomed off on a dangerous ride.

I couldn't stop obsessing over her picture. I stared at it for a full fifteen minutes before realizing I still needed to shower for work. I analyzed every centimeter of her face, every angle of the sparkle in her eye, and every reflection of the light playing out on the waves in her hair.

I braved further. I clicked onto Becca's fan page and hovered over the like button for several long seconds before deciding not to like it. Bonnie would see that activity. Becca had posted a blog in her newsfeed, so I clicked on it and landed on her website. It housed her photos, her tour dates, her biography, and a ton of videos containing soliloquies from her concerts where she spoke about her inspiration for writing each of her songs.

Aside from her beautiful, lyrical tone, fans adored her soliloquies. She'd disclose tidbits of her life to fans as she sat on a stool leaning against her guitar. She connected to her fans on an intimate level. From the looks of it, those soliloquies became her specialty, her mark, and the thing that separated her from the days of backing up Kara.

What a brilliant idea. She needed a shift from that scene. She needed something that set her apart from who she was and who she had become. Sometimes she spoke for five minutes then would break into an acapella song. Sometimes she'd speak for fifteen minutes about her favorite television show or an article she just read and tie it to a song. She enjoyed bringing light to things happening in the news. She reveled in exciting, intellectual discussions. Her fans adored her all the more for that part of her when she brought them into her secret, private world, if even for a five minute span of time in a crowded hall.

When I listened to those speeches through ear buds, the room disappeared around me. Only Becca's intimate rants and raves on life remained. She spoke about people she met, lessons learned, fun times experienced, and new friends.

She lived her life way past the point of moving on from us. She drank up the delicious juice of life's sweet moments. She took action. While I busied myself watching episodes of lesbians living exciting lives, Becca lived that life. She faced fear head on, pushing it out of her way. She cleared a path towards a world where the sun shone brighter, the grass grew greener, and the flowers bloomed more beautifully. Like some kind of martyr, people flocked behind her to catch a ride on her colorful, cheerful, and dynamic journey.

A weird jealousy wrapped itself around me.

For the weeks that followed, I continued to sit on the couch with my computer in my lap, reading Becca's blog or her Facebook page. I read about her latest song project or her latest adventure out at a restaurant, and each time, I'd cringe with jealousy.

Why did I torture myself so?

Because she intrigued me. Her life intrigued me. The way she ran after her dreams and stopped at nothing to achieve them, intrigued me. I lived vicariously through my ex-girlfriend, sitting on a couch that was way too cushy and eating way too many tortilla chips to be any good for my growing waistline.

I needed to stop the fanatical obsession, so I decided to leave the laptop in the bedroom. I sat for two nights with Bonnie, trying to get back into the television-watching ritual that I used to enjoy. It killed me to keep still. The commercials drove me wacky. My mind wandered from one worry point to another. I worried about bills. I worried about where my life was going. I worried about whether my car would start in the morning. I worried about things I had no interest in worrying about.

Before long, I started checking Becca's Facebook page every morning. Then, I moved on to checking it every lunch and dinner. Eventually, I scrambled to get online to check it at weird hours, like when I bathed or brushed my teeth. I just had to know what Becca was up to.

She'd post status updates about relationships, love, friends, moving on, and reaching goals. On the days I cried over the apathy strangling my inner child, she spoke about tears. On the days when the sun didn't shine, she spoke about sadness. My psyche warped at times, wondering if she knew I was listening to her. Did she discover how many times I visited her page? I panicked and wiped out all trace of my cookies and history, as if that simple act would erase my virtual footsteps.

My heart ached whenever she posted a new picture of herself enjoying simple things like a cup of tea, a chocolate, or a walk in the park in the freshly

79

fallen leaves. She went on with her life, and I still hadn't taken a step forward. Something had to change.

# #

I needed to jumpstart my career. My engine had restarted, and I wanted to open up and let her roar.

I woke up on a Monday morning and decided that would be the day I'd march into Matt's office with my butterfly shots and ask him to consider them for the garden section. I'd offer them for free. In exchange, I'd get exposure. I would be willing to start at the bottom. Nothing said the bottom more than free.

I sat in front of him at his desk, watching his flat expression. My stomach growled, and he acted like he didn't even hear it. He just flipped through my portfolio book, skipping right past the shot I loved most—my yellow butterfly, sipping on the nectar of a flower.

I closed in on myself as he neared the end much too fast to grasp the hard work I had poured into them.

He closed the portfolio cover and handed it back to me. "Thank you, Kelly, but I'm not going to be able to use any of them."

"Why not?"

"I'm going to be frank with you." He folded his hands in front of him. His desk clock ticked. His computer dinged, alerting him to a new email. My stomach growled again. "Your work is amateurish."

I gulped, stunned by the blow. "I see."

"That's why I told you to take some classes back when you applied for the photographer position. Have you?"

"I haven't had the time." My mind stalled, snagged on his description of amateur. "Why is my work amateurish?"

80

He tightened his hands so they whitened. "It lacks an underlying compositional order."

I winced at the insult. A slap across the face with a hot poker would've hurt less.

"Take the classes. You'll understand what I mean." He stood up. "Kelly, I'm sorry to run out on you, but I have to get to a meeting."

#

On the drive home, I told Bonnie I wanted to look for a new job.

"You've got it good here. It's a short commute. The days are flexible. We can take lunch when we want. We don't have stress." Her words tumbled out of her in a panicked heap.

"Matt may as well have spit on my photos."

She reached for my hand. "Don't let him rattle you. You have a great position. And, you're so good at it."

Bonnie wanted me to play it safe, always.

I stared ahead at the traffic light, willing it to turn green. When it did, I shook her hand off. "It's green."

"I don't care." Bonnie continued to watch me. The car behind us honked. "Look at me, please."

I snapped my gaze to her.

"You're a good photographer. Don't let anyone tell you otherwise."

"I'm going to start looking for something new."

"Just don't rush it." She squeezed my hand.

The car behind us honked again.

"You should go before this guy jumps out of his car and tries to beat us up," I said.

She chuckled and sped off, tapping the steering wheel to a country song that blasted way past a comfortable range.

# #

I needed to hear the truth from someone I trusted. So, the next day, I met up with Margie.

"Tell me what's wrong with this photograph." I dropped the butterfly image down in front of her.

She picked up the photo and examined it. "It's a butterfly. How can anything be wrong with it?" She handed it back to me.

Margie wouldn't lie to me. "Do you want it?"

She glanced at it again. "I've got a similar one hanging in my home office already." She reached into her cupboard and pulled out a few baby bottles.

"How come you've never asked me to photograph the baby?"

She opened the lids to the baby bottles. "I never want to mix business with pleasure. It's a hard and fast rule that I live by."

I reached above me for a wine glass. "You married your business partner."

She reached for a wine bottle, shooting me a dirty look. "We almost got divorced. Remember?"

I stole the bottle from her and unscrewed the top. "It's a photograph. Not a business transaction."

She pulled out a giant pot and began to fill it with water. "If I hate it, then what? How do I tell you?"

"So you're already presuming that you'll hate it."

"I just don't want you coming to me with some gigantic, forty-eight by sixty inch canvas wrapped photo and expect me to hang it up in my foyer. Art is subjective."

"Not only does my creative director not have faith in my ability, but now my best friend too?"

She turned the faucet on higher. "What's going on here?"

"I'm at a crossroads."

She narrowed her eyes and shut off the water. "Tell me more."

"Everyone around me is happy with their lives and with what they're doing. I'm not. I want things to start moving forward, but no one is buying."

"Are you willing to take some friendly advice?"

I dropped my head back, exacerbated.

"I see that as a no." She carried the pot of water over to the stove and turned on the burner.

I squeezed my fingers and toes, hoping that small action would curb my desire to punch a wall. "Tell me."

"Your photos are not unlike any other photos I see on my Facebook timeline." Margie wiped her wet hands on her skinny jeans.

I grabbed the counter, catching my balance from the blow.

"I'm sorry. But it's true. If you want to carve your mark out there, you have to be willing to grow and develop your talent even more. Your stuff is good, but it lacks an edge. You need a gripping signature so that when people see your stuff, they say, oh yeah, that's Kelly Copeland's work."

Blindsided, I tripped over the voice in my head that told me to stay quiet. "You're saying I'm ordinary?"

"No." She shook her head and began separating the nipples from the bottle tops. "You've got heart and passion. You possess a quality that exceeds ordinary. But, even that painter who paints those cottages, what the hell is his name?" She rounded up the bottle pieces on a towel.

"Kincaid."

"Right." Margie carried the towel over to the counter near the stove. "Kincaid had to take criticism at some point. His art didn't just happen on its own. He pushed it. He looked for ways to stand out from the crowd. When he figured it out, how to add those details to areas no bigger than my freaking fingernail, he won hearts." She turned back around to face me. "You knew that when you were viewing a cottage with minute details that stood out three-dimensionally on a canvas, that you were viewing a Kincaid original." She pointed her finger. "That's what you need to figure out for yourself. What details will draw people to your photos? What will be your signature?"

I needed to put my ego aside and take solid advice from someone successful. "How do you propose I do this?"

"You work your ass off. You get out there into the world and experiment. You analyze works of art and figure out what elements jump out at you and make them works of art."

"I can do that."

"Hell yeah. Of course you can." She shooed me towards the living room. "Now go upstairs and look at my peaceful angel. She's wearing the onesie you and Bonnie gave her."

Later on, long after I cuddled with baby Mackenzie and helped Margie sterilize and reassemble a dozen bottles, I skipped down her front walk with a fire under my feet. I blazed all the way home, and that blaze erupted into an all-out inferno overnight. I couldn't sleep. I lay awake, dreaming up my plan for the next day. I would figure it out. I would get my butterfly in the garden section of our magazine. I would study and practice my butt off until I figured out my signature.

I would become the Becca James of the photography world.

# #

"Instead of getting a new job, I decided I'm going to start a photography business," I said to Bonnie on our drive into work that next morning.

She stopped singing with the song on the radio.

"Now, I know what you're thinking. I'm not going to quit my job. I'm not going to just cut all ties to a stable paycheck and assume enough clients will knock on my door and hand me thousands of dollars to photograph their weddings. I'm not going to ruin our life. I'm just going to dip my feet into this pond and see what bites."

Bonnie's eye twitched. I had never seen that reaction before.

"Relax." I placed my hand on her arm. "I know I've got a great opportunity here. I can work full time at this stress-free job and then focus on my photography skills and business on the side."

"It's going to require a lot of time apart."

"Yeah? So?" The sarcasm shot out of my mouth like a cannon.

She exhaled. "That's my own selfishness talking. I'm sorry."

"You can do it with me."

She nodded and continued to drive forward. "Yeah. Maybe I should consider that."

I reached out for her hand. "We can do this. We can be successful."

"I thought we already were."

I patted her hand. "You know what I mean."

She blinked. "Yeah. Of course I do."

# #

Instead of drinking coffee with Bonnie and the sales assistants that morning, I surfed the Internet for website hosts.

I could make it happen. *We* could make it happen.

At ten o'clock, I received a call from Natalie in human resources, asking me to report to her office. "Is this about my insurance paperwork? If it is, I have it at home. So, can I bring it to you tomorrow?"

"This isn't about insurance."

"Oh," I said. "Is something wrong?" The blood drained from my face.

"I just need to see you right now."

I clamped down on my teeth, and drew in deeply as I stood up. "I'll be right down."

I headed straight for Bonnie. I landed at her cubicle, and she wasn't there. Her light gray sweater was draped over her chair, indicating she was probably just in the bathroom. She never went into a meeting room without it because of the drafts.

I turned out of her cubicle and broke into a long stride towards human resources. Nausea gnawed at my stomach. I turned the corner out of Marketing and spotted Bonnie walking towards me. She didn't look up until I called out her name, at which point her tear-stained eyes met mine. Her face hung. Her eyes drooped. Her skin paled.

"What happened?"

"I was just laid off."

My ears rung. "What? Why?"

"Magazine sales and subscriptions are way down," she said, her voice inching out of her lips.

My tongue fought for space in my mouth. "I was just called to human resources."

# #

When we returned home with our layoff notices, Bonnie drew me a bath. "After this, we'll rent a movie, pop some popcorn, and have some beer." She patted my back and nudged me down the hall.

Anger seared through me, burning every single solitary cell in my body. The last thing I wanted to do was feed my anger with food and beer. I was laid off. Me. The one who worked hard. The one who aspired to bring her photography to the next level. The one who volunteered for projects. The one who did lunch runs when sales couldn't leave their desks. The one who focused on the task at hand while at work instead of chatting with colleagues all day like most did. Yet, I had lost my job.

"It's not fair," I said, gritting my teeth as I walked down the hallway.

She wrapped her arm around me and escorted me. "I know."

I wanted to yell at her and tell her we didn't deserve the layoffs. But a part of me wondered if maybe we did deserve that blow. We certainly didn't work to our true abilities. "I can't believe we got laid off."

"The rest have been there longer. That's what it comes down to. It's not fair. I know."

I couldn't listen to a saving grace speech. I stepped into the bathroom and blocked her at the door. "I need to be alone."

"Okay."

I closed the door on her.

I didn't want to soak. I didn't trust that the bubbles and the echo of soft jazz percussion would protect me from the torrential downpour of anxiety building up in my cloudy mind. So, I unplugged the drain and turned on the shower to its hottest setting.

Two seconds later, Bonnie entered. "Are you okay?"

"I'll be fine," I said. "I just really need to be alone."

She left me to battle my inner voice. It raked me over, scratching at my sensitivity. It flipped and dragged me against the rocky surface of reason. I bled under the rage of its stronghold, crying out for mercy. It flung me up against a new wall, a wall that blocked me from a future I had dreamed up. It stole the light from my path. It grew taller with each step I took. It stopped all momentum and grace.

Angered, I stepped out from under the hot water, wrapped a towel around my red-hot skin, and walked out of the bathroom to bring Bonnie into my battle. I turned the corner to the kitchen, ready to drop my pity-me attitude on her, when I saw her standing by the kitchen sink, sobbing and holding a soapy sponge. Her shoulders hunched and bobbed up and down.

Saddened by what I saw, which was a woman covering up her true feelings for the sake of saving mine, I inched backwards to the bathroom. I climbed back under the hot water to wash away my selfish residue.

# #

After my layoff, I applied to every single marketing and publishing firm within a fifty-mile radius. My days consisted of reading every help wanted ad in every newspaper and online classified site I could find. I uploaded my resume to every job-hunting site and created job alerts.

Bonnie got a job right away as a client service representative in an investment firm's call center. She went in at nine o'clock every morning and left for home at five o'clock on the dot every night. She loved it, even though her salary was slashed by five thousand dollars a year.

I didn't want to settle. Sure, I wanted to start my own business, but I needed funding for that. So, I applied to as many creative positions that I could find. I wanted to land a job that I loved.

While I waited for the phone calls, I read every book written on the subject of photography. I wanted to walk into my interviews as a professional, not an amateur.

After a month of sipping coffee in bookstore cafes, digesting every photography technique out there, and sending out resumes without any interviews, I panicked.

When we approached the end of month two and no one responded to follow up emails I had sent, Bonnie sat me down and begged me to go work with her.

"I've got some leads out there. I just need more time."

"Kelly, we're running out of time. The bills are out of control. Plus, we still owe my parents for Cliff's lessons."

Cliff's lessons. Her parents went on cruises to the Caribbean every year, but they refused to purchase thirty-dollar weekly lessons for their autistic son who thrived on music. "Another month. That's all I'm asking for."

"I worry about you. You worked so hard to get the photographer job at the publishing company and they crushed your dream. How will you cope if this dream of landing a new photography job doesn't pan out either?"

The insult shot through me, stealing my ground. "You don't believe my work is valuable, do you?"

"I didn't say that. I'm just trying to be realistic."

I stood up and walked away from the laptop. I needed to get out of the condo. I grabbed my keys and headed to the door. I opened it and closed it, and Bonnie didn't try to stop me. That hurt me more than anything.

# #

When I returned later on that night, after circling Howard County and Baltimore County a few times, Bonnie apologized for hurting me.

My body and brain hurt. I was exhausted and emotionally drained. What could she say now to improve things? Nothing. "I just want to go to sleep and forget tonight. Can we do that?"

Relief washed over her face. "Yes. God, yes. Let's get you into bed and start fresh tomorrow."

She placed her hand on the small of my back and ushered me to our bedroom where I pretended to fall asleep faster than she could brush her teeth and slide in beside me.

# #

In the month that followed, we sat on the couch, watching reruns. We engaged in frivolous small talk. During commercials, she'd talk with Zoey, asking about her day and what she enjoyed most about lunch. I talked back for her, saying things like, "Oh, well, Mommy, I enjoyed my day. I chased back and forth through the house to catch glimpses of those pesky landscape people. They were mowing the grass and blowing the scraps all over our front walk. Oh, and I loved my lunch. Ask Mommy Kelly what she cooked for me. Go ahead. Ask her."

Bonnie would turn to me and laugh, and I'd reciprocate.

She talked to Zoey. "I bet Mommy drizzled extra fish oil on your lunch because she knows how much you love it." She scratched behind Zoey's ears. "She added more chicken than rice too, didn't she?"

I enjoyed that ridiculous habit we formed of talking through Zoey to lighten the mood. "Yes, I did. And you're revealing all my secrets," I said to Zoey.

The light mood finally broke one day when Bonnie turned on the air conditioner and it didn't work. "We're going to need to call someone."

"I'll take care of it."

90

"I'll ask your dad if he knows anyone when I see him on Saturday."

"Sounds good." They went shopping at yard sales every Saturday. My dad used to drag me along with him, and I hated rummaging through people's stuff. Bonnie loved to. So, she took over that role.

She folded a towel and placed it on the counter. "We'll have to put it on the credit card. We have just enough to pay the rent this month, and maybe to pay the full amount on the electricity bill."

"I'm trying," I said. "Okay? I'm trying. I've got my resume all over the freaking place and not one phone call has come in." I sounded like a whiney kid. I had to stop that behavior, but didn't know how.

She pulled out another towel from the laundry basket, folding her bottom lip in tight. "Babe, maybe you should look for something else in the meantime."

I tossed the shirt I just folded back into the basket. "I'll start applying to other things."

"Come work with me. It's not that bad."

I didn't want a job that she labeled as 'not that bad.' "I can't do finance. I can't."

"What about asking Margie for a job?"

"Doing what?"

"Maybe she needs help managing the place."

My fiancée flushed my creative and professional value down the drain with one quick and powerful thrust on the handle of life. "I'll ask."

"It's worth a shot. Then we can work on your photography business on the side."

Even though she came at me from a nurturing place, I couldn't help but feel like she placated to me like a mother soothing her bullied child.

I picked up a clean towel and wiped the sweat off my forehead. The summer would drag on forever if I didn't get a job soon.

#

Two days later, unable to tolerate the broken air conditioner, I sat in front of Margie and Marc, trying to convince them why they needed me to help manage their already remarkable business. I'd do anything to avoid having to work with Bonnie at the investment firm and answering telephone calls from angry shareholders. I'd also take the bruise to my pride over having to walk into the unemployment office one more time to tell some woman who treated me like a number that I actively sought employment just so I could continue to collect my unemployment benefits.

Chapter Eight

Present Day 2013

"Time check," Bonnie yelled down the hall to me. "You've got twenty minutes to decide on your outfit."

"Fine," I yelled back. I shuffled around our bedroom in search of my black camisole, tossing the bed sheets up in the air to get a good look under the bed. Then, I rummaged through the laundry basket to see if it fell in with the clean clothes yet to be folded. I came up empty-handed. I couldn't wear the red top without it, and I couldn't imagine showing up to Mackenzie's second birthday bash wearing anything less.

I invited Becca. You two will just have to figure out a way to get along on your own. I'll be too busy helping my little one act polite to all of her guests.

Wonderful, Margie. Nice of her to tell me that thirty minutes before the party. Becca would probably show up with some beautiful woman on her arm. God knew she had her pick of them. I couldn't open up an internet browser without some headline about her with another woman.

I stole a glance at my hair. It hung lifeless down the middle of my back. My face had grown pudgy over the years. Where did that wrinkle near my eye come from? I leaned in closer. Bad idea. I looked like a frump.

I couldn't go to the party. I couldn't let Becca see me that way, twenty pounds heavier, no layers in my hair, and chapped lips.

I stormed out of the bedroom and down the hall. Bonnie stood, clamping her wallet in her hand, ready to go. "Why are you still in your pajamas?"

I cradled my stomach. "I just threw up."

She placed her wallet on top of the couch. "We're not going anywhere, then."

"Nope." I put on my best queasy face. "I just want to relax."

She wrapped her arm around me and led me to the bedroom. "Let's get you to bed."

#

A few hours later, long after Bonnie had fallen asleep, I sat in the dark pantry on a bulk-sized bag of Taste of the Wild dog kibble. "Talk to me," I whispered to Margie. "Did she bring someone else with her?"

"Why do you care?"

I wish I knew. "I just wanted to know if you liked her date or not."

"Yes. Her name is Dina. She's about five feet, six inches tall. She has short, textured hair and big brown, expressive eyes. She likes racing cars on the side. She's a cop." She paused. "Anything else you want me to stab you with?"

I pulled a granola bar out of its box and chomped on it. Salt and sweet blended together in my mouth. I took another bite. "Hmm. I don't feel inadequate at all," I teased.

"I can tell you that Dina freaked Marc out. She's hardcore with her questioning. She interrogated him the whole night."

I loved Marc. "So did she like you?"

"Women hate me. You know that. Bonnie is a prime example."

"She doesn't hate you. She's just busy when we get together."

94

"I'm fine with it. Ever since I grew boobs, women have hated me unless I'm their hairstylist. Then they love me. I'm fine with that, too. I prefer it. I have you and Marc, and occasionally when Becca rolls into town, her. You three are all I need in this world. Everyone else can go kiss my ass if they're bothered by my enthusiasm."

More like her obsession with controlling everyone and everything.

"Well, I'm glad I survived the cut."

After my layoff, she hired me as her salon manager, and I'd been picked, stabbed, and burned by her demands ever since. No one wanted to deal with her dictator-like personality, hence the vacancy I slid right into.

I could see through her tough exterior, though, and reach that softness inside of her where fear and insecurity remained well protected. She let few in there. And those that she did, remained loyal and understanding when she veered off into her unfiltered rants.

"I have to go. I hear Mackenzie banging the crib. That girl never sleeps!"

We hung up, and I tore another granola bar out of the box and opened it.

There I sat, in a dark closet, sneaking granola bars, still embarrassed of my life.

# #

Three days after I sat in my pantry and devoured an entire box of granola bars, my life changed.

On my way over to Margie's house, I stopped at Rite Aid to pick up some diapers for Mackenzie. I riffled through the aisles for bargains, clutching the diapers in one arm and sipping a Starbucks coffee with my free hand. I came across a steal on cough medicine, buy two and get two free.

While reaching out for the cherry flavor, I caught the sound of someone laughing in the next aisle over. I glanced through the aligned rows of cherry and grape flavors and my heart clenched.

Becca.

She stood in front of a sea of greeting cards in the 'love' section. From my angle, I could see the gentle slope of her nose and the delicate curve of her cheek as she lingered over the text. She had curled her hair in big waves. The ends bounced around the collar of her jean jacket. I traveled down to her torso and admired the way her jeans still accentuated her hips and lengthened her thighs. She wore a pair of sporty hiking sneakers, the kind with the chunky treads.

I stood watching her, hiding behind the cough medicine. With my jaw dropped, heart racing, and eyes unblinking, I braced against a series of anxious assaults attacking my logic. How would I escape unseen? Ditch the diapers and run?

She couldn't see me like that. I was dressed in a baggy sweatshirt, sporting a messy ponytail, and wearing nothing but mascara on my otherwise naked eyes. The strings to my yoga pants hung untied down the front of my crotch, and the sneaker on my right foot had a hole in it. My pink sock glared through the mesh hole.

She glanced up and laughed towards the ceiling.

The way she tilted her jawbone, her whole being shined like she was someone important. The way her fingers curled up around the edges of the card, and her hips rocked forward in a sexy pitch, screamed happy and confident. Two things I was not.

She looked even more beautiful than she did on those magazine pages. Her dimple rested in the apple of her cheek and her skin shimmered as if she just emerged from a day at the spa. Becca James, the famous folk musician with a fan following that dwarfed most major NFL teams, was about to purchase a greeting card just like any other ordinary person.

She selected a new card. Hearts circled around a cute, animated bunny. She tilted her head and then brushed back her layers. How many times had I twirled my finger around that hair and taken it for granted?

Stagnant air rattled in my chest, burdened by a lack of space to circulate. I challenged my better judgment and squinted to get a better view of her expression. Then, I saw her necklace. I gave her the sapphire pendant necklace on her twenty-sixth birthday, the same night she sang the first song she ever wrote for me. It enhanced her neck and flirted with her collarbone as it draped down to that sweet spot in her cleavage.

She continued reading the greeting card, and then she traced her fingers along the platinum chain and down to the sapphire.

I moaned.

She turned around.

I ducked, crouching behind a wall of thermometers and Band-Aid boxes. I stopped all airflow into my lungs. Then, my tummy growled. I squeezed my arms over it, but that just intensified the range of the growls.

I watched her feet shuffle to the right then to the left. She paused.

My stomach growled louder.

In a last ditch attempt to escape unscathed, I dropped to the ground, pushed up on my toes, and launched forward in a duck crawl.

Then, her phone rang. "Hey you," she said in her raspy voice. "Yeah, I was just thinking of you, actually." A tease pulled at the end of her words.

I stopped crawling and backed up to get a better listen.

She giggled. "I'll be there in less than half an hour," she said to the lucky person on the other end of that call. "I'll be careful. Yes, yes. It's rain, not a tornado."

I stood up, unable to support my ankles under the strain of such a load.

"You bet," she whispered.

My heart flew off the edge of that cliff she had carved in my life two years prior. I didn't want to hear anymore.

I turned to run, but then the sleeve of my baggy sweatshirt got caught on a cough medicine bottle. Before I knew it, bottles fell like dominoes off the shelf and down to my feet.

I dropped to my knees again, and bolted up the aisle like a chicken running from a cleaver knife. I tripped over my yoga pants and fell on my face, scraping my skin on the rough carpeting. I pushed forward anyway, carried by the panic of being caught.

When I reached the end of the aisle, I sprang to my feet and bolted out the store entrance. The sky had opened up, and rain poured down. Drops the size of quarters pelted the ground and formed pond-sized puddles. I walked to the far end of the store's overhang, planning my escape into the wild, wet parking lot.

I looked down, realizing I still had the diapers.

The damn diapers.

"Miss," a man called out from behind me. I looked over my shoulder at him. He wore a security uniform. He rushed up to me, saying something into the walkie-talkie, looking too much like a cop ready to fling himself on top of me and wrestle me to the ground.

I flung my hands up in the air. The diapers dropped to my feet. "I wasn't stealing them," I yelled out. "I promise."

An old man smoking a cigarette on a bench a few feet from me scoffed. I looked down at him. He stared up at me like I had just murdered his only son. "I didn't do anything wrong."

He scoffed again.

Smoke billowed out of his mouth like a dirty chimney and polluted the air with its noxious fumes. The stench burned my nostrils, causing me to cough.

The rent-a-cop's shoes crushed against the cement as he inched closer to me.

The old man drew on his cigarette and looked up at the guard.

I forced myself to look at him too. A sarcastic grin sat on his face, the likes of which I'd imagine an older brother to wear when finding his little sister playing with matches or sneaking a cigarette.

My little escape act would surely serve as the highlight of his day, perhaps even week.

"I didn't steal them," I pleaded.

He picked them up, and examined them as if he'd never laid eyes on a pack of diapers before. He snarled his upper lip, and said, "You're going to need to follow me." He gripped my elbow and yanked.

The old man laughed.

I glared at him.

He waved his finger at me.

I chucked him the bird. That earned me a firmer yank.

The guard led me towards the store entrance. I resisted like a child afraid of a public spanking. As we neared the entrance, my heart raced. I couldn't go back in there like that. "Please," I whispered, pulling on his vinyl coat sleeve. "Can we just settle this out here?"

He pulled me harder. "That old man's cigarette is making me queasy. So no."

He pulled open the door, and I drew in a long sigh as if it would be my last mouthful of sustenance. Once inside, he let go of my arm and stared down at the diapers. "We take shoplifting seriously here. We prosecute."

My body stood erect, at full alert. I scanned the store for signs of Becca, and sure enough, she was walking up the greeting card aisle, straight towards us. I tugged at the security guard's coat and pulled him to the right. "Please, can we go this way?"

He stopped and adjusted his wire-framed eyeglasses, staring down at me. "The embarrassment is part of the consequence."

"I can explain," I said, shifting to the right a bit more to block myself. I leaned into him. "I wasn't stealing."

He grabbed onto my arm again. "That's what everyone says when they get caught." He fidgeted, scratching his ankle with the bottom of his hard, shiny shoe.

I looked back over to the greeting card aisle. Becca's eyes flew open and her cheeks reddened. Then her voice, her beautiful raspy voice, reached out to me. "Kelly?"

Every single capillary in my face filled with blood. The heat alone could've melted an ice cube within minutes. Her eyes wandered down to the security guard's grip on my elbow. "Oh, just kill me now."

"You're Becca James," the security guard said, dropping his hand.

She moved in, staring straight into my eyes and ignoring him.

"Hi." My voice shrunk in the shadow of the security guard.

She stood right in front of me, and placed her hand on my arm, caressing it with her warmth. "It's so good to see you."

The security guard stepped back, but his strong energy still stole the moment. "I just saw you last month at Ram's Head in the city," he said.

She ignored him, and continued to focus on me with her soft, warm touch. "How have you been?"

I couldn't find my voice. I shrugged, licked my lips, and motioned my eyes towards the security guard.

She glanced his way then back at me. "What did you do?"

"Simple misunderstanding," I said. "I forgot I had diapers in my hand when I left the store."

"Diapers?" she asked. A tinge of red coated her usual golden face.

"For Mackenzie."

She nodded and gazed over to the security guard. "If I autograph something for you, will you let her go?"

He stared at Becca with dreamy eyes. "I'm willing to work that out."

She dropped her hand from my arm. "Do you have a pen and something for me to autograph?"

He pulled out a pad and pen and handed it to her. "My name's Tony." He tossed my diapers at me.

One autograph, a cell phone pic and a stern warning later, he finally walked away with a stagger in his gait, whispering into his walkie-talkie.

We turned back to each other. "So…," she said, tightening the grip on her greeting card.

I eyed it. Oversized, glittery, a Hallmark for sure. "So."

"Shoplifting diapers for Margie now?"

"I'm living on the edge." I cocked my head. "Margie has that effect on my life."

"I was just there for her party. Mackenzie is a doll. "

"Yeah, she is some doll, for sure."

"Why didn't you and Bonnie go?"

"Eh, you know. Life is crazy busy these days."

She narrowed her eyes and nodded.

"I fought a stomach bug that night. I didn't want to get anyone sick."

She twisted her smile the way she always did when she caught on to my lie. "So, how's life?"

"I can't complain."

"How's the photography coming along?"

"It's fine." I shifted my feet, straightened my shoulders, and cleared my throat. "You know, just taking photos whenever I can." My face burned.

"Any more photos in *The Post* or have you moved on to even bigger things?"

The Post. My quintessential moment as a photographer right after meeting Bonnie...never to be relived again. "I've been dabbling with plans to open a photography studio instead of sticking with publications."

Her eyes glittered under the lights. "I knew you'd be a success story."

I plastered a smile on my face while swallowing the bitter taste of my lie.

She leaned and whispered, "I adore your humility."

She smelled like coconut cream. My stomach flipped.

"I don't know what you're talking about." A genuine smile spread across my face.

She caught it, and hers grew even bigger than mine. There we stood, the two of us, face-to-face again, smiling like we just shared our first kiss and didn't know how to walk away from it.

"I hear from Margie life's treating you pretty awesome." I left out the part about seeing her in magazines and every internet browser.

"I've had some lucky breaks along the way."

I bet she had. "I'd love to hear about them one day."

She nodded and gazed into my eyes. "I'd love that. Let's do that one day."

"One day it is," I said with surprising confidence.

She latched onto that confidence and flashed playful eyes at me. "How's Bonnie?"

She's not you, I wanted to say. I settled on, "She's doing great too."

"That's fantastic to hear." She nodded on quick tempo. "I'm happy for you. I really am."

102

Always happy for Bonnie and me. "Well, I should get going. You know how Margie gets if you're late."

She reached out to me for a hug. I fell into her arms and indulged in her warm embrace, lingering perhaps a moment too long. She kissed the top of my head as she always used to do, and my body eased against her more. She whispered, "I still miss you."

I hugged her tighter before the security guard came back with another autograph request for the cashier.

I walked towards the register to pay for the diapers, saying goodbye with a wave and wink.

She blew me a kiss, and I tucked that kiss deep into my heart where Bonnie could never see it.

Chapter Nine

I handed Margie the diapers as I walked in her front door. "I just had an interesting time getting those out of the store."

She propped her hand on her hip. "I heard."

I flung my pocketbook onto the credenza. "What do you mean, you heard?"

She tilted her head and scanned my face. "You're blushing."

I punched her upper arm. "She called you?"

A small grin crept across her face. "How was it seeing her?"

"No big deal."

She scoffed and headed for the living room. I followed her like a puppy dog.

"Tell me what she said on the phone."

"Why do you suddenly care what she has to say?"

I pulled at her arm, desperate for a jolt. "Tell me."

She whipped her head and met my eyes. "She said you stole diapers for me, and then we had a good laugh over it."

"That's it? I stole diapers?"

"Did you want her to say more?"

Of course I did. I wanted her to tell Margie how much she missed me, and how seeing me reminded her how she still cared for me. I wanted her to tell

Margie that her heart fluttered and her fingers went numb when she saw me standing with the security guard. "It's been two years since we've seen each other. She called you to tell you she ran into me. So, yes, is it so wrong that I expected a little more?"

She pulled away and walked over to the couch, plopping down on it. She spread her legs out in front of her and rested her head back against the cushion, acting as if she'd just worked a day in the hot fields, tending to crops. "She said she misses you."

My heart twirled and my knees buckled. "She does?" I grabbed for the couch and sat down beside her.

She picked up a throw pillow and cradled it on her lap. "Why are you so surprised?"

"Because for the past two years, you never once talked to me about her. I just assumed she forgot about me."

She snickered. "Just because I never told you, doesn't mean she didn't ask."

"So she's asked about me?"

Margie looked down to the pillow in her lap. "Every time we talk, she asks about you."

"What have you told her?"

She looked back up at me. "I fill her in on the important details."

"Like?"

"Like your photography accomplishments."

"I don't have any."

She shrugged. "Does it reignite a spark in you to start gathering them again?"

"Stop it," I said, tossing another pillow at her. "I'm happy working for you."

She rolled her eyes. "She loves your pink socks."

I propped my feet up on her coffee table and stared at my pink sock through my sneaker hole. "That's embarrassing."

"Indeed." Margie bent over to pick up one of Mackenzie's dolls. "Of course, Becca has always found your comfy side adorable."

I swallowed the giddy rush bubbling up in me.

"If I told you that Becca said you looked adorable today, that wouldn't mess up your heart, would it?"

My heart beat to life. My face flushed. The sweet lure of adrenaline pumped through my veins. "Not at all."

"Well, she did. She loves when you wear your hair in a ponytail. She said it's always been her favorite look on you."

I wanted to hear more. "She looked adorable herself."

Margie tossed the doll into an overflowing bin of stuffed animals, plastic kitchenware and coloring books. She tied her hair back in a messy ponytail before bending back down to grab Mackenzie's dog slippers. "Honestly, will my child ever learn to pick up after herself?"

"She's two."

Margie was an excellent hairdresser. She was an excellent friend. She catered to her husband the way any good spouse would. But, Margie was not the doting mother. When Mackenzie was one month old, she begged Marc to get a vasectomy, citing she could never do that stage again. Now that Mackenzie was getting out of babyhood and into toddlerhood, Margie eased up on the whining and embraced playtime and book reading.

Margie sat down beside me again, dog slippers in hand. "Do you hear that?" She tilted her head to the side.

I followed her lead. "I don't hear a thing."

"Exactly." She fell back against her pillows. "Such peace when she falls asleep. I used to dread coming home to an empty house before we had her. I'd get this gnawing pain in the pit of my stomach. Now, the quiet is the most beautiful sound to my ears." She turned to me. "Never take it for granted. Because once you and Bonnie start having babies, there'll be little of this."

I leaned back against the pillows too and stared at the empty space between the high ceilings and us. Bonnie and babies were the last things I wanted to discuss. I wanted Becca details. Did she like the messy pieces framing my face? Did she notice my new highlights? Did she like my side part? "So what else did Becca say?"

She twisted her head my way. "You definitely shouldn't be having babies with Bonnie."

"Why? Because I'm flattered by Becca's comment?"

"So you are?"

I think she enjoyed feeding my malnourished ego.

"Do you think I'd be a good mom?"

"Having a baby changes everything. Your life is no longer yours."

"You make it sound like a jail sentence."

She continued looking up at the ceiling. "I wouldn't trade it for anything. I adore Mackenzie. I can't imagine life without her now that she's here. But, there's a big difference between you and me."

"Like?"

"I'm in love with Marc."

I sat up. "And I'm in love with Bonnie."

"No, you're not."

"Fuck you."

She turned and met my eye. "You still care way too much about how Becca views you."

108

"I couldn't care less what she thinks of me."

"Your eyes haven't sparkled like they've been sparkling tonight since you first told me about her. So don't feed me that bullshit."

I stood up and walked over to the toy bin. I rearranged the stuffed animals for something to do. "Give me a break. Neither do your eyes when you talk about Marc."

"You're not happy."

"Of course, I'm not happy," I said. "Would you be if you were in my shoes and lost the only job with a connection to your passion?"

"You should ask Becca about her new project. She needs a photographer."

"Don't do that." I pointed at her.

Margie tossed the slipper at me. I tossed it back to her. We went back and forth like that until she flung it into the overfilled bin.

"You're too good to waste your life in my spa, earning money to live a life you don't want to live. You need to get your head out of your ass and stop feeling so sorry for yourself. You got laid off. So have millions of people. Deal with it."

"By working for my ex-girlfriend on a project?"

"Why not? You work for your best friend right now. How much worse can it get?"

"I haven't had a photography gig in ages."

"So, fake it til you make it. That's how I landed where I am. That's how Marc climbed to the top of his game. That's how Becca rose to her stardom."

Her words sunk in, filling me with an indescribable clarity. "I should fake it."

She arched her eyebrow, not disagreeing.

"You have the seedlings to all the life you need and deserve. You just have to be willing to water and nurture them, and allow some light into you."

109

"Tell me more about her project."

Margie sat tall and pulled out her ponytail. Her golden mane cascaded down past her shoulders. "No. She should tell you more about it."

Suddenly, my dream caught back up to me. It hit me upside the head, waking me from a stupor that caused me to coast through the past year of my life in a dead-end job, dragging around pity like a sack of my worldly possessions. The room grew larger with the new energy swirling around me. I took off towards the kitchen. "Do you have any wine left from last week?"

She followed me. "Plenty."

When we entered the kitchen, she walked around the counter and pulled out the red wine from the rack. When she reached up for the wine glasses, she flashed me a matter-of-fact look. "I have a friend at *Howard County Home and Garden Magazine* in Columbia. If you can toughen up and allow her to see some of your work, she'll critique it and help you figure out how to get to the next level."

I worked to keep my voice balanced and nonchalant. "Why would she go to that trouble?"

"Because we all enjoy having our egos stroked."

"Even if I had a shot in hell and got my skills back up to par, Bonnie would never go for me working with Becca."

"If you're as tight with her as you insist, this shouldn't matter. She'd want you to do what makes you happy. If she understood what the project was about, she might be more open to agreeing."

"Tell me."

She regarded me with a sly grin. "Ah, the ears are perked now."

"Just tell me."

She poured red wine into a glass and handed it to me, all the while sporting a straight face. "Becca started this charity a while back to help school

110

kids get instruments. Someone approached her about doing a documentary that would show her on tour and interacting with the recipients of the instruments." She paused and poured herself a healthy serving of wine. "I imagine Bonnie understands how important music is to a child?" Her eyes twinkled.

"Of course. But, Becca must know a ton of photographers." I paused, and we just stared across the tops of our wine glasses at each other. "So, why would she consider me?"

"She's close to securing one, but then she saw you tonight and asked what your deal was these days."

A smile snuck on my face, one that evolved out of the pure adrenaline that comes from a dream reopening its roof to let the sun shine in. "My deal?"

Margie laughed and sipped her wine. "I can see the wheels cranking."

The wheels were cranking, for sure. I gripped the counter to steady the dizzying effect. "Let me soak it all up." I sipped more wine and peeked up at Margie over the rim of my glass, fending off a desire to tell her just how hard my heart was beating.

# #

I pulled into my parking spot and turned off the car. Golden light warmed the living room, which meant Bonnie was waiting up for me.

I opened the car door, climbed out, and slammed it shut.

The crickets chirped their relentless song into the night, reminding me of all of those nights I spent pining over Becca in the dark pathways of Lake Elkhorn.

What was I thinking? I couldn't bring that back into my life again. Why would I want to do that? That would not be a smart move.

I headed towards the steps, determined to leave all trace of that nonsense right out there in the dark parking lot. Under no circumstance would working with her bring anything of value to my life. It would disrupt everything.

I had Bonnie now. Bonnie was so good to me. She never left my side. She never hurt me. She would never discard me.

A moment later, I unlocked the front door, smiling. "I'm home." Zoey galloped up to me, wagging her tail. She curled her body up into a circle, and then she stopped in front of me. "How's my girly, huh?" She whined and curled up tighter.

I walked in and found Bonnie flipping through the television channels. "Hey," she said, looking up at me. She blew me a kiss before continuing her surf through television land.

"Hey," I said back. I walked past her and marched to our bedroom and into our walk-in closet. I stepped up on the footstool and reached for my camera case.

I sat on the edge of our bed and stared at it, running my fingers over its black surface. I played out a scene where I sat beside Bonnie and told her I had a new gig starting that would take me away from her for a little while. Oh, by the way, it would be taking pictures for Becca.

I placed my camera back in its case and returned it to the top shelf above my sweaters, realizing how daft I was for even entertaining the idea of exposing my vulnerability to Becca again and opening up a wormhole of chaos for Bonnie and I.

Bonnie wandered into the room with sleepy eyes. "How did it go tonight? Another counseling session for her or was it a pure Mackenzie visit this time?"

"We talked about Mackenzie." I looked into her face, trying to find that magic we so needed after tonight.

"You're a good person." She winked at me then walked towards the bathroom.

I was still, wasn't I?

# #

The next morning, after breakfast, I pulled out my camera again. I walked into the kitchen and adjusted the lens, taking a picture of Bonnie eating her last bite of toast. "What brings that thing out of hiding?"

"I'm craving photography this morning."

She smiled at the camera. "Did you get my good side?"

I clicked again, giggling. "Got it." I moved in front of her and snapped another angle. "God, how I've missed this."

I had spent too much time crying and pitying myself since my layoff. "I need to get back into it. It's so much fun."

She continued posing for me, making silly faces.

I continued adjusting my lens and snapping away. "I'm just going to tread back in and see where it takes me."

She wiped the crumbs from her plate with her finger. "Why now? Why all of a sudden?"

"I figure that now is a good time. I'm in a great place, emotionally. Besides, I need to do more than answer phone calls from clients at Margie's spa. I can't sweep up hair for the rest of my life and be satisfied. It's torture."

Bonnie blinked. "You feel tortured?"

I approached her and rubbed her shoulders. "Sort of. Yeah."

She shrugged me off. "Sorry," she said. "Sorry you feel so tortured by your life." She stood and walked out of the kitchen.

I watched her walk away, stunned by her reaction.

I turned to the window to escape the mixed bag of anguish, fear, and disappointment I just created in the room. The rising sun looked too large in the morning sky, shining a light on me that I didn't want.

I just wanted to photograph again, not upset her.

I dashed off to find her.

I found her leaning against the bathroom sink, playing with water. "I'm sorry," she said, not looking up at me. "I'm just scared because I don't want you to go down that obsessive road again. You deserve to be happy, and I don't understand why the rest of the world doesn't see what I see when I look at your work."

I placed my hand on the small of her back and leaned into her, kissing her bare shoulder. "Thank you."

"You need to photograph." Her simple, yet weighty, words etched in my soul.

I whispered into her ear. "That means the world."

"What can I do to help?"

The path to a new venture opened up before me suddenly. Bonnie waved me through the open door with a smile. I didn't need Becca. I could start my own business with Bonnie's help. Such a venture could be a great opportunity to further enhance our life.

"Well, I need to make a website. Can you help me find suitable photos from my collections to upload into a portfolio section?"

"Consider it done."

Hope swelled in me. The room brightened, as if a veil had been lifted.

# #

Later that night, Bonnie busied herself with a game of solitaire on the computer. I walked past her to grab a cup of water. "I'm on a roll," she said.

114

"You don't say?" I shimmied around her to grab a mug.

I poured myself some water from the pitcher. "So, did you have a chance to review my photos today?"

She grinned at the computer. "I'm good."

"Bonnie?"

"Yeah." She looked up.

"You said you'd look at my photos. Did you?"

She twisted her mouth. "Oh, I'm so sorry. Not yet. I didn't realize you needed them today."

I walked past her with my water, glaring at the computer as if it had any part in her misplaced loyalty.

"This is important to me."

She closed her laptop. "Babe, take it easy. It hasn't even been a day, and you're already obsessing."

Her crooked expression rubbed me the wrong way.

"I just want to get this started."

She drew a breath and stood up. "You will. In good time. It will happen. You just need to be careful with your expectations." She stepped closer. "I don't want you to get disappointed if the rest of the world doesn't respond right away."

The day before, my dreams were tucked away, sealed off from light, and not able to poke their temptation into my life. Then, just one day later, they emerged like ripened seedlings, poking their first bit of green out of the soil to seek sun and nourishment, unsatisfied with living another second buried under the darkness that enslaved them.

They wouldn't be denied sun. They grew at a rapid rate. By the time I finished my water, they had grown to the height of actual plants with leaves and all and were dying to bloom.

I couldn't contain their explosive power. They blew right through the protective netting that kept them at bay, and sprang to life, overpowering any obstacle that dared get in their way. The pull of their desire sent me spiraling up into the sky where I could see the beauty of my dreams playing out plain as day. They danced before me, splaying the air with every color of the rainbow, freed from the captivity of my fear, and reenergized to do whatever it took to continue their rightful dance.

If I relied on Bonnie to set my dreams assail, I'd be one hell of a disappointed person. Some things just needed to be done alone. She'd never understand healthy obsession the way I did.

I dashed off towards the bathroom, closed the door, and called Margie. She answered on a single ring. "Tell Becca I want her to call me and tell me more about her project."

"Consider it already done."

A nervous tingle coursed through me, bringing me to life. A new energy formed, one that spun me around in delightful swirls and lifted me to a fun new level. "Okay," I said with a shrill I couldn't contain.

I walked back out to Bonnie who had moved on to a game of Spider Solitaire.

"Why are you smiling?" she asked.

Not even falling down and breaking my leg at that moment could calm the adrenaline rush. "It just struck me that you're right. It will happen, and all in good time."

Chapter Ten

I left Margie's spa early that night to meet with Becca. I wanted to hear more about her project.

I drove down Little Patuxent Parkway, applying lip liner and listening to *Healing Through the Chakras* to help balance my nerves. I drove over bumps the size of small hillsides, yet somehow managed to create a perfect silhouette around my lips with the rose color. I dabbed them with matching lipstick and piled on a layer of gloss. I stole a peek in my rearview mirror before speeding through the traffic light en route to meet my ex.

I just wanted to learn more.

# #

I sat in my car, trying to still my nerves. I panted like I just ran a road race. It was Becca. The same Becca who used to go shopping with me. The same Becca who would take trips to Margie and Marc's with me. The same Becca who used to hold my hand, kiss me, and make love to me. The one who still persuaded me to chase my dreams.

We weren't going on a date. We were meeting to discuss a project. A worthy project. A project of great purpose.

I wondered if she was just as nervous.

I wanted to walk into the meeting and discover that I didn't want anything to happen. I wanted her to tell me details that would spin me around in the opposite direction of the idea; things like 'you'll have to hang upside down from wires on stage' or 'you'll have to stand in a pit of snakes and get shots of me with them wrapping around my arms and waist.' Those were about the only things that would keep me away.

Maybe.

I didn't want to love what she had to say.

I didn't want to add chaos into my life.

I didn't want to have an uncomfortable conversation with Bonnie.

I wanted it to all be one big mistake that we'd laugh about in a few minutes, and then have her send me off with a friendly tap on the back and wishes for a great life.

Then again, I didn't want my new surge of life to go away. That new surge already powered me into taking out my camera again and imagining the thrill of that chase for the perfect photograph.

Hell.

I didn't know what I wanted.

I opened the backdoor to the nightclub. I charged forward, armed with the energy of a thousand butterflies taking up flight.

The narrow hallway opened up into an intimate room with black leather sofas, a television, and a few tables with jackets tossed on them. A skinny man, wearing a black t-shirt and a scruffy beard, sat on a couch. I cleared my throat, and he looked up from the magazine he was reading.

"Hey," he said before looking back down. "The rest of the band is in the next room."

I walked past him like I belonged backstage. "Becca's back there too?"

He nodded.

I approached the door. My hand rested on the handle when he said, "She's

118

not in a good mood."

I turned back to him. "No?"

"If you're looking for a quality interview from her, you might want to come back for tomorrow's show. She's playing again."

I dropped my hand from the doorknob. "I'm not here to interview her."

He tossed his magazine to the side. "Oh, I just assumed you were. Most of the press walk in here like you did, like they own the joint."

I smirked at the reference. "I'm a friend."

"Then you'll understand why she's in a pissed off mood. Kara was supposed to show up and didn't." He stretched his eyes up wide so his eyebrows arched towards his scarce hairline.

Her name still drove through me like a dull knife. I clamped down on the inside of my cheek, edging away from the door. "She's still playing with Kara?"

His lips narrowed into a straight line. "Every once in a while. I told her it was suicide. Kara might've gone to rehab, but she's still the same old reckless girl, sans the liquor bottle and pills."

I had to get out of there. I had about as much interest in rehashing that past, as I did in getting a root canal. Some things would never change. I would never put Bonnie through the tour if Kara had anything to do with it. No way. I pulled my pocketbook strap over my shoulder and turned to go. "I'll just come back another time."

"Come back tomorrow." He picked up his magazine again and thumbed through it.

I never should've come. I should've been sitting on the couch with my fiancée, watching *Modern Family* like we did every week. I shouldn't have been chasing down an old girlfriend just to massage my photography ego.

119

"Okay, yeah. I'll be back tomorrow." I swung around to the exit and marched towards it.

I stood a mere foot from freedom when I heard the scrawny guy say, "Hey, you've got a visitor."

I froze, staring at the exit and wishing I could just erase the last ten seconds of my life and fast forward to when my feet hit the parking lot with a clear-cut path to my car.

"Hey, you," Becca called out.

I turned to her. "He said you were busy, and I didn't want to disturb you. I can come back some other time."

"Drummers, what do they know?" She punched his arm as she walked by him. "This is a perfect time." She turned to the scrawny guy and tossed a towel at him.

"Listen, when you're bitchy, I stay away and warn everyone else to do the same," he said.

She walked up to me. "You know me by now. I don't bite."

I regarded her with a half-smile. "Shall we talk outside?"

"No way." She turned to the guy. "Can we have a few minutes alone?"

He stood up. "Suit yourself." He walked away while still reading the magazine. "By the way, Margie called while you were in the bathroom. She's going to be late tonight."

"You're seeing Margie tonight?" I asked.

"You know Margie. She wants to hear every last detail about our meeting."

I laughed. "Sounds just like her."

Becca mirrored my laugh. Her whole face glowed.

She was too pretty.

She placed her hand on the small of my back and guided me to the couch where the scrawny guy had been sitting. Her hand created a halo of heat on my back.

We sat down and our knees brushed. She didn't move over. Neither did I.

I steadied my breathing. "So."

She relaxed against the back of the couch, keeping her knee pressed against mine. "So." Her eyes flexed into an easy gaze.

"I hear you have a project," I said in a way too animated voice.

"I do. It's a documentary to bring awareness to the foundation I started."

"You started a foundation?"

"The CRE8 Music Foundation."

My eyes circled her face. "Tell me about it."

She smiled. "Have you ever heard of the Mozart Effect?"

I shook my head.

"The Mozart Effect was a research experiment performed on college students to test the effects of music on learning. Students were given the chance to listen to ten minutes of a piano sonata before taking a test. The results showed that for those who chose to listen to the sonata, their performance was higher than those who didn't. The experiment suggests that music can have a direct effect on a person's learning."

"Go on."

"Well, it turns out that in several more studies and surveys, it's been demonstrated that students' academic scores, especially in math, improved when they participated in some form of music education program."

"Interesting," I said, trying to keep balance with my rapid heartbeat.

"There are so many kids out there who could benefit from musical education, and of course, with funding issues, schools are often forced to cut that program first. In other words, the very element that can help build a brighter future for our kids is being taken away from them because the resources are just not there."

My heart swelled. Becca had come so far from her selfish, egotistical self.

"Kids who have access to musical educational programs tend to change their outlook on learning. They see themselves as more successful because they're developing skills that are not only enjoyable, but are pragmatic and tangible. This provides great advantages to those kids with low self-esteem, truancy issues, and behavioral problems."

"And we wonder why our kids are dropping out at unprecedented rates," I said, returning a professional volley.

"Exactly. With all the evidence pointing to the benefits of music education, it's hard to sit back and watch school administrators continue to downplay the subject, and in some cases, remove the program from its curriculum. My charity seeks to dissolve this issue by providing the funding and donated instruments to school systems across the country."

I sat back and stared into her gleaming eyes, mesmerized by the depth of purpose resting in them. I craved to touch the purpose and twirl with its magic and power. "Has it been successful?"

"I'm just getting started. I have so much work to do. I need more awareness. People don't understand what's happening to the music programs or that there's even a need. I don't want to sit on a stage and preach to people, so I needed to come up with a better way. I approached *Music Life Magazine* about doing an article on it, and they countered with an even better vehicle— a documentary. They're producing it, funding it, and going to help me promote it to their national audience."

She wanted something, and she went after it. She didn't let a wall block her. She climbed over it. "What an incredible time for you."

"They've agreed to finance several film shoots along my tour. They'll gather clips from each and create the documentary from them. This is huge. We have the chance to generate massive awareness for an important cause."

I wanted to be a part of it, and I didn't even know exactly what would be in store for me. She spoke with the kind of enthusiasm and passion she used to have when she spoke about her early days of sitting on her rooftop and practicing Barry Manilow songs for her mother. She used to dream of how one day she would perform them for real.

Her zest pulled at me, and I reached out for it by opening the door to my heart and letting her settle back in that area she had once taken up. "I want to help."

Her eyes twinkled. "Can you send me a few of your best photos?"

"What are you looking for in terms of context?"

"Gabby is looking for someone with an edge. Someone who can capture inspiring candid moments."

"Gabby?" Gabby was her former manager and whipped her like a sled dog from what I remembered. She was a leather-faced woman, just short of six feet tall, and had a body like a pencil from the two hours she worked out on her tread climber every morning.

"Uh hmm." She studied me for a moment. "Yeah. She's a great manager. I need to focus on the music, and she helps me do that."

"Does that mean you're back with Kara?"

She wagged her finger. "She manages Kara separately."

"Are the tours local?" I asked.

"Only two. The first and last stop. They're all going to be within just a few months though. It'll be quick, but powerful."

I arched an eye. "I'll have to see if it'll work with my schedule."

She placed her hand on my wrist and leaned in close. "Margie told me you needed this."

I flushed. "She told you that?"

Her eyes flickered. "Don't be embarrassed. It's me."

I seared under her gaze. "I don't need a charity handout."

"Gabby doesn't do anything just for charity. She seeks opportunities to build her credibility. Her name is on this. She's not going to just bring you on board because I ask. Your work alone will stand for itself. This opportunity for more experience isn't a handout."

Tiny prickles coursed through my veins, realizing how far out of my league I would be. "This isn't a good idea."

"Don't say no yet. Submit your photos by the weekend. Let's just see what Gabby says. We'll take it from there."

"I'll see what I can put together."

She wrapped her hand around my wrist again. "Don't pass this up. This could be big for you."

Her confidence in my ability lifted me. She understood about dreams, and knew how to live them. She didn't waste her time by sitting in front of television sets, dulling her mind with programs about derelict people fighting about their personal lives to millions of strangers. She wanted to be a musician, and she became one. I admired that.

A power emanated from her, one that pulled at me like a magnet, sending an urgent plea to my soul to get up off the couch that had stolen my passion and take some photos.

Chapter Eleven

I walked into the condo and Bonnie was fast asleep on the couch and covered up with a fluffy pink blanket. Zoey jumped up from the spot next to her and barked, causing Bonnie to leap off the couch with a look of panic.

"It's just me."

Dazed, she sat back down and tossed her head in her hands. "What time is it?"

"It's nine."

She lifted her head from her hands. "Oh?"

"I'm starved." I walked to the kitchen to avoid the talk I needed to have with her. I looked in the fridge for leftovers. "What did you eat for dinner?"

She followed me. "Oh, I just had some cereal." She opened her arms to me. "Want me to get you some?"

I walked into her open arms. "I'll just toast some bread. Don't worry about it."

She kissed my forehead. "Okay, then. I'm going to lie back down."

I stood in the kitchen, staring up at the ceiling fan, itching to do something more important than burn toast in my red kitchen.

My chance played out before me, aerating the space with new energy.

Zoey circled around my legs. I bent down to pet her and whispered into her thick fur, "It's going to be fine. It's just a job. It's just a few tour stops. I need this. We all need this."

Zoey ran out of my arms and towards the living room, as if cueing me into my moment. I tilted my chin up and walked over to my fiancée.

I grabbed her hands. "I have to tell you something."

She eyed me with caution.

I wanted to throw up. I wanted to take my words back already.

"Tell me already."

Once I released the rest of my words, I would not be able to take them back. It was now or never. "I ran into Becca at Rite Aid the night I visited Margie."

Her eyes hiccupped a blink. "Oh?"

"It was no big deal. I just figured you should know." I squeezed her hands.

"I knew you were hiding something." She tossed me a long gaze. "Should I be worried?"

I leaned in closer. "No. She means nothing to me."

"Then why didn't you just tell me?"

"I didn't want you to worry."

"How did she look?"

"The same." I swung my arms up in the air in a stretch, trying to balance the awkward vibe against an equally awkward move.

"Who approached who first?"

"Well, it's kind of a crazy story." I giggled.

She didn't. She just arched her eyebrow, waiting on my next line.

I stumbled into it, ill prepared to turn my honesty into anything resembling innocence. "I didn't want to have to say hi, so I took off down a parallel aisle and headed out of the store altogether. Only, I forgot I had diapers in my hand for Margie." I paused, waiting on a reaction.

She remained still.

"So, anyway, a security guard chased after me and this whole crazy stupid scene ensued. The security guard wanted to take me into the store for questioning. I tried to tell him I wasn't stealing, and he didn't believe me. Then, Becca emerged."

"Becca to the rescue?"

"Well, she did get me out of being arrested."

Bonnie wrestled with a half-smile.

"Apparently, the guard is a fan and wanted an autograph. I just stood in his way to gaining access to her, so he listened to Becca vouch for me and he let me go."

Extending my hand to lift her from the surprise shake to our foundation, I added, "You know Becca. She's all about her fame and what it can do for her."

"Then what?"

I shrugged and stumbled through the tense air. "We just continued to talk, and she told me about an opportunity."

"An opportunity?" Her eyes scanned my face, leaving traces of concern in every spot.

"Now look." I raised my hands up in front of us. "You know I've been feeling lost since my layoff, and I've been trying to get back out there and get my balance again. It's been hard. Opportunities aren't exactly abundant in the photography world. I can't pick up the newspaper and look up photographer for a job category."

Her face grew longer with each word. "What is this opportunity?"

I bit the inside of my cheek until I tasted blood. That empowered me with clarity and a boldness I needed to launch forward with my news. "It's a photography project."

She bent over, shaking her head back and forth. "This is like a damned nightmare."

I reached out to touch her shoulder. She shook it off. "I need this break."

She flung me a look. "You're actually considering it?"

"It's a great opportunity, and if we're ever going to get on with our lives and our plans for kids and that white picket fence, then I need to do something other than work for Margie. Besides, it's just a few tour dates within a few months."

She scoffed.

Bonnie never scoffed.

"It's just a gig. A few tour stops and I'm done."

"Tour stops?" Devastation and fright hung from every pore on her face.

"It's for a charity that supports music education. Without music, can you imagine what Cliff would've turned out like?"

"You're going to bring Cliff into this?"

I searched for peace in her eyes and came up empty. "I'm just trying to show you why I'm considering it. It means something. People will be affected in a positive way by my contributions. It's something I can be proud to say, hey I had a part in that."

The pain only dug deeper into the fine lines on her face.

"We need this."

"We?" She stood up and flung her hands in the air.

I stood tall to meet her. "I'm not happy. I hate that I have to walk through that spa door every day and work for my best friend. When she hands me my paycheck, I want to cry because it hangs like a noose around my neck. With each passing week, it tightens a little more. I fear one of these weeks, the weight of it will finally strangle me for good."

"And this is the solution?"

"It's the only solution that's presented itself." Tears spewed out of my eyes. "I can't work for Margie for the rest of my life. I won't. You have to understand that I love photography, and I can't let this kind of opportunity fly by."

She blinked as if I'd slapped her across the face. We stood with hands on our hips, heads bowed, gasping. "If spending time with your ex is what you want to do, then who am I to stop you?"

I wanted to hide from the conversation. I wanted to bury my head under the blankets and pretend it never happened. "If I wanted to be with her, I would be. Am I? No. I'm sitting here with you, in our comfy condo with our lovable Zoey because this is where I want to be at the end of the day. But…"

"But?"

"But, I need a break. And she's offering me one."

"Then you should do it." She shook her head and walked out of the living room.

I figured I should wait for a more opportune time to tell her I just spent the last two hours with Becca.

# #

The next morning, I found Bonnie watching the Saturday edition of *The Today Show.*

"I'm going out to take some photos. Do you want to come?"

"No. I'm going to do a little cleaning."

Bonnie rarely cleaned the house.

I walked up to her and kissed the top of her head. "Okay, I'll be back in a few hours."

I spent the day strolling in the park, snapping pictures of old men fishing, couples holding hands, and dogs chasing balls. I needed something that screamed dynamic. I needed that compositional factor, that element of surprise. I walked towards the tennis courts and watched as an older couple volleyed back and forth. I imagined what a cool shot it would be to get the woman's face just as she slammed the ball over the net. I'd have to be bold. I'd have to get out of my comfort zone. I'd have to do something crazy.

I wanted that shot.

I needed the picture perfect shot to prove to Bonnie, Becca, and Gabby that I deserved the opportunity. I walked onto their court, and they stopped volleying.

"Can I get a picture of you in action? It's for a school project."

The man shrugged. "Sure. Why not?"

The woman walked towards me, straightening her hair. "Where do you want us?"

"I need candid. I need in the moment. Just pretend I'm not here."

"So we should just keep playing?" the woman asked.

"Just keep playing."

They walked off to their respective spots and continued their game. Meanwhile, braving all, I laid down at the net, angled my lens through the holes at the woman, and waited for my perfect shot.

# #

When I returned home, Bonnie was steeping tea. "I don't ever want to keep you from your dream," she said without looking at me.

I cornered her against the counter. "I want to do this project, and not because it's Becca's."

"Then why?"

"Because it's worthwhile."

She dug her hand against the counter. "Go on."

I gathered my patience on a long exhale. "Well, we know from Cliff how important music is to learning. Music has saved children from dropping out of school, from failing grades, and from boredom. The work I do for this project can impact others on a profound level. It's my chance to walk a path that matters and to get out there and do something important. I can finally make a difference."

She stared at the camera still dangling from my neck. "You're not going to let this go, are you?"

I placed my hand on her shoulder. "It's something I really want to do."

"How does Becca fit into this equation?"

"She's just my work partner in this."

Bonnie groaned. "She's just so famous and beautiful."

"If I wanted to be with Becca, I'd be with her."

She placed her hand on mine and leaned her head down against it. "I'm scared of losing you."

I should've reassured her that she would not lose me. Instead, I settled on, "I need this purpose in my life or I'll lose myself."

"This is where you'll find it?"

"There are no other options knocking on my door." My voice bounced off the walls, creating an eerie echo.

"Only you know what's best for you." She turned away from me. "I'm going to get dinner started."

The rest of the night we dodged the subject. We ate and talked about Zoey and her adventure to the dog park. We watched television. Then we brushed our teeth and went to bed.

An hour into our sleep, I snuck out of bed and edited my photos under the dim light of my laptop and the glow from our digital photo album.

# #

The next morning, I sent off my photos to Becca. She called me an hour later. "Gabby wants to meet up about the pictures."

I leapt across the room and squeezed my fists in quiet celebration. "When?"

"Can you come down to my studio tomorrow afternoon around three?"

"I'll be there."

# #

As I opened the door to her studio, I smelled wood and musk. My eyes landed on Becca, sitting idle behind a Baldwin Acrosonic piano. She played a soft melody and looked up at me with a knowing, loving glance.

"That's beautiful," I whispered.

"Hmm." She didn't look away, and neither did I.

She scooted over on the bench, welcoming me to sit next to her.

I sat down and placed my fingers on the piano, still looking into her unwavering eyes.

"Gabby will be here any minute. Don't let her freak you out. She can be a little rough around the edges."

"I can handle her." I stared hard, willing her to keep that playful flicker in her chocolate eyes. I should've looked away. I should've never contributed to the intensity, but her spirit had a way of wrapping itself around my being like a lasso and pulling me towards it, helpless to whatever undercurrents weakened my better reasoning. Locking into her gaze comforted me, grounded me, and brought me right back to that place of beauty we enjoyed before the fame swept in and blew it all away.

132

She looked away first. "Don't say I didn't warn you." She fingered the keys, playing the first few notes of "Let it Be"—a favorite of mine. "I need to ask you something before Gabby arrives," she said, continuing to play and hum the melody.

I clamped my hand over her wrist and she stopped playing. "You know I've never been good with suspense."

She turned her body to me and cupped her hands over mine. "Am I going to mess up your life by offering you this gig?"

I wanted the gig. "I'd say it's quite the opposite."

"Is Bonnie alright with it?"

"She's encouraging me," I said with such confidence.

She reddened and looked down at our hands before pulling them away. "Of course she is. I didn't mean to imply that she wouldn't be okay with it."

A strange vibe wrapped itself around us. "Well, of course, maybe she's a little concerned. I mean, you're famous and rich, and well, she's not."

"Everyone has this false idea that because I'm famous, I'm automatically a spoiled brat with no morals or rules to follow. People assume that I'm a hellion, barreling down the road to success without a care of who I knock off as I pedal fast off into the sunset." She looked up at me. "I'm not like that. I respect you and her, and I hope she understands that."

I stared at her, at the necklace I gave her still hanging around her neck, and at the happiness for me dripping off the corners of her mouth. "We'll make sure she does," I whispered.

She looked at me and filled the air with even more weight. "I'm not the same old Becca I was when all this fame first hit me. I would never want to be that same person again. That person wouldn't have cared about anyone else's feelings but her own." She stood up and circled the room like she had a cape attached to her back. "Fame is so shallow and lonely. It took me a long

133

time to figure out who I can trust. And, that list isn't very long. If I had known back then about how this would all come to a lonely head—"

"You never would've changed it."

She stopped circling and agreed with a strong tilt to her head. Then, she sat back down.

We landed in comfortable silence, enveloped in the space and time dedicated solely to us.

I closed my eyes and took in the relaxing beat of my heart, circling back to a moment in time when we enjoyed the same cadence under a canopy of trees, blue skies, and beautiful butterflies.

"You know what the hardest part of fame is?" she asked.

I opened my eyes and found solace in hers. "Enlighten me."

"I can't talk about how I wish I could walk through a mall with a friend, enjoying an ice cream cone while window shopping, without having to wear big sunglasses and a hat. I can't complain about the stress of eating out at restaurants every night while on the road. I can't cry about the pain of not having fun with friends. No one feels sorry for a person who seemingly has everything." Pain etched on the shallow lines edging her tired eyes.

"Seemingly?" My voice twisted in concern.

"Most people think I have no right to complain because someone who has fans, money, connections, and fringe benefits others might die for, shouldn't have the right to complain."

"It's not a world most people understand, Becca. You're living a dream most of us only get to when we're in REM sleep."

"Few people are real to me in this world. You're one of them. Margie's another."

"And Kara?"

"Yes, even Kara. In fact, she gets it. The difference is, she loves it. She loves having a different girl every night if she wants. She'll never be happy settling down with one person. Whoever she ends up with is going to have to understand that she's shared goods."

"Picture perfect life there."

"You still don't like her," she said, chuckling.

"She stole you away from yourself."

"No." She traced her finger across the keys, lingering close to mine. "I did that all on my own."

I clung to the hum of the portable heater unit, not sure what to make of her intimate confession. "All great things come at a price, don't they?"

"They do." She stared off to the corner of the room. "Bonnie sure is a lucky woman. I hope she realizes it."

"She does." I fought through the stab of her uninvited support for my relationship with someone other than her, and forced a smile.

"That's why I asked that question earlier. I don't want our working together to put strain on your relationship."

I glanced at the piano, looking to it for stability. "I need this gig to help me and Bonnie get our lives started." I craned my neck to the textured, faded, plaster ceiling. "Things have been kind of rough for us the past year. We were laid off. She's pretending to be happy as a financial service rep, and I'm working for Margie."

She caressed my cold arm with her warm hand and sent me a careful smile. A flicker danced in her eyes, as if she discovered a hidden doorway that beckoned for her to enter. Finally, she said, "I was so surprised to hear you haven't been working as a photographer for a few years."

"I take it Margie enjoys talking about me when I'm not around?"

She wrinkled her nose. "Quite the opposite. I have to dig."

My heart twirled. She dug for me. I moved in closer. "So, did you dig until she couldn't refuse your inquisition?"

Her face straightened. "Something like that."

I studied her eyes, trying to uncover her next move, but she remained mysterious.

"Photography jobs are few." I spoke to her as though she had no clue about rejection and scarcity.

She turned her gaze back towards the piano and feathered her slender fingers over the dusty white keys. "I'm sad for you."

Her sudden pity pressed against my chest. It hurt to draw a breath. "Don't say that."

"What are you doing with your life, Bumbles?"

I closed my eyes and drank in the sweetness of my pet name. It swaddled me in nostalgia and longing for those days when life stood before me, naked and waiting for me to fill it with hope and joy. Her words challenged me. I needed to be challenged.

I hugged my arms to my chest, swallowing back emotions that I didn't even realize were piled up in the back of my throat.

She embraced my wrist again. The familiar comfort of her hand delivered a soft kiss to my unchallenged soul. "You're too talented to answer calls for Margie all day. What happened to your dreams?"

My rebuttal sat front and center on my tongue, but I couldn't open my mouth out of fear that I'd break down into messy sobs. I pursed my lips and hugged myself tighter until I could speak without moaning, whining, or producing ugly guttural cries. "Life happened," was all I could manage.

She tugged at my sleeve.

I looked into her eyes, and for the first time in a long time, saw remnants of the girl I once loved, my old friend, a woman I suddenly couldn't imagine not having in my life again.

"Trust me. Your buried dreams can't stay buried forever. They'll haunt you until you breathe life into them again. They need you to thrive." She spoke in clear, punctuated beats. "You need them to thrive. If the dream dies, a part of you dies. You're in a symbiotic relationship that can't be quelled."

The urgency in her words, and in the rapid rise and fall of her chest, convinced me I needed to step up onto that stone she placed before me. I needed to climb up out of the valley that swallowed me and get onto the promising path that she could offer me. "I need to photograph again."

"You've just taken the first step," she said, peppering me with confidence. "Hang on because the next one could change everything for you and Bonnie."

I blinked through the clear air, agreeing with a nod that I had indeed just taken a step and a necessary sharp turn onto a new road.

"If you and Gabby agree to bring me on board for this, I'll need to get Bonnie to agree. I'm not sure how to do that."

"Let's have dinner. The four of us."

"Four?"

"I'll bring the woman I've been dating."

"Fantastic," I said, tucking the disappointment deep into the three syllables.

# #

That night, I arrived home to find Bonnie sitting at the table with a pile of papers spread out in front of her. "How was your day?"

"Fine." I circled around to her. "What's all of this?" I asked as I kissed the top of her head.

She folded her hands and sat up like a businessperson, wearing polka dotted pajamas and about to toss out a brilliant idea. "I have a proposition for you."

I pulled out a chair, shoved the pile of books and old newspapers onto the floor, and sat down. I scanned the paperwork for a clue. She covered up the pile well. "Go on."

"We both want something in life that will complete us, right?" Her eyes pleaded for my agreement.

I leaned in closer. "You're not complete, either?"

She rolled her naked eyes. "You know what I'm yearning for, and so far, you haven't budged."

I fidgeted with the edge of the cushioned chair, digging my fingernails into its squishy pad. "A baby."

She sat taller, stretching her neck and projecting an air of authority over me. The collar of her cotton pajamas bunched up in a haphazard fold at her neck. "More than just a baby." She stretched out the suspense with a slow and steady arch to her eye. "A special needs baby."

My mind screeched to a halt. "Special needs?"

She reached out for my hands. "If Cliff didn't have the support system he has with us, can you imagine how far behind he might be in life? Because of us, he's come so far. Imagine if we could bring that same magic into another child's life?" She clutched my hands. "This is our purpose."

I couldn't even wrap my brain around raising a healthy baby. How would I ever raise a special needs one? I stood up and walked over to the sink that was overflowing with dirty dishes from the night before and breakfast that morning, for no other reason than to get away from the conversation.

She came up behind me and wrapped her arms around my waist, snuggling up against my neck. "I know you're scared. But, you're going to be a beautiful mommy."

I turned on the faucet and soaped up the sponge. "I'm petrified."

She swung me around. The soap dripped to our feet. "Just sign the paperwork. Trust in this important step we take together, just as I trust in you with this project thing."

My heart dropped and I couldn't swallow.

I should've wanted a baby with the woman I planned to spend my life with. I should've been just as caring in wanting to help a special needs baby. I should've dreamed of us embracing a baby, staring at her with the admiration of a parents' glow, and needing nothing more than that baby's coo to lift our hearts into the stratosphere for eternity. I should've wanted that structure in my life, and I should've wanted to create that structure for a needy child.

I should *not* have been craving for the gate to my future to open up for me to run through like a wild horse, escaping my new prison. But suddenly, I couldn't even see Bonnie's dark eyes, her ivory skin, or her rose petal lips anymore. Tears blinded me. They were not tears of joy, but of sheer fright.

The woman wanted to have a baby with me. She wanted to dig a hole, pour cement into it, level it out, and pile a life onto it that consisted of babies, wedding rings, joint bank accounts, trips to Disney World, play dates, car seats, swing sets, bins of toys, and years of birthday parties.

What would happen if I stumbled over even one of those elements? Could we survive the crumble that would ensue? Could we save our world? Would I be happier in the hope of rising up and escaping the pile of debris or would I rebuild it? How did one know?

I wanted an entrepreneurial adventure, not a baby who needed special care.

I didn't want responsibility, dirty diapers, or trips to the doctors for inoculations. I wanted to fill photo albums with pictures of exotic places, animals, insects, and people. Not baby toes, first steps, and rides on tricycles.

I didn't want to go on play dates, buy clothes in the children's department, or cook chicken soup when everyone got sick with a cold.

The spokes of Bonnie's eyes flickered with the fire of a woman on a mission. Could I be that person to her? Could I be a good mother? What did she see in me that caused her tongue to move in such a way that she uttered the words: *yes, this is the mother of my child*?

Adopting a baby could be the first truly important thing I did in my life.

I tossed the soapy sponge back into the sink and wiped my hands on her polka dots. I circled a pink polka dot with my finger. "Go through the paperwork, and when you're ready for me, I'll sign it."

Her face brightened. "We're going to make great parents."

"Yes," I said, shaking off a dreaded chill.

She patted my arm. "I'm going to get started on it."

"Bon?" I reached up for her hand, embracing the strength of the intimate moment. "How do you feel about having dinner with Becca so we can learn more about the project?"

Her mouth hung open, and anguish tugged at her cheeks.

"With her girlfriend," I added.

She closed her mouth and offered me a nod.

# #

As we entered the small, hole-in-the-wall café, I wrapped my hand in Bonnie's. I wanted her to start off the meeting with a deep sense of belonging and confidence. The heat from the bread ovens, the sweetness of the nutty coffee, and the buzz of happy chatter thawed my nerves instantly.

I spotted Becca towards the back, standing near an oversized print of wild flowers. Her hand lounged on the shoulder of a handsome woman wearing a paramedic uniform.

140

I led the way through a maze of tables filled with friends who were chattering through the steam of their flavored coffees. I almost tripped over a young redheaded girl with freckles who was rushing past us, giggling and carrying a small plate with a sugar coated muffin.

When we landed in front of Becca and her new lover, they greeted us with smiles. Becca hugged Bonnie first. "It's nice to see you again."

Bonnie reacted like she'd just stepped through the security gates at the airport after a long, extended trip overseas. "It's so good to finally see you again too."

The last time they saw each other was well over two years prior when Becca attempted to put her life back together after her fall down fame's unforgiving slope. She slyly showed up at the dog park we took Zoey to with her neighbor's dog. Just as back then, they stood now with superficial grins, pretending that sharing space was perfectly normal.

When Becca turned to me, I extended my hand. "Thanks for agreeing to meet up with us." We shook hands like a couple of important businesswomen meeting in a Manhattan office on the fiftieth floor of a skyscraper.

She reached for her girlfriend. Becca cupped her arm around the woman's thick waist. "This is Dina. This is Kelly and her fiancée, Bonnie."

She shook our hands like a politician, firm and hearty.

"Is this table alright?" Becca asked, waving her hand to the only table with four chairs.

Bonnie sat first. "This is perfect."

Dina sat like a dude, resting her arm along the back of Becca's chair. Was she her new type?

Becca started right into the conversation by telling Bonnie all about the foundation and the incredible community support for it. She kept referring to 'them.' The possessive pronoun over their coupling chilled me. My stomach

141

felt all cold and shocked, like I swallowed a glass of ice cubes without chewing them. Trembling, I placed my hands under my thighs and hunched my shoulders forward.

The more Becca flung that pronoun around, the more comfortable Bonnie became. Soon, she mirrored Dina's position and placed her arm around the back of my chair.

"So why did you choose Kelly for this project?" Bonnie asked.

"Well, because she asked to be a part of it."

The room swayed around me.

Bonnie struggled through the silence that followed with a furrowed frown, stopping only to stir her coffee. Her fingers trembled.

I needed to interject and fix the waves of uncertainty obviously taking the balance out of Bonnie's footing. "So how long have you two been together?" I asked, suddenly jolted back to life, to protective mode, to saving face mode.

They glanced at each other as if reminiscing about their first kiss. I wanted to throw up. "Four months yesterday," Becca said, not taking her eyes off Dina.

"Where did you meet?" I asked, shoveling more dirt to step on to get Bonnie and me out of the awkward hole of distrust I created when I asked my ex-girlfriend for a job.

"I fell off the steps coming down from a stage one night. She responded to the rescue call and wrapped my ankle for me."

Dina squeezed Becca's shoulder in silent possession.

"So will you be going on this documentary tour, too?" Bonnie asked Dina.

"The parts that are within driving distance. I still have to report to work while this thing is happening."

"How exactly is this thing going to work?" Bonnie asked.

Becca sat up in her seat, and Dina's hand fell from her shoulder. "We'll be filming several stops along my tour over a three month period that starts in March. The first and last ones will take place right here in the Mid-Atlantic. The others will be spread equally across the country to gain the exposure we need."

"What will my fiancée's responsibilities need to be?"

She spoke about me as though I were a piece of personal property. Even Becca struggled to keep smiling.

"We'll fly her out to each tour stop so she can photograph the show and the moments when we donate instruments to the schools. We'll then use those photographs to promote awareness for the documentary as well as the foundation."

"How much will you be paying her for her time?"

Becca's jaw dropped. "It's pro bono." She turned to face me. "I assumed you knew that?"

Silence suffocated our table. I placed my hand on Bonnie's leg. "Getting paid for this would take away from the very reason I'm doing it."

"Which is?"

"Personal fulfillment."

"If money's an issue," Becca said. "I'm sure I can get Gabby to agree to a stipend."

"No," I said. "It's not an issue at all."

Bonnie cleared her throat, and then she asked Becca, "How's Gabby's beautiful sister, Kara, these days?"

"Surprisingly, she's doing well. She's got a new duo formed."

The waitress popped over to our table. "I'll be right with you folks."

Take your time," Becca said.

The waitress dropped her jaw. "Becca James?"

143

Becca placed her finger up to her lips and nodded.

The waitress caught on and giggled. "Oh wow." She bounced in place like a teenager being asked to prom. "I'll be right back."

Bonnie put her foot back on the pedal to her line of questioning. "Will Kara be joining you on this tour?"

"She'll be at one of our shows," Becca said.

"The girl can draw a crowd, for sure," Dina said, taking a sip of her coffee.

Her coolness in the wake of Kara's name sent tiny shards of debris ravaging through me. I took a sip of my black coffee. Its bitterness turned my stomach and sat in it like a pile of rocks for the remainder of our meeting.

# #

On the drive home, Bonnie sang and acted like we just enjoyed an afternoon walk in the park. As we turned into our parking spot, and before Bonnie shut off the engine, she turned to me and said, "This is a great opportunity."

Just as the sun so diligently cleared away rain clouds, a new light dawned its way into my life.

"Do you really think so?" I beamed.

"I do. Becca's grown up a lot, and she seems happy with Dina. It's only a few gigs, and the experience you'll gain will be good for us. It'll give you what you crave. It'll give me pleasure knowing you're happy." She smoothed my ponytail. "I'm okay with this. I really am. This is a fantastic opportunity for you."

Sitting before me was a woman who loved me, trusted me, and encouraged me to go out there and live with purpose. I had everything I needed to be happy and fulfilled. "For us."

She reached out and hugged me. "Our future starts now."

Chapter Twelve

During the two months leading up to the documentary, I photographed clients at Margie's salon. I played with different lighting, angles, and focal elements. I searched the Internet for as much creative knowledge as I could find so I could add some pizazz to those photos. After studying many examples, I played around with the new techniques. Eventually, I added my own flavor and signature to every photo I edited.

I bloomed to life.

Bonnie survived my learning period by tackling household projects that we'd put off since the day we moved in together. She organized our canned goods and household products, and even started cleaning the house, regularly.

As I studied and practiced, she cleaned and organized, as if on a mission.

About a week before the first tour stop of the documentary, I met with Gabby and Becca to discuss logistics. I listened to them plan her lineup for the upcoming dates. She wanted to introduce her fans to Charlie, a young man who inspired her to start the foundation, but they disagreed on how to introduce him. Becca suggested he enter the room from the back of the hall, surprising the crowd with a solo violin concerto as he approached the stage. Gabby balked at that, wanting to keep it real and educational.

Gabby pulled up clips from past shows to illustrate her point. She pointed to her laptop, critiquing and complimenting certain parts. They analyzed

Becca's show the way a football team analyzed past games, selecting parts where the crowds went crazy and when they sat nonplussed.

I was mesmerized, soaking up her passion as she accepted Gabby's criticisms with eager nods.

Becca charged after her dreams the way a dog lunged out of an open gate, with arms and legs opened wide, not fearing that the gate could close at any moment. Nothing stopped her. What she wanted, she got. If she feared something, she faced it, extinguishing whatever power it possessed. Nothing stood between her and the epicenter of her joy. She controlled her music, bringing life to flat notes, laughter to a solemn room, and order to a restless crowd.

The fans adored her. She reached down to touch their hands, offering them flirty winks. Gabby wanted more of that.

Her stage fright had evaporated. Becca commanded that stage.

She attracted people to her music because her words rang true. They sparkled with a rare brilliance, blinding a person to anything but that moment in time when Becca's voice sang out over the radio, in a concert hall, or in an outdoor arena. Her songs played out like stories, showering people in that ah-ha moment, as if she composed the songs specifically around their lives.

I couldn't wait to get the documentary started.

At the end of our meeting, Gabby asked about my dream equipment. Two days before the first tour stop, I opened my door to a UPS deliveryman handing over each and every item I mentioned to her.

Armed with my new equipment, Bonnie and I arrived at the first concert.

Bonnie hit it off with Dina. The two of them chatted about online security and identity theft as I waited for Margie to finish styling Becca's hair. She sprayed her locks with Shaper Plus hairspray then tore off her styling cape. I snapped a photo of them as they hugged.

Several minutes later, I stood in the middle of the crowded room, taking pictures of fans as they applauded the opening singer, a pretty folk/bluesy musician with blonde hair and small town charm.

As soon as she waved to the crowd and walked down the steps to the stage, they whistled and stomped their feet, calling out for Becca.

The hall blazed to life when she appeared on stage. She ran out with her back up guitarists and scrawny drummer, and they all bowed down to their ankles, holding hands. They bowed three times then she hushed the crowd with a few strokes of her guitar. She tossed out a couple guitar picks and riled up the crowd by cranking out one of her and Kara's songs, "I Can Presume." Her fans went nuts, swinging their arms overhead, whistling, shouting out hoots and hollers. She played to them, jamming hard on her guitar, banging her head back and forth in spastic thrusts, and then coming to a halt at the mic where she whispered the first few words in a slow, seductive cobra style.

They danced along with Becca's intense travels up and down her fret board, cheering as she dashed from one octave to another. Their cheers added fuel to her fingers.

I looked around, and in between laughter, flirts, and chiding, people stared at Becca the way you'd suspect someone would stare at the northern lights. Recognition played out in their eyes and a calm reverie smoothed over the creased foreheads, the dropping jowls, and the worry lines around eyes. Her music soothed souls, blanketing people in nostalgia and sweet new memories. Couples hugged and swayed together, enjoying the gift of her voice.

I snapped my camera perfectly on cue with a girl who rolled her eyes in ecstasy when Becca hit a beauty of a note, carrying it like silk over the crowd and leaving them breathless. I glanced at Dina and Bonnie. Dina danced in place, swinging her wide hips and swaying her head back and forth, completely immersed in Becca.

149

How did Dina deal with all those women raising Becca up on a super-human pedestal? Did her inadequacy for rising to the same level eat at her? How could someone ever compete with thousands of fans?

I couldn't survive it.

I stared at Bonnie and admired her down-to-earth attitude. She put all anxiety aside for me. A comfort swaddled me knowing she loved me.

Becca ended the song on a sweet, melodic note that raised the hairs on my arm. I scanned the crowd and saw awe. Becca stirred the crowd and created magic. She set the backdrop to many a person's greatest moments with those they loved. She crafted the entire scene the way a novelist would plan pivotal, dramatic moments in stories so powerful they earned literary genius awards. She understood how to pace her fans, bringing them to that point of elation only after she led them on an unpredictable journey of fast and slow, push and pull, and rise and fall. Then, she opened up the door to nirvana when her voice floated to a sweet, soft end.

Becca James was a true artist.

She continued to entertain us for an hour more. She ended the last song of the set on a wave then reached out for her mic. "As many of you might already know, tonight marks a special beginning to a project that is near and dear to my heart. I have a special guest here tonight that I'd like to bring on stage to help me explain it to you."

Becca moved closer to the front of the stage and scanned the crowd as if she were surveying a sunny beach, capping her hand above her eyes to shield the brightness.

"Charlie." She reached out her arm to a teenaged boy with short hair and a Yankees cap who was standing in the front row with a violin in hand. "Come on up here."

I snapped a series of pictures as he moseyed away from a doting woman with cropped blonde hair. She pulled him back and removed his cap. Then, with a nudge, sent him on his way to the side of the stage where Gabby stood. She chauffeured him up to Becca.

Becca welcomed him to the front of the stage. He stood by her side, cradling his violin. I captured her pride and the excitement edging the tip of her lips as she steadied to highlight the young man's story. Like everyone else, I stood anxious to hear what the young man would reveal to our beautiful Becca James, the queen of getting people to open up and spill their heart wrenching, inspiring stories.

She wrapped her arm around his shoulders. "Charlie is the reason I started the CRE8 Foundation." She spoke with clarity and placed emphasis on each word. "He, like so many other young men and women, is inspired by music."

"Music is my life," he said.

The crowd quieted to a murmur that vibrated against the farthest reaches of the hall. Becca handled her fans the way a skilled surgeon handled a scalpel to tender skin. She knew just when to touch the delicate layer that separated fiction from reality and just when to reach in and nurse over the things that needed care and attention.

There I stood as a fan, just like everyone else, eager to be touched by her magnetic spirit and compassion. How could I not admire such brilliance?

She held the mic out to him. "Care to tell them your story?"

He twisted his mouth. "Two years ago, I was a freshman in high school and heading down the wrong path. I failed every subject. I smoked. I drank. I experimented with drugs. I vandalized mailboxes with M80 explosives. And, I got suspended from school. A lot."

Becca urged him to continue by squeezing his shoulders.

"I used to get away with it. My mother never knew. I'd sign the notices they sent home with me. I'd dodge the phone calls and have my friend step in. She'd pretend she was my mom. Then one day, I was eating breakfast with my mother when someone knocked on our door." He paused. "It was Becca."

Becca cleared her throat. "I was out walking my neighbor's dog and saw a note on the ground. I opened it up and read the note from Howard High School. It was addressed to Charlie's mom, who by the way is here with us tonight." She waved to the woman with blonde cropped hair.

"It disclosed that Charlie had been suspended again and would not be allowed back in school for three days." She paused. "So, what did I do?" She tightened her grip on his shoulder again.

He remained still.

"I marched right up to their front door and hand delivered the note to his mom."

The crowd booed her.

"That was rough," Charlie said, flashing us a smirk.

She defended with a quick raise of her hands. "Now wait a minute. If I were Charlie's mom, I'd want to know. I couldn't help him otherwise."

Charlie pressed his hands together and balanced them against his chin as if ready to launch into a serious rebuttal. "She's right. The last person on the planet I wanted to disappoint was my mother. But, I got in with the wrong crowd and school offered me nothing more than a chance to play pranks on other kids. I had no direction or purpose."

"That is, until I came along." Becca tilted her head up on a chuckle. "I asked him point blank why he was such a menace." She peeked over at him. "Care to tell them what you told me that day?"

He wriggled his face, contorting it so his eyes reached far up to the midpoint of the ceiling above. "I told her it was because I was bored."

"Bored," Becca yelled out.

152

"She bribed me. She told me if I could prove in one month that I was a good student who required no disciplinary action, she would pay for me to take guitar lessons for an entire year."

"What did you say to that?" They exchanged a stare. "Go on, tell them." She waved her arm out at the crowd. They responded with a cheer.

"I told her I'd rather learn the violin."

She nodded to the crowd. "Honest to God. He wanted to play the violin over the guitar."

"I raised my grades that month from failing to a C."

I looked around at the crowd, and their eyes waited in anxious anticipation. Becca and Charlie's banter worked just as Gabby predicted it would.

"So, I arrived at his house ready to help him decide on a good music teacher when he tells me he didn't need the lessons anymore."

"I joined the school band instead."

"Would you be a good sport and show this audience what two years of school band can do for a mischievous young man like yourself?"

"If they'll have me."

Becca opened up her arms to the crowd. "Friends, will you have him?"

Applause shattered the silence.

"Shall we?" She raised her hand up at him.

He put his chin to his violin. "Whenever you're ready."

They broke out into a soft melody. Their music coated the room in a rich and complex haze of highs and lows. Joy etched on the young man's face. Passion stretched the folds of his eyelids. The sound he created glided into the air like delicate doves, swooping in and out of the currents. Becca fingered her guitar, watching him with awe as he told his story with the pressure of his fingertips and bow. He carved out intense notes. Amongst the soft lights and

153

murmur of fans, I witnessed something rare and cosmic.

I rushed up to the front of the stage and snapped picture after picture of the young man mesmerizing a room full of folk loving fans with his dichotomous dainty and bold performance. The story he told on that stage was of pure and simple joy with a tinge of pain and sorrow trailing behind it. The result pinched that far corner of my senses, stirring up pride for a young man I'd never met. He displayed courage and honor. He spoke to us in measured time and in a language far too beautiful and pristine to be abused by ordinary hands. He played a song rippling with undefined parameters. It rang clear of tradition and took on a path all its own, like expensive wine, only to be understood and appreciated by musical connoisseurs.

I snapped a final picture of him ending on the verge of a raw emotion where his face pulled in tight and he released a deep, rich breath. He bent over in a bow, and the crowd went crazy. Becca beamed like a proud mother, watching that teenager transform into a man under the bright lights of earned exposure.

Charlie passed his violin to a stage handler. Becca placed her guitar back down on its stand and walked over to Charlie. He stood like a stiff board, front and center, a sharp contrast to his grandiose presence while he played his music.

"Charlie practices for hours daily. He's determined to get into the University of Maryland's School of Music. Without school band, kids like Charlie wouldn't have such an opportunity."

"If it wasn't for the school band," Charlie said, "I'd probably be addicted to drugs." He looked up at Becca. "Music saved my life."

Becca turned to him. "Tell them what's happening at the end of this school year, Charlie."

"They may have to cut the music program from our school."

Becca projected her voice without a microphone. "Without music, our world would be flat, dull, and lack originality, flavor, and interest. We need musicians just as much as we need doctors, engineers, and scientists. Music brings out some of our best qualities. It connects us. It inspires us. It allows us to grow deeper roots into the human experience."

Charlie nodded at every point.

"Just by being here tonight, you're helping. Part of the proceeds of this tour will be donated to a charitable fund we set up to help raise awareness of the importance of music education programs and to get instruments into schools. Music injects hope back into kids. It opens their spirit and energizes them and those around them. Imagine if Charlie had never stepped into that music classroom?"

Charlie tipped his chin up to Becca as if on cue. "I'd be a mess." He turned to us. "That's why Becca needs your help."

Becca pulled him into a tighter hug. "Future politician here," she said. "I want to thank you for being a part of this great cause, and for giving kids like Charlie a fighting chance to add some pretty spectacular magic to our world."

The crowd broke out into a thunderous clap.

"Now what do you say we get this place rocking?"

Whistles and screams bellowed out of the mouths of eager fans. Becca hugged Charlie one last time, and then she watched him walk off the stage. He carried himself with great confidence.

I looked down at the last image I had captured of him. He was caught up in the moment of his art, and I saw the birth of a story that needed to be told.

A surge of energy lifted me, and I floated up beyond those walls, up where blue skies stretched on to infinity.

# #

Later that night, after I'd brushed my teeth, drank some water, and dressed in my pajamas, I plopped down next to Bonnie on our bed with my camera in hand.

"I want to show you some of the shots I got tonight." I clicked into the review mode of my camera and shifted up closer to her. She tore off her glasses and placed them on her bedside table. "Can I look at them tomorrow? My eyes are so tired."

I leaned in closer, clicking on the picture of Charlie playing the violin. "Just this one. You've got to see it."

"I've got a huge headache." She groaned.

I put my camera down and climbed to my knees. "Let me take care of that." I massaged her temples. "How does that feel?"

She lowered her shoulders and relaxed into my hands. "That feels good."

I circled my fingers around her forehead, kneading away the strain. "Sorry it was such a late night."

"I didn't think the show would ever end," she mumbled under my touch.

I slowed my massaging. "You didn't like it?"

"Becca sounded off tonight. That's why I have a headache."

Her criticism stung. I blinked into the light from her bedside lamp. "I thought she sounded great."

"Her speech was a bit cheesy too."

I could hear my argument spilling in my brain as I defended her. "Why? Why was it cheesy?"

"She put that poor kid on display like he was a golden ticket to big donations."

156

"The whole point of this tour is to get more donations." Her insult tasted bitter. "It's not like she's personally benefiting from this."

"It's press."

I stopped rubbing her temples altogether now.

"She's doing this for the right reasons."

"Why are you defending her?"

"Because like it or not, I'm associated with this project now. By you picking on it, you're picking on me."

She snapped her gaze away from me. "I thought I'd be okay with this whole gig, but, honestly, I'm feeling a little jealous."

I crawled up closer to her and lifted her chin. "You have no reason to be jealous."

Her chin quivered.

I sighed, unsure how to assure her.

She pulled away, rolled over, and shut off her lamp.

I lay paralyzed under the weight of her discontent. It suffocated me in its gritty goo, leaking into every cell in my body.

Chapter Thirteen

The next morning, Bonnie made me coffee. She handed it to me with an apology written all over her face. "I felt jealous last night. I'm sorry."

The gritty goo from the night before evaporated. I could once again draw a relaxed breath. "Thank God. You freaked me out."

She leaned against the cold granite counter with me. "It was harder than I expected."

"Why?" I sipped the French vanilla coffee.

"Becca is one sexy woman."

"You do trust me, right?"

"Of course."

"I'm focused on the task at hand."

"You did seem to be enjoying yourself," she said.

"I belonged there." A smile took over my face. "I didn't want it to end because I felt alive."

We both stood in silence for a moment, staring at each other. Finally, she eased up on her gaze, offering me a half-smile. "That's all that matters."

"Something occurred to me last night after I snapped a cool picture of Charlie."

Bonnie sipped her coffee. "Tell me."

"I took this picture of him with the violin in the forefront, and when I look at it, I see a story."

"Your pictures always tell stories."

"This one is different. He poured his soul into that song, and it was like he and the violin were a unified spirit. Take away the violin and the young man is incomplete. Remove him and the violin is nothing more than polished wood without a song."

"Hmm."

"The picture tells the story without words."

Bonnie squinted.

I powered through. "That story is exactly what the CRE8 Foundation needs to get it more attention."

Bonnie's face turned white.

"Imagine the awareness it could build?"

Bonnie put down her coffee mug. "Slow down there, grasshopper." She reached for my mug and placed it down, too. "Remember, we've got big plans after this." She opened up her arms to me, and I slipped into them.

I pressed my face against her shoulder. "I know," I mumbled, straddling the fine line of empathy and self-regard.

"I love you." She continued to rock me and pressed me harder, as if afraid I'd run away.

For the first time since we met, I choked under her duress and didn't say it back.

# #

Two days later, Gabby hired me to take some pictures of Becca in the park to use for her social media sites.

160

Becca agreed to meet me at ten o'clock at the south gate entrance to the park. She was standing outside of her car, looking out over the pond. I waved as I pulled up next to her. Her fingers dangled from her front jean pockets. The necklace I gave her shimmered in the mid-morning glow. A family of geese flew overhead, flapping their wings with great enthusiasm as if rising with the excitement that built below them.

Adrenaline pumped through my veins. I took a long swallow from my water bottle, and then I climbed out of my car. I inhaled the fresh smell that marked so many of those early moments when Becca and I first fell in love with each other. She remained leaning up against her car with her fingers tucked in the crook of her pockets, tilting her head, and taking me in with one of her signature long glances, the kind that curled my toes and buckled my knees.

"Hi there," I said.

"Hi." She rose from her relaxed lean. "I love when you wear your hair in a ponytail."

I ran my fingers through the end of it, blushing at the compliment. "I worked hours on it." I winked.

She laughed and her cheeks reddened. "Let me help you gather your stuff." She reached out to me, and the lapels from her shirt spread apart, exposing her cleavage.

I handed her my camera case and reached into my backseat for a blanket that I planned to use to create some texture in a few shots. I learned that trick from an online course.

"That was some show the other night." I kicked random rocks as we strolled down the path.

"Gabby told me I talked too long." She bent down, picked up a rock, and tossed it in front of us.

161

"Bonnie thought you did too."

She threw her head back and laughed. "I still don't know what the hell I'm doing up there on that stage."

I reached out for her wrist and stopped her, gazing straight into her eyes. "I loved it. You talked for the perfect amount of time."

She fixed her eyes on me, and then she turned away with a shy grin. "Charlie had a good time up there. That's all that matters to me. That justified my lengthy break from playing more music."

I nodded in agreement.

"I've listened to so many of your soliloquies."

She laughed again. "Is that what people are calling them?"

"Do you ever read the comments on YouTube?"

She shrugged. "I used to. But after a while I started to realize, good or bad, the comments always affected my music, and not in a good way. I can't focus too much on what I'm doing because it trips me up. So, I just play and have fun."

"So humble." I nudged her.

She nudged me back.

We did that until we fell into a comfortable silence.

We walked towards a waterfall, and our arms kept brushing. With each sweep of her shirt against mine, my heart revved.

I loved that side of Becca, the silly girl without a spotlight, without a guitar, and without thousands of screaming fans turning her face a few shades of red.

I spent two hours posing her against rock formations and the railings of the bridge, then against the backdrop of waterfalls, cliffs, and fields of blooming wildflowers. She dazzled the forefront of each photo with her sometimes serious gaze and other times with her all-out dazzling love for life.

162

By the time we arrived back at our cars, my face hurt from smiling and laughing so much. "This was fun," I said, dumping my camera and tripod into the trunk of my car.

Becca leaned up against her car, looking every bit as fresh as she did the moment I arrived. "So, I wanted to ask you…" She lingered on me. "About Bonnie."

My skin tingled. "What about her?"

"Is she okay with everything?"

I weighed telling the truth or lying. "She's a little jealous of you."

"That's what Dina said too."

I approached her with a cautious stride. "Really?"

She shook her head and kicked the dirt.

"Is Dina jealous?"

"We're not exclusive, so there's no reason for her to be jealous."

I closed in on her. "Your choice or hers?"

"It wouldn't be fair to be in a relationship with anyone exclusively. My life is complicated. You know how it is."

I lingered on her friendly gaze. "Oh, I do." I kicked my heel against the ground, dislodging imaginary dirt.

She opened her mouth as if about to say something, and then she closed it settling on a tilt of her head instead.

I took that as my turn to depart from the scene. "I'll have these edited and ready for you and Gabby to review within a few days. Does that work for you?"

She remained leaning against my car. "Are you two happy together?"

The wind blew across the pond and circled around us, sealing us into the small space. "Yeah."

She remained silent, as if demanding more from me.

163

"She's good to me." I hesitated to say more but I couldn't resist her soft, waiting eyes. "She's afraid of what I might find outside of our safety bubble."

"It's a big world, for sure."

"Yes. She likes things just as they are and doesn't enjoy change. So, this is kind of freaking her out a little."

"How so?"

Becca's calmness relaxed me the way a gentle rain calmed a stifling day. "I told her about this amazing shot I took of Charlie playing his violin, and instead of embracing that moment with me, she turned away from it."

"Hmm." She looked up to the sky, and then she lanced back at me. "You're an artist. The quiet celebration can be lonely."

I moved in even closer. "It hurts a little."

She lifted my chin with the tip of her finger. "I, for one, can't wait to see that amazing shot."

I peeled her finger away and lowered it in one slow, graceful sweep back to her front jean pocket. I slipped my hand away.

"I, for one, can't wait to show it to you," I said in a lofty note before walking away. "I'll see you soon."

I winked over my shoulder at her and climbed into my car.

I backed out of the spot and drove away, watching her stand there with her finger in her front pocket and looking every bit as sweet and innocent as I remembered her looking years before she became the famous Becca James.

# #

I sat at the kitchen counter, editing the photos from the first tour stop and the photo shoot in the park. Bonnie vacuumed around me. I lifted my feet when she pushed the vacuum cleaner under the counter. "Thank you," she said all official.

"No problem." I continued focusing on my work while she slammed the vacuum cleaner into walls and grunted as she picked up furniture to get underneath it. The banging rattled against my last nerve.

Once she finished vacuuming, she tackled the bathroom. She scrubbed the tub and shower, and then she huffed and puffed around me. She carried the trashcan and the cleaners as if being forced to do chores. "Is something wrong?" I finally asked.

She faced me. "I don't want to bother you while you're working."

I pushed my laptop away and offered her my full attention. "Tell me why you're upset."

"I'm frustrated." Her forehead wrinkled. "I don't know what to do with myself now that you're busy outside of us."

"I want to share this joy with you," I said, standing up and grabbing her shoulders. "Don't you see? I want you to be just as excited about this opportunity as me. I want you to embrace this chance. I want you to be happy for me, and for us."

"It's hard when you're finding happiness outside of us. It's like you stopped caring about our plans."

"Just because I don't watch television with you or vacuum the rugs, doesn't mean I don't care about you or our future. That's not even logical." I shook her. "I have to work harder."

"But, every night?"

"It's in my blood. I can't help it. I have to develop my skills. I need to beat it over and over again into my brain. I can't do that while watching television."

She picked up a towel and wiped the counter. "You can't keep up this pace. You're going to kill yourself and us in the process." She pushed the towel around the clean counter with unnatural force, as if trying to wipe the glossy finish from it.

"Please don't pile guilt on me for working hard and for working on something I truly love."

Her fingers whitened as she continued pushing the towel around my laptop. "You're never here with me anymore. Even when you're sitting next to me, you're a million miles away."

"The photos need to be taken and the story needs to be told."

She flung the towel to the floor, picked up the broom, and tossed it over her shoulder. "Then, don't let me stop you. Tell the story." Her voice leaked with sarcasm. "I'll keep myself entertained." She swung away and walked off to the bathroom again. Dust balls from the broom fell to the floor with each stomp she took.

I stood up and followed her. I tore the broom out of her hands. "Fine. You want to relax? Let's go relax on the couch together."

"You'll put away your laptop?"

I ground my teeth together. "No. I love what I'm doing, so if you want to cuddle on the couch, I'm going to have my laptop with me while we do it."

She tightened her lips. "Just forget it then."

"Forget it?"

"Just do what you have to do. We'll catch up one day when you're done with the project."

# #

The next tour date arrived quickly. On the morning of my flight, Bonnie dropped me off at the airport two hours ahead of my departure. She stepped out of the car and helped me get my bag from the trunk.

"Just get back soon," she said, hugging me close.

I pulled away. "I won't be long."

She offered me a crooked smile. "Bring me back a souvenir."

"I'm not going to be sightseeing. I'm going straight to the hotel to check in, and then I'm heading off to the show to take pictures."

She exhaled and her whole body lifted and dropped with it.

"I'll call you when I land." I kissed her and waved goodbye, looking forward to some alone time.

A few minutes later, once past security, I breathed a sigh of relief at my thirty-six hours of freedom waiting for me.

Two hours later, I landed and headed straight over to the baggage carousel. Gabby stood waiting for me with her arms folded across her flat chest. She marched over to me. "I've got forty-five minutes to get you to the hotel. That's it. I'm on a tight schedule. After that, Kara's flight comes in so I have to circle back."

"Kara's coming to the show?"

"She sure is. Now come on, we don't have time to jibber jabber. Let's get your suitcase and get you out of here." Her heels clacked against the floor in angry beats.

I followed her lead, fighting an uprising in the pit of my stomach.

"By the way, I got your pictures from the first concert. I loved the close-up picture you took of Charlie with the violin. We need more like that."

My heart quickened. "Really?"

Her heels continued to pound the floor. "It blew me away."

I pulled at her arm. "That means the world to me."

She pressed onward. "We have to walk faster."

We skirted around families pulling their luggage and airport handlers chauffeuring people around on the back of battery-powered carts. She marched past an elderly couple holding hands as they traversed the polished

167

floors leading to the parking garage. When the man dropped his cane, she passed right by him. She could be such a bitch. I stopped to hand the poor guy his cane, and then I sprinted to catch up with her.

"By the way," she said, "can you please get better angles on Becca tonight?"

My heart dropped. "What was wrong with the angles?"

"Becca said something about how the light did funny things to her face and neck. She prefers shots that don't draw attention to lines forming around her mouth these days."

I walked beside her, raw and exposed, like an unglazed painting that was vulnerable to the sun.

# #

By the time Gabby picked me up at the hotel and got me to the venue later on, my confidence sat at my feet.

We walked into the small backroom of the hall where Becca was cradling her guitar and warming up. The film crew swarmed around her, asking her questions about life on the road. She tossed me a smile when I brushed past her.

I looked away from her, escaping into my camera as I checked its settings. She continued answering questions about when inspiration sprang up in her life. I took the opportunity to get some candid photos of her, ones she'd hopefully like this time around.

Just as I knelt down to get a sharp angle of her with her guitar as the focal point, I heard Kara's sultry voice curl up behind me.

"Hey, pretty lady." She curved around Becca and hugged her from behind, kissing her cheek and leaving the fine outline of lips on her skin.

I clicked a shot and caught Becca's flush. I maneuvered around them, snapping picture after picture as they laughed about Kara's ride over to the venue. "My sister yelled at a little old lady for crossing into our lane."

"She's brutal." Becca pushed a piece of hair behind her ear and snuck a look my way. I stuck the camera in her face and snapped another photo.

"Kara, you remember Kelly?"

Kara swayed her hips forward and curled her lips up in their typical sultry pose. She traveled her eyes around my face like she had the right to it. "Of course."

No hello. No hug. No kiss on the cheek. Just of course.

"Don't mind me," I said. "Just pretend I'm not here."

She dropped her hands from her hips. "Okay, sweetie." She curled back up to Becca, running her fingers through Becca's hair. "So when do I get to talk on camera and tell them how great you are?"

Becca didn't even bother to shift away from her.

Some things never changed.

# #

When Becca took the stage, she did so wearing a sporty white tank top covered by a tanked style black jacket. She wore my necklace, along with a long braided necklace that hung down below her breasts. She curled her hair in big waves and swept sexy side bangs across her left eye.

She played to the crowd, rocking out with her guitar, feeding off their energy as if it were a drug. Random people yelled out above the cheers about how they loved her. She played back with them, blowing kisses and giggling.

No wonder she stayed single. How would she ever appreciate the simplicity of just one woman loving her?

She sat on her stool and picked up the mic. "So today I got a chance to

169

visit the beach, and I have a question."

The crowd stilled, waiting on her words.

"How do you get any work done in this city? I'd be sitting on that beach with a Corona every day if I lived here."

Whistles broke through the hush.

She laughed and slid her fingers down the strings, crafting a beautiful whistle. "Tomorrow, a few of us will be taking a break from the beach to visit a high school where we'll be dropping off thirty instruments that were purchased for the CRE8 Foundation. Thanks to you all, we get to put smiles on some faces."

Kara strolled onto the stage at that point, and the crowd went nuts. She spoke into her cordless mic. "I knew I loved this woman for a reason. Isn't she spectacular? She's not only gorgeous and talented, but charitable too."

I rolled my eyes.

She cradled her arm around Becca's shoulder and sealed her eyes closed. Becca kissed her cheek.

"How about we talk a little less, and play a little more?" Kara whispered into her mic.

"Alright," Becca said, placing her mic back in its stand.

They lit up the stage, singing in harmony, and welcoming the crowd to join them in clapping out beats. The fans danced and drank up the ingenious and uncensored moves and notes. At one point, Becca outplayed Kara on the guitar, leaving her to hang back. Becca embraced the front and center position she had earned.

I scanned the crowd, and all eyes were on Becca, not Kara. As sexy and showy as Kara was, she couldn't command the musical stage presence that Becca could. Becca had become the star of the show. Kara fumbled to stand in her light. All the flirting and strutting in the world could never substitute what she lacked in talent.

Kara was just another pretty face.

After they finished their song, Kara spoke to the crowd. "This woman right here," she said, pointing to Becca, "she's the real deal. What she's doing is important. Please open your hearts and consider donating an instrument or writing a check to the CRE8 foundation. Every little bit helps."

Becca slid in beside her and placed her arm around Kara's waist. She kissed her cheek and then raised up her hands to get the crowd cheering. "Let's give her a hand, folks. Ms. Kara Travers!"

# #

After the show, Darra, the film director, sat down to interview Becca. "You speak with your fans. You dig deep into intimate parts of your life, and the fans love it. It's like they get front row seats to your life where you open up bits and pieces about you as a person. Doesn't that put you in a vulnerable position?"

"It does," she said, pulling on a string from her shirt.

"So why do it?"

"Why not do it?" Becca grinned.

"Well, some speculate that you do it as a gimmick. It's become your signature. Is that why you do it? To separate yourself from the rest of the acts?"

She leaned forward. "Frankly, I don't care what the rest of the acts are doing. I'm not after the same things they are."

"Which is?"

"The gimmick." She laughed.

Darra laughed.

I hugged my arms across my chest, taking in that sweet side of Becca.

171

"You like the connection, don't you?"

In Becca's smile sat a pain I hadn't seen before.

"Music has always grounded me. But when the stage came along, it stole the nostalgia. The stage separates me from what's real. When I sit on the stool and just talk with people, I feel real again. I feel safe. I become a part of the conversation and experience." She glanced down at her fingers. "I feel a little less lonely."

A reverent silence followed. Becca showered us all in her vulnerability, opening a private window to her soul and allowing us to step inside her cozy home, take off our shoes, and snuggle up under a warm blanket with her for a few precious moments.

# #

After the film crew finished their interview, Kara and Gabby invited everyone out for drinks. "I'm just going to head back to my hotel," Becca said. "I'm a little drained."

I adored that little cry for solace.

I declined as well.

I called Bonnie upon returning to my hotel room.

"I missed you tonight. Zoey and I watched *Zoolander* and ate popcorn."

I looked around my solitary hotel room. "I hope you had fun."

"Not without you."

"I'll be home soon."

"Go get some rest," she said.

"You bet," I said, trying to shake off the strain between us.

I hung up and opened my laptop. I didn't want to sleep. I couldn't wait to dive into editing the photos I took. I stayed up the entire night working on them, refining each one with meticulous detail. My heart soared as I rose to

172

the challenge of developing and growing as a photographer.

The next morning, I pulled them up on my laptop as we waited for the school gymnasium to fill with the students who would receive the instruments. I stood back as Gabby and Becca reviewed them. Becca's sparkling eyes proved that my two hours of sleep was well worth it. "These are great," Becca said.

"They're missing something still," Gabby said.

I lurched forward. "What's missing?"

"I could have taken these with my cell phone." She stormed away, leaving me to wrestle with my red face and bashed ego.

Becca cradled my arm. "I told you she could be tough."

I agreed with a scoff. I placed my hand on my laptop, hesitating to close it until Becca offered her opinion. When she didn't, I dropped the lid. "I'm going to get set up for the event."

I traveled way out of my league. I prayed I wasn't going to ruin the opportunity for her.

Chapter Fourteen

I was folding towels in the backroom of the spa when Margie popped her head in. "You have to come meet my client."

Curiosity trumped towel folding. I followed her out to her hair station where a lady sat with a head full of foils. She was sipping tea and flipping through *People Magazine*.

"Donna, this is Kelly."

Tin foil blocked my view of her eyes. I didn't recognize her. I extended my hand, and she shook it. "Margie tells me you're photographing Becca James' documentary right now."

"Yes, I am." I eyed Margie, and she offered me a sly grin.

"I'm the creative director for *Howard County Home and Garden Magazine*."

My heart leapt. "I've always admired your magazine. I have every issue back to the year two thousand."

"One of my local photographers just quit to take a job overseas for *National Geographic*. So, if you'd like to send me some samples of your work, I'd love to take a look."

A warmth trickled through my veins. "I'll get right on it."

One of the foils tilted and poked at her eye. "Send them along. Margie will give you my email."

I headed back to the pile of unfolded towels. The room looked brighter. The smell of lilac fabric softener tickled my senses. The soft, fuzzy texture wrapped me in a pleasure that lifted me to the upper extremes of joy, to that place where clouds were fluffier, skies were bluer, grass was greener, and dreams regardless of their size, came true.

I cut out early that day to get my portfolio in its best shape. I reexamined the butterfly pictures that plagued me before and understood why Margie didn't want any of them hanging on a canvas the size of her wall. They lacked that critical focal point that my violin picture captured so eloquently.

I thought about sending her some of the documentary shots, but after Gabby's critique, I decided to hit the backyard of the condo complex. I would spend an hour amongst the trees, lying down on my back and shooting pictures of tree trunks from the viewpoint of an ant. It was for a nature magazine after all.

In one shot, I caught a squirrel hanging on the edge of a tree branch, nibbling on an acorn. I zoomed in on the squirrel's tiny claws digging into it and captured it.

As I lay back against the ground that afternoon, capturing moments of nature at play, I longed for Becca to be hanging off the tree, smiling at my camera, allowing me to capture her spirit at play. My interest in photographing squirrels eating nuts and ants crawling up the sides of tree trunks suddenly paled in comparison to portraits now.

Later on, long after I sent my new photos and resume to Donna at the magazine, I was soaping up my tummy and circling my navel, when Bonnie climbed into the shower with me. She took the soap from me and lathered it on my back. "How was the spa?" she asked.

I tilted my neck when she circled the soap towards it. "Fine." The potential job opportunity sat on my tongue, ready to seal the deal on our future as spouses and parents. Instead of releasing us from the perils of instability, I chose to swallow the words and bury them in me for the night.

I feared losing my opportunity to photograph Becca. Taking a job at the magazine would remove my access to Becca's friendship and toss me straight into the path of marriage and babyhood. I feared that unknown. Didn't everyone? Many people feared marriage and babies. Surely, time would erase the anxiety and replace it with a sense of certainty.

I banked on that.

I clung to the towel holder while Bonnie deflowered my skin with her bare hands. She warmed up to me, moaning and traveling on to pursuits that caused me to flinch.

"Fine, huh?" she whispered into my ear, stopping to nibble on it.

"Yup. Just another ordinary day folding towels, listening to Margie talk her clients into expensive shampoos, and cashing out clients who pay more for their hair than most people spend on their groceries in a week."

She spun me to face her and spread the bubbles across my shoulders and down to my breast. We hadn't been intimate in months. We needed to bond. I closed my eyes and grounded myself in the moment. As she circled and teased, I tensed. "What's wrong, babe?" she asked.

She needed me to be there with her. "Not a thing." I kissed her, attempting to bring her in close to my heart. Her tongue pushed against mine. I twirled mine with hers, hoping to relax her, but it only caused her to push against mine harder. The wind that I always trusted to set our hearts sailing, suddenly capsized beneath the new gust that blew into my life in the form of promise, hope, and purpose. I opened my mind's eyes and a tidal wave barreled down on us, threatening to sweep us up into a current way too powerful to survive. The rage of water blocked out the sun, the blue skies, and the thrill of an adventure gone wrong.

"Kelly, I want you so badly right now," she whispered. She reached down to the inside of my thighs and pulled my legs apart with her fist then plunged her fingers into me. "I love you so much," she moaned.

I opened my eyes to connect with her, only to lose further sight of the woman standing naked with me under the hot water. I wanted to run. I wanted to hide under my blankets and protect her from my restless heart. She continued to finger me, and with each flick, I cringed.

I closed my eyes and tried to imagine our souls connecting under the rush of steamy water. I pictured warm breath on my neck, strong arms lifting me, and soft skin melding together with mine. I saw Becca's lips caressing my skin, her tongue taking pleasure in my taste, and her heart beating against mine. I imagined seeking out her warmth, landing in that special place where she moaned under the tease of my touch, buckled in my arms, and clung to me in breathless ecstasy as she escaped into my love and surrendered her heart to me. Within moments of that beautiful escape, my body floated off to that sweet place of nirvana that no pill, no picture, and no other woman in the world could match.

# #

Becca and her crew came to town for an impromptu interview with a local radio station about promoting the documentary at a folk festival. I met her at her old studio, Vibrations. The music store cleared the main instrument sales floor and set up a few rows of chairs for students and parents from a local school. Local television stations were there to interview her about her foundation.

She, along with her drummer and back up guitarists, were jamming when I entered. A few minutes later, they took questions from the children, who asked things like how she got started, how they can become famous too, how many years of lessons they needed to take, and how often they should practice to be as good as her.

Becca answered the kids with an endearing quality. They ate her up, as did everyone. Her cheeks shined, her eyes sparkled, and she giggled like a schoolgirl herself.

Later on, as I was leaving, Becca asked if she could walk out with me. It was raining, and we had no cover. "I should go," I said. "I told Bonnie I'd be home by now."

She grabbed my arm. "Come sit in my car for a few minutes."

Raindrops fell on her face and rolled down her skin, gathering on her soft lips. "I shouldn't."

"Just a few minutes. I want to talk about the documentary."

I looked down at my watch. "I suppose a few minutes can't hurt."

I climbed into her front seat.

We chatted about the needs of the documentary, and what kind of shots she'd like for me to still get. That led to a conversation about Kara and her rehab. She was doing great with it. "She's like a different person without the influence of drugs and alcohol."

"She doesn't like me."

"She very insecure," she said. "You intimidate her."

"Me?"

She chuckled. "You're sweet and loyal, and it might be hard to see under her disguise, but she admires those qualities."

I wriggled around the compliment, bouncing it from hand-to-hand, unsure how to interpret or respond to it. I changed the subject. "So are you still seeing Dina?"

She looked away and out the window. "Things are tense. She wants more than I can give her. She's not crazy about me being on the road all the time."

179

"Doesn't that come with the territory?"

"Everyone thinks they can handle it until it becomes a part of their life."

Everyone. I wondered just how many people that consisted of. "It's not easy, is it?"

"Being on the road is fun. Fame is definitely not. I can't have one without the other."

"Hmm."

"It gets lonely. It's hard to trust who's real and who's just out for a ride. That's why I don't even bother anymore. When I'm not on stage, I just want simplicity." She closed her eyes. "Just simple."

I stared at her closed eyelids and wanted to kiss them.

She opened them and caught me staring at her. "It's coming down hard," she said, turning away.

I still loved her. I loved her even more than before. The new aura of simplicity was so attractive.

I needed to break from that thought. I needed to put on my professional hat. So, I tiptoed to the edge of a question that would do the trick and pull me back to sanity. "Gabby told me you didn't like the angle I got on you. Why didn't you just tell me yourself?"

She played with her steering wheel, smoothing her hands back and forth over it. The overhead parking lights casted a glow on her profile, exposing her neck and a deep swallow. "It was one picture I referred to, and I was talking about my own flaw, not your work."

I searched the curves in her profile for the truth. I looked for the infidelity on the tips of her shiny hair, on the frequency of her blinks, and then on the slight tremble of her pinky finger. "You can tell me if you're not happy."

She pulled in her bottom lip and laughed. "Everything does not have to be perfect, Bumbles."

"I wanted to be perfect for this."

She lifted my chin. "I don't want perfect."

I became aware of our inflated breaths and of our synched heartbeats.

I shifted away, and her finger fell to my arm.

"You're always pitch perfect on stage. Don't you strive for that?"

"When I do, I almost always screw it up." She laughed.

"If we don't strive for perfection, then we're mediocre."

"There's no such thing as picture perfect. Everything being perfectly in order is boring. It leads to disappointment. A displaced object in a frame... now that's more interesting." She drummed her fingers on the steering wheel. "That's where real living happens. Stick an oddball box in the forefront of a shot and people will stop and stare at it and find the beauty. Like that amazing picture you took of Charlie."

My spirit lightened under the twinkle in her eye. "You liked it?"

"I loved it." She looked into my eyes. "You're incredibly talented. I hope you realize just how much."

I blushed.

"That photo speaks a powerful message."

I locked onto her eyes. "I have this idea," I said, vetting out the first droplets of what I imagined could turn into a gushing river of opportunity that could forever change the landscape to our future.

She leaned in closer. "Go on."

"That picture I took tells a story. People latch onto stories. They don't latch onto the idea of money, donations, or tangible goods. They connect to stories. Like the stories you tell on stage. People connect to you through them. What if your foundation offered people the chance to be photographed in the same context of Charlie's picture, but with their own instrument? The photographs could be staged in such a way that is consistent, so when people see them, their brains automatically connect it to the CRE8 Foundation and its powerful mission. You could charge people for these photographs, and the proceeds would go to purchase more instruments and to fund more awareness campaigns to keep music in schools."

Her eyes lit up. "That's perfect."

"You said perfect was boring."

She laughed then opened her window and stuck her hand out. "In every other case it is." She splashed rain on her face. "Rain is the perfect imperfection. It ruins a pretty, sunny day. It turns the ground muddy. It destroys a good hair day. Yet, despite these imperfections, it's magical."

She cupped the rain and splashed it at me. I jumped back and squealed. I opened my window and did the same. We splashed water back and forth on each other several times until she grabbed the door handle and jumped out of her car.

"Where are you going," I called after her.

"To dance," she yelled back before slamming the door shut. I ran out to meet her. The headlights shined on us like stage spotlights. She spun in wide circles with her arms outstretched. I joined her, catching the buzz of fun and the sweet escape.

We spun together, grasping onto each other's wrists and letting ourselves move with the flow of a turbine. I stretched my head backwards and opened my mouth to catch the raindrops on my tongue. Drops poured down, pelting my face and transporting me right back in time to when she and I would run in the rain at Patapsco. We didn't care if we got soaked. We didn't care now either. She swung me around square dance style. We danced to a beat all our own, giggling and free.

At one point, she stopped dancing and let go of me. She opened her arms up to the dark skies and inhaled a long stream of air. I'd never seen her look more peaceful and beautiful before. Instinctively, I reached out for her. I curled up behind her and rested my head on the crook of her shoulder. She swayed under my embrace as I cradled my arms around her waist. She fit perfectly in my arms. I matched her slow rock of the hips, pressing my belly against the small of her back and burying myself into that moment. I wanted to remember how great it felt to snuggle up against her so close again. I smelled her musky vanilla scent and my head spun, drunk on her.

I breathed, she breathed. We clung together under the weight of raindrops, as one source, one being, and one soul united. She reached down for my hands on her navel and softened up to them. Her desire traveled through me like hot tea on a cold, bitter day, wiping away everything that wasn't comforting and intoxicating.

I turned inward to her soft skin, to the curve in her neck that always set my heart racing, and craved to plant soft, feathery kisses on her. She reached up to my cheek and circled her fingers. A deep hunger grew in me. My eyes landed on her soft lips. Her warm breath blanketed my face. Dizzy, I pushed her towards the hood of her car and leaned into her, craving for her to let go and kiss me.

Our wet clothes clung to us. Our hair tangled across our neck, shoulders, and faces.

"I shouldn't be this close to you," I whispered.

She clung tighter to me. "We should back away from each other before someone gets hurt."

"Yes," I said, not budging.

Suddenly, a long casted trail of white lights closed in on us. I jumped off her and wrapped my arms around my soaked chest.

The vehicle approached. Its lights brightened and widened the area around us, exposing our wilted clothes, hair, and flushed faces.

Becca reached out for my arm and pulled me in close to her again. She stood tall and rigid, even while shivering.

We stood in front of the headlights like two drowned fools. The car door opened and out jumped Bonnie. "What are you doing out in this rain? Get in the car."

My heart zoomed. As my feet moved, I realized I was pulling Becca along. I racked my mind for excuses that would fit, that would save Bonnie from the hurt of knowing her fiancée was just about ready to cross the line of no return and break the sacred trust she offered to me.

We ran to her car. I dropped into the front seat and Becca, waterlogged and dripping, plopped on the back seat on top of some carpet samples Bonnie had just picked up for us. "I'm sorry." She tossed them to the side. "They're soaked now too."

We all exhaled in unison. "What a freaking night," Becca said, her voice sounding like more of an echo. "First, we almost forget my guitar. Then we almost forgot her camera. Then some asshole tells me I have a flat tire."

I flashed my eyes at her, searching for my next line. She ignored me and continued. "I don't even know if I have a spare tire."

"Do you have any roadside assistance?" Bonnie asked her, clearly annoyed.

"No."

Becca tapped her fingers against the rain-streaked window. "This is why Dina gets annoyed with me."

Dina. Just hearing her name caused my stomach to flex up and fight me. Like I suddenly had a claim on Becca.

"You should have it." Bonnie put on her wipers. "What were you planning on doing out in this rain? Were you seriously considering changing the tire?" She sounded so condescending.

184

"I'm sure she could manage," I said, all defenses rising on my inflection.

Bonnie snapped a look at me, and then she turned back to Becca. "I'll call my roadside guys and have them change it." She opened up her pocketbook and took out her wallet. She plucked out her trusty roadside assistance card and began dialing their number.

I looked back at Becca, arching my eyes at her and willing her to get us out of the lie in one piece.

"Let me get my cell from my car." She opened up her door and jumped out.

"I'm on hold." Bonnie eyed me. "Do you want to tell me what's going on?"

I flapped like a fish on land under her stare. With no flat tire and my head and heart twisted in unrecognizable ways, I sank into my seat, ill prepared to shuck out another lie. "The guy said she had a flat tire. What was I going to do? Let her sit idle in the rain?"

"Why were you in front of her car and not investigating the tire?"

"We were trying to figure out what to do. Neither one of us has changed a tire before."

"You jumped when I pulled up." She shifted her cell to her other ear.

"It's pouring outside," I said. "I'm cold. I'm shivering. I'm trying to figure out how to help her."

"Why didn't you just call me?"

"I figured you were asleep by now."

"You're two hours late."

I looked her straight in the eye. "These gigs don't operate on a tight schedule. I warned you about this." I reached out for her free hand. She pulled away from me.

Becca jumped back in the car. "It's totally flat. I'm going to call Gabby

185

and have her sit here with me so you girls can get on your way. Gabby's got coverage."

"We're here now," Bonnie said. "Don't be silly."

I opened my mouth, about to join Bonnie on her offer to sit for as long as it took, when Bonnie pointed her finger up. "Yes," she said into her cell. "I've got a flat tire and need some roadside assistance with it."

Bonnie had a habit of not being able to talk on her cell and focus on anything else. So, she buried her head against her steering wheel, blocking her free ear with her hand.

Now cocooned into her own world, I turned back to Becca and probed her with a stare.

She motioned a jab with her hand.

She cut a hole in her tire for me.

"It's really flat?" I asked her.

"Gone, sliced, dead." She winked before looking away out at the stormy, relentless night.

Chapter Fifteen

Typically, the only time Bonnie went out was when she visited with Cliff, went on yard sale hunts with my father, or took me out for dinner. The night after the parking lot incident, she called me from work and told me some coworkers invited her out for happy hour. I cheered with a silent fist pump. That would allow me time to edit and upload photos without guilt pinching me and reminding me that I should've been paying more attention to her than my laptop.

She told me she'd be home by nine o'clock.

She arrived home at seven forty-five with two carryout boxes. "Cheesecake," she said, carrying them into the kitchen.

I hadn't finished my work yet. I didn't want to put it aside and eat cheesecake. I kept working on a close up of Becca's fingers curled around Tangerine Twist, ignoring the clanking of glasses rising from the kitchen.

I had just gotten the curve setting the way I wanted on the photo when she barged into the living room carrying the two boxes under one arm and two glasses of milk in the other.

Reluctantly, I placed my laptop down on the coffee table and took a box and a glass off her hands.

"Happy hour ended early?" I asked.

She assumed her position next to me on the couch. "I wanted to be home with you." She dug her fork into the cheesecake.

I escaped into mine.

"Is everything okay?" she asked. "You seem a little stressed."

I pushed the cheesecake around, taking out my frustrations on it. "I'm fine. I was just in work mode."

She snapped her eyes at me. "Sorry. I didn't mean to intrude on you."

I sighed, probably heavier and more dramatically than one should under the distress of someone else. I shook off my irritation. "I'm sorry. I just need a minute to snap out of photographer mode."

We ate our cheesecake in silence, each pushing it around in our respective boxes, every once in a while surfacing with an apologetic nod.

"You know what," she said rising. "I'm going to watch television in the bedroom. You finish what you were doing."

I pulled at her arm, branded by disgust for being such a self-absorbed person. "No, stay."

She glanced at my laptop and the image of Becca's fingers on her guitar. "I'm kind of tired anyway. It's better if I just leave you alone."

My hand slipped from her arm as she pulled away. She placed her half-eaten cheesecake on the coffee table and walked out of the room.

# #

As my next leg of the tour approached, I dug deeper into padding my portfolio for Donna at *Howard County Home and Garden Magazine*. She called and asked me to come down to speak with her and the creative team in two weeks. "Between you and me, it's competitive. There are lots of people who want full time photography jobs. So, I'd recommend bringing in more dynamic pictures to wow the team."

I stressed about how I'd manage to get new photos, continue working on

Becca's stuff, and put in my hours at Margie's spa so we could still pay our bills and put food on the table.

I had just hung up with Donna when Bonnie and Zoey walked into the room. "Zoey and I have an appointment to meet with the director of Pet Therapy Academy. Want to come?"

"Pet therapy?"

"My mother told me about it. A few pet therapy dogs visited her school one day, and she had Cliff with her. Well, I guess Cliff fell in love with the dogs so he begged me to get him a job as a pet therapy handler."

"He has an interview?"

"No. But, why not let him work with Zoey? She's calm, and he's so good with her."

"That's fantastic." My heart skipped at the entrepreneurial outburst.

"Come with us."

"I can't." I pointed my eyes at my computer.

"Seriously? More work?"

The time had come to let her in on my magazine opportunity. "I have a shot at a full-time photography position with *Howard County Home and Garden Magazine*. Margie set it up for me. I have two weeks to get my portfolio in order."

Her eyes lit up, and she leapt to my side for a hug. "Oh, that's such great news."

"I'm going to need to focus." My voice got lost in the folds of her t-shirt.

She applauded the idea with a reassuring nod. "Of course. I'll get out of your way in a few minutes."

In the days that followed, Gabby called a meeting and told me she wanted to test out the CRE8 photo shoot idea on the next tour date. She already began marketing to the local community and on the website that photos would start three hours before the scheduled opening act. My idea had value, and that set my heart racing with the fuel of purpose.

I started brainstorming ideas of how I could shoot photos of people with their instruments so that each one could tell its own story. Ideas about colors, poses, backdrops, and focal points would come to me while walking around the neighborhood, and I'd struggle to open my iPhone and get them down. As Zoey pulled me with one arm, I typed with the other. Bonnie would toss me annoyed looks.

By the end of the week, she grew antsy. She begged me to spend time with her, Zoey, and Cliff. "Just come sit for a few minutes." She patted the couch.

I pulled away from my work and sat next to her.

She flicked on the Netflix channel and settled in for an episode of *Orange is the New Black*.

I tried to relax. I tried to watch the show. I tried not to focus on the clock advance on the cable box, reminding me how much time I wasted on that passive activity. Honestly, I tried. But, as I sat there on the couch with Zoey on one side, and Bonnie on the other, my body shook as if experiencing withdrawals.

I was not unlike a runner being asked to stop mid stride and stroll for the rest of the race. I had my eye on the finish line, and I didn't want to stop and pick flowers along the side of the road. I wanted to keep pushing forward, keep feeling the pavement under my feet, keep smiling and waving to the bystanders counting on me to finish what I started.

My heart began to dance again, and I didn't want to sit it out. I had done that for too long.

"I'm sorry. I can't just sit here idle." I stood up, and Bonnie cocked her head in defeat.

The night before I was set to take off on the next leg of the tour, I was sitting on the couch with my laptop. I had ten hours to edit over one hundred photos and upload them to Becca's site.

Meanwhile, Bonnie walked into the living room with a rag and furniture polish in hand. I looked up at her. "I'll help you in a few minutes. I just have to get through some of these edits."

She walked past me, swiping the rag along the arm of the leather recliner. Since my taking on the documentary, she turned into a cleaning Nazi, shoving her hard work in my face as if to punish me for doing something outside of us.

She walked over to the loveseat and started pulling off the pillows and blankets, tossing them on the ground. She pulled off the cushions and scoffed. "We're going to get cockroaches in this place." She stormed off into the linen closet and pulled out the vacuum cleaner.

"You just sit there." She turned on the vacuum cleaner and began sucking up the crumbs from the couch not more than ten feet away from me.

She pushed the vacuum around with anger, pulling and yanking that cord, as if single-handedly taking on the battle of a lifetime against crumbs while her fiancée sat and played with photos.

I closed my laptop and stood up. "How can I help?" I yelled out over the noise.

She snapped her eyes to me. "Oh, don't worry about it. You continue to do what you're doing, and I'll clean the house." She didn't smile. She didn't blink. She closed in on herself and acted like a servant, dutifully pushing the head of the vacuum around the areas between us.

I couldn't work like that. I bent over and turned off the vacuum cleaner. "You're making me feel guilty."

She stood tall now, bracing her hands on her hips in a power stance.

191

"You've got an important job to do. So do it."

"If you wait an hour, I'll help you."

"There's too much to do to wait an hour. Just go work in the office. I'll deal with this mess." She clicked the vacuum back on and proceeded to push the head of it around my feet.

I watched her tackle the carpet, one angry sweep at a time. Her energy pounded against me like a jackhammer. It poked and pricked the air around us, creating a dust cloud that choked any positive and creative air from the room. Unbelievable. I picked up my laptop and stormed down the hall to the office. I slammed the door shut, fuming and finding it hard to find balance. I sat down to face the photos of Becca interacting with children from a school visit. Bonnie thumped and banged her way through the house. Glass broke. Doors slammed. Feet pounded.

I stood, yanked the office door open and glared at her as she moved the television console by herself. "What are you doing?" I yelled at her.

"What does it look like I'm doing?"

"It sounds like you're tearing down the house."

"Well, one of us has to do it. I suppose that someone is me by default now."

She groaned as she pushed the heavy piece of furniture out of its grooves in the carpet.

I couldn't take her passive aggressive behavior a moment longer. "Stop forcing this guilt on me for working on my dream."

She stopped pushing and stood up tall. "I knew that by taking this project on, this is exactly what would happen. You'd become so overwhelmed and busy that you'd spend your free time outside of work on your laptop. I'd get stuck doing all the dirty work."

"That's not fair."

"Exactly." She flung her hands up in the air.

"I have to work on these photos. I don't have a team of assistants doing it for me."

"Is any of this really worth it?"

I'd never been more in my element. "Of course it is."

She clicked her tongue. "I'm not even a part of your life anymore."

"It's just a few more weeks of hard work."

"Then what?"

"Then we go back to our life as it was." As the words droned out of me, my heart shriveled up like a dead leaf. "I get this new job, and we live happily ever after."

"You know what scares me?" she asked, fighting her quivering chin.

I hated when she cried. I opened my arms to her, and she folded into them. "Nothing should scare you."

"Your mind has been stretched by this whole project. You're happier. You're motivated to get out of bed at four in the morning. Once all of this ends, I don't know how I'm going to be enough for you."

I patted her back. "Well, if I get the job at *Howard County Home and Garden Magazine*, I'll have everything I need to be happy and fulfilled."

"What if you don't get it?"

"Then, I'll find another opportunity." I hugged her tighter, taking the higher road of responsibility over my selfish desires. "Problem solved."

Her body fell limp against mine, as if defeated.

# #

I texted Bonnie the moment I landed to let her know I arrived safely. "Guess what else just arrived?" she asked.

"Tell me."

"A phone call from the adoption agency. Apparently, they want to do a home inspection." Her voice rang high, reaching up to that place where fate met up with its purpose.

I should've responded with the same enthusiastic tone, but somewhere between adoption and home inspection, I panicked. "A home inspection? Already?"

"I didn't think we'd get an appointment this quickly," she said.

I didn't think she'd get the paperwork done that quickly.

I heard Becca calling my name. I looked past the luggage carousel and spotted her. She was wearing her big sunglasses and a fedora hat.

"I've got to go," I said to Bonnie. "My luggage is coming out of the carousel now."

"I love you," she said.

"Me too."

I slipped my cellphone into my pocketbook and walked up to Becca. "Aren't you supposed to be resting up for tonight?"

"Gabby's got her hands full prepping for the CRE8 photo shoot, so she asked my drummer to pick you up. I jumped in to rescue you."

"That scrawny guy?"

"Yup. That scrawny guy."

"Thank you," I said dramatically.

She smiled. "Besides, I wanted an opportunity to see you alone first." She cocked her head. "Is everything still cool between us?"

"Why wouldn't it be?"

"Well, I slashed my tire to fend off your fiancée last time we met up."

"You can take it out of my imaginary earnings."

She laughed.

We walked to the parking garage in silence. When we got to the payment

194

machine, she inserted her credit card, and we waited in uncomfortable silence. She stretched out her fingers at the credit card slot, as if willing for it to come shooting back out at her. The machine cranked out whirs and groans, and finally returned her card and receipt. She folded it into neat triangles, pressing down on each edge. The lights above us hummed, horns honked and cars drove over bumps, creating loud thuds, and still the awkward silence reigned over us.

"I don't want you to get the wrong idea," she said. "I wouldn't have crossed the line."

Her words poked at my heart. "Don't be silly. I get it. Nothing happened. No one got hurt. We're good." I sounded choppy and nervous.

She nodded. "Great. I'm glad you feel the same way."

She tucked her folded receipt in her front pocket, lowered her hat, and led me to her parked car. For the entire car ride over to the hotel, the sting of her not wanting to cross the line with me never went away. It just drove deeper, claiming its power over me.

# #

Becca and Gabby walked towards me with coffee, brushing through the crowd that came to honor the test of my idea. Kids and adults scrambled the room with their instruments, vying for their turn for their CRE8 photo.

I stood on top of a chair and focused in on the crowd. I snapped wide-angle shots with my cellphone, capturing the buzz and excitement, and then forwarded them to Gabby to post on Becca's fan page. People wore their prescribed monochromatic outfits.

"This is way too chaotic," Gabby said, handing me a coffee.

"Isn't that a good thing?" I asked, taking a sip.

"No." She spun around to face the swarm. "We need order. We need lines.

We need a system. It'll never work this way. People are going to get annoyed and kill the buzz. All it takes is one obnoxious person to tweet out to their followers that this scene sucked, and bam, we're done."

Despite the fact that I'd been worrying about the same thing, I stood up to her. "I never expected such a crowd. So, I'm pleased either way. Those teens out there," I pointed to a group with their noses in their cells, "they love crowds and chaos."

"I'm going to take care of this." She marched out of the lobby and down the hallway towards the administrative offices.

"She knows what she's doing," Becca said, still dressed in disguise, folding her arms across her chest and staring out into the crowd. "If Kara and I had listened to her back in our wild days, we could've saved ourselves a lot of headaches."

I stared out at the restless crowd. "How do you do it?"

"Do what?"

"Enjoy being in front of all these people all the time?"

Becca lifted her face to me. I could see my reflection in her eyeglasses, and I hated that I wore my hair in a ponytail for her.

"I find one or two people in the crowd who look like they need lifting and I connect with them. I pretend they need music to heal from something. It's never about the entire crowd. It's about individuals. It's about the goal. It's about the purpose of the music. My goal, every time I perform, is to offer someone the healing elements of the music. If I can lift one person by the end of a song, then I've done my job."

Her chest rose and fell as she spoke. "When you look out at this crowd, don't focus on the blur of them all together. Zero in on that one person you are helping in that one moment. Imagine her story and struggle to get there on that stool in front of you. What did she go through to get there? What can she

196

teach others through her artistic ability? Reach into her story and pull out the inspiration to help you enjoy this incredible opportunity; an opportunity to bring light to the world through the gift of music. Each time you snap that camera, you are helping to keep music alive. Without it, we're dead, lifeless, colorless, and unimpressionable."

I wanted to hear more, and I knew she had even more of a story inside her to keep going for the entire day. But, Gabby reappeared with a cordless microphone and four men carrying two rectangular tables. They cleared the crowd from in front of my backdrop and set up the tables. Gabby placed four sets of spreadsheets and pens down, and the men proceeded to sit. Gabby turned to the crowd, tapped the microphone, and ordered the room to quiet with the notice of an important announcement.

She spoke with power and explained how the day would work. "You'll need to check in at the table by last name, and then you'll be handed a number. When we call your number, you'll need to line up to the right of the photo set." She opened her arms up wide. "Now, let's get started and create some buzz," she said. The crowd cheered.

She turned to me. "Don't just stand here. Go." She pointed to my setup, and I ran towards it, afraid that if I didn't, I'd be poked and prodded with her fiery eyes.

She scared the shit out of me, but I loved it. I needed her. From the pleased look on her face as she watched the chaos start to fold into a well-orchestrated plan, I surmised she needed me too.

I had never felt more alive.

Becca followed me and helped straighten the backdrop one last time. My stomach knotted up, anticipating the rush of adrenaline.

Becca curled her arm around my elbow and whispered, "Relax, the nerves are natural. They'll subside as soon as you start clicking that camera." She

197

kissed my cheek and strolled off towards the side of the setup.

Her warmth lingered on my cheek.

Ten people were already lined up and waiting for their turn to get their CRE8 picture taken. A ten-year old girl named Molly carried her flute and a reserved smile to me. I propped her against the backdrop on a sharp right angle to my camera. She looked too stiff and unnatural. So, I had her tilt into her instrument and stare straight at my lens. I told her to imagine my lens as her music drifting away from her. The harder she stared at it, the more her eyes cradled the critical passion I sought. I snapped three photos of her and of everyone else who came through the line that day.

By the end of the day, I had snapped over one thousand photos of people and their instruments, all coming to me with a message of hope that together we would be able to keep music alive and thriving.

I closed my eyes once the crowds cleared and saw my purpose laid out before me. It stood regal, blinding me with its beauty, shining with the brilliance of rare jewels freshly harvested and waiting on their value to be shared.

# #

Later on, as usual, the applause ran through the venue like a speeding train. Then, in one sweeping, peaceful brush of Becca's fingers against the strings of her guitar, the crowd halted. That action worked like a charm each time. She controlled the stage now.

She picked up the microphone and shaded her eyes from the lights, as she scanned the crowd. "I see we've got some Red Sox fans in the house tonight."

The crowd roared to life again. She waited on their pause. Eventually, when it returned, she continued, "I've been to Boston a few times. That's where my parents met. They enjoyed their first date at a downtown tennis court."

Whistles ignited.

She bowed her head and chuckled as if hearing a private joke whispered into her ear.

She picked up a bottle of water from the floor and sipped some, and then she wiped her mouth on her sleeve. I loved that down-to-earth action.

Then, she broke out into one of her big hits, massaging the crowd over in her ingenious rhythm. At the end of her song, she sat down on a stool and adjusted her mic.

She strolled into a peaceful melody, looking up at us with a sly grin. "This next song I'm going to play, I wrote while on the road to Denver. It's about temptation."

She scanned the crowd. "Temptations lurk everywhere. We know we shouldn't indulge, but we want to so badly. We bargain with ourselves to let our guard down, just this once. What could it hurt? We'll go right back to being strict with ourselves tomorrow."

She scanned the crowd. "I'm so guilty of choosing hastily. French fries or salad? Sleep or exercise? To kiss or not to kiss?" Her eyes reached out to the crowd, and her lips curled up. The crowd jumped, clapped, and hooted. She laughed.

"I've been to that place many times where I've ignored that logical part of my brain as tempting choices have danced provocatively for me, conjuring up all sorts of flutters. I've experienced times when my heart was racing, my nerves were firing up, and my neurons were exploding and priming me for what was about to come."

The crowd held their breath.

"Yeah, the good stuff. Right?" She chuckled on a dramatic exhale. "Maybe." She reflected on the crowd. "The duel between right and wrong progresses fast. Just a nudge in either direction could change our course for good," she paused, "or for bad."

Was I 'the bad'?

"I'll kiss you Becca," someone yelled.

"I'm next in line," another woman screamed.

"I've been there. Maybe some of you have too. A flip of the switch in one direction could mean the difference between light and darkness."

Was I 'the darkness'?

"There's no darkness with you, Becca," someone yelled.

She looked at me, cradling her guitar. "Temptation is universal. It can set us back for the short-term or can wreak havoc on the rest of our lives. Thankfully, we get to choose our actions. I've never seen someone disappointed with taking the higher road."

She bowed her head and waited for the perfect moment to break into another melody that soothed over her words and transported us from a state of reverie to a new state of clarity.

Temptation knocked on my heart, begging me to open it and let it in. It wanted to steep in there and tease me with gluttonous helpings of the delicious vulnerability that served itself up front and center before me.

I wondered at what point I had become the havoc that landed her on the higher road, and landed me on the one below, looking up at her like a stupid fan.

# #

I turned down Gabby's invite to join everyone for drinks after the concert, citing a headache. And, the next day, when we donated instruments to a local school, I acted professional and hid behind my camera lens.

Later that day, I arrived home with a goal to act more like myself with

Bonnie, a person who belonged in a safe and secure bubble of a life where havoc had no chance at ruining me. Bonnie respected me. I needed to respect her too. I needed to snap out of my euphoric fantasies and stand firm in my resolve to face my promises with steel eyes, logical thoughts, and unshakable restraint.

I cooked her favorite meal, spaghetti and meatballs. We sipped wine, listened to romantic piano music, and giggled over how Zoey sat on the couch like a human being and stared at us. In between giggling over that, a silent beat stole the stage. We tried to fill the void with small talk about angry customer service calls and horrible food in the hotel I stayed at, but none of it grew into substantial dialogue.

We needed that night to work. We needed to come back together—united and stronger.

I turned to trusty Zoey for help. "Zoey, pretty girl, what did you and Mommy do while I was gone?"

"Mommy and I went for walks, cleaned the house, and met up with a nice lady from the adoption center," Bonnie said, in her high-pitched Zoey voice.

"You already met with her?"

Bonnie poured herself more merlot. "I wanted to get the ball rolling."

Dazed, I tossed my fork down. "Shouldn't I be part of the ball rolling?" All defenses rose.

"Relax. It was just to submit the paperwork. Now we wait while they review it, call our references, you know, those kinds of things." She circled her fork in the air like I should've known that stuff.

I picked up my fork again and focused on my spaghetti.

"So Mommy K," Bonnie said in her high-pitched Zoey voice. "Tell us about these photos we're seeing all over Facebook today from the CRE8 tour."

I twirled my spaghetti, sticking a forkful in my mouth so I could contemplate how to explain that one.

Bonnie reached out for my wrist, lowering my fork. "Seriously," she said in her own voice. "People were talking about it like it's a new part of the foundation. Is it?"

I nodded and my belly flipped just like it used to do when my parents sat me down to talk about a bad grade. "Remember I wanted to show you a picture the night after the first concert?"

She shook her head.

"You had a headache." I paused, waiting for her to remember. "Anyway, Gabby loved it and thought the picture told a story that needs telling. So, she organized a public photo shoot for people to bring their instruments and get their photos taken. They have stories to tell."

Bonnie bit her cheek and shifted. "And you want to tell it?" Panic rested in the tiny wrinkles lining her eyes.

"They haven't asked me to. The other night was just a test."

"What if you passed the test?" She swallowed hard.

I wet my lips, trying to capture some moisture. "I will tell them I just accepted a job with *Howard County Home and Garden Magazine*, of course."

She stretched her eyes, and they danced with a new joy I'd yet to see in them. "You got the job?"

"Not yet. But I will."

Her breathing turned shallow and her chest bobbed dangerously out of rhythm. "If you don't?"

Her disbelief in my ability filled me with a coldness that stole the strength of my voice. "I will."

She cradled her folded hands under her chin. "Everything is changing for us, isn't it?"

202

I opened my mouth, and closed it back up. I certainly couldn't go back to the life I lived prior to that project. "Change is a good thing. It means we're growing."

"I hope not apart."

Apart. The reality of that one word splintered through me. It dug into my heart, threatening the hope that I could somehow remain untarnished by my lack of self-control over my desires for a life that added up to more than adopting a baby.

I stared into her eyes, and searched for a way to prove to her that she could trust her heart in mine. But, I couldn't prove that any more than I would be able to cultivate peace in a blender.

"Don't say that." I leaned into her. "Don't ever say that."

She released a relieved sigh and opened her arms to me. "Are you sure?"

Her heart beat fast against my chest. I cradled her in close, trying my best to protect her from my dangerous dreams. "Everything will work out as it should."

# #

I met with the creative team of *Howard County Home and Garden Magazine* and blew them away. They stared at my photos with open mouths, pointing to the details I had suffered to create while I went hours upon hours without food, sunlight, and sleep. They told me they'd be in touch within a week.

I had waited forever to receive such recognition from a team of accomplished professionals. I had dreamed up ideas of how such a compliment would sit in my heart, and never did I imagine it would lift me up the way it did.

I called Bonnie right away to tell her the good news. "I'll pick up Chinese food and beer on my way home. We're going to celebrate!"

When I returned home, I sat on the couch with Zoey and let that small victory settle in. The sunlight had finally found its way into my life and illuminated the path I had sought since the day Becca broke my heart. I'd have my dream job, earning the kind of salary that would allow me to buy us a bigger place with a backyard where we could put a swing set for our future kids. Once the marriage bill got approved in Maryland, Bonnie and I could legalize our commitment, and grow old together. I would never have to worry about a life lived on the edge of the unknown, working for my best friend, and volunteering my time for my ex-girlfriend.

Yes, that made sense. That made total sense.

I repeated that mantra over and over again until it felt a little less foreign.

I hugged Zoey. "I'll keep saying this until the day I die—I have everything I need to be happy and fulfilled."

Later on, I stood in the kitchen, stirring instant coffee into boiling water when Gabby called.

"We netted over forty thousand dollars from that one photo shoot," she said.

"That's incredible."

"That's seventy-five percent more than we take in from the percentage of each ticket. Do you realize how big the potential is for this? Can you imagine how many instruments we'll be able to purchase and the awareness we'll generate?"

"It sounds like you and Becca found a winning ticket."

"What? No. It's not just us. You're the reason. You're the ticket."

"I'm just a photographer. Anyone can replicate what I did."

"No," she said. "There's something about your photos that's unique. I can't quite put my finger on it, but there's definitely something magical going on there."

My ego swelled. "I thought you had a problem with my photography. You know, those weird angles."

"Those weird angles are your signature. Don't always listen to me. I don't always know what I'm talking about. What the hell do I know about photography?"

I had a signature. "Well, I'll keep that in mind for my future work."

"You've got a future with us if you want it."

Purpose and destiny melded together and formed a new base for my feet, lifting me higher than anything, even the magazine, Bonnie, our future big house and babies. "Seriously? You're offering me a job?"

"It's more than a job. You'd be contributing to an important cause and making a huge difference to many people."

I pulled myself up on the counter and let my legs dangle. "How would this work exactly?"

"We'd plan a similar event for each concert. Becca is booked for seven months after this documentary finishes. And who knows from there. We could arrange events separate from concerts after the tour stops and keep the funds rolling in."

"So I'd be on the road constantly?"

"Well, yeah. Becca's got fans throughout the country now."

"I've got a life here. I can't just pack up and leave it."

"Sleep on it. Trust me, you'll feel differently in the morning."

# #

Bonnie and I ate Chinese food while watching her new favorite show, *Terra Nova*. In between fumbling to pick up a piece of rice with my chopsticks and slipping it into my mouth, I glanced over at her. I focused on her fixated gaze on the television, and tried to envision our life six months, a year, five years ahead. Would it just be more Chinese food and *Terra Nova*? Would we ever challenge ourselves to take up sailing or crafts or start our own foundation?

No. With Bonnie I got what I asked for. I got a future laid out for me that included safety, security, loyalty, and lots of television and fried rice.

How could I ever ask her to accept my idea of going on the road with Becca to fulfill some deep yearning to feed a life purpose?

To be a part of it, I'd have to leave Bonnie.

How could I leave her after all she'd put up with for me? She wanted to offer me a life full of security, love, and family.

I'd never find that on the road.

Didn't I want that?

She interrupted my trek down that confusing path by asking me, "So when are you going to hear back from them?" She bit into an egg roll. Pieces of cabbage and carrots spilled down to her lap.

"I'm not sure," I said, keeping our future a mystery until I could wrap my brain around it.

\# \#

One day later, Donna called me and offered me the position. "When can you start?"

Her question should've brought tears of joy and grand leaps. Instead, I bit my nails, seeking refuge from the crack between where I stood and where I wanted to stand. "I'm in the middle of photographing that documentary tour. Can I have until the end of the month to start?"

"We'll certainly wait for you. You dazzled the team. Congratulations. We're thrilled to welcome you aboard."

206

I should've called Bonnie right away. I should've cemented our future, and our children's future, with a hearty leap around the living room, jumping onto and off the couch in complete exhilaration.

Instead, I called Becca and asked her if she could swing by Maryland to have a chat.

"I'm actually visiting Margie and Mackenzie now."

#

Margie left us alone in one of her many living rooms while she went off into the playroom with Makenzie.

"Are you ever going to have kids?" I asked.

"Not with my life the way it is. That would be so unfair."

"Bonnie wants a kid now, and I'm freaking out."

She looked up. "I thought you always wanted a big family?"

I did. I dreamed of having a family with Becca before she became famous. "It scares me now."

"How so?"

My eyes wandered down to her lips as she asked the question. I traveled back up to her soft, waiting eyes. "I feel like we would just be adding a child to our life to fill a personal void."

"A child can do that. It worked for Margie."

"I don't want to use a child as a band aid." I spoke those words, and they shocked my ears.

"Go on." Becca swung her body towards me.

"Bonnie is unfulfilled. She's seeking this baby to fill that gap instead of searching outside of herself for what the real issue is."

"The real issue being?"

"She's afraid."

"Of?"

"Of losing me. I'm all she has. She stopped dreaming the day we met. She used to be filled with dreams of her own. She wanted to travel, learn Spanish and Hindi, and volunteer in a third world country where she could teach photography to little kids."

"What happened?"

"She became comfortable with us. The camera went into the closet along with her dreams, and out came endless hours of television marathons. You know, at first, I enjoyed it because I used to obsess over my work to the point of driving myself crazy."

"Yes, I remember." She pointed her eyes at me. "Just like me."

"When I first hooked up with her, we spent the first few months relaxing. This refreshed my spirit. I slid right into this lazy, comfortable lifestyle because I needed that at the time."

"I hear a 'but' coming."

"But, then that got old. I saw how everyone else got on with life, and I fell backwards, getting lazy and fat. So, I turned back to work. Now, I don't know how not to work anymore. Is it normal to want to constantly work at my skill?"

"You're asking me?"

"I'm not happy sitting idle. My mind races when I'm still. I have so much energy running through me now. I can't take a walk without jotting down an idea for setting up shots and a story. I'm sitting in front of Bonnie eating breakfast, and all I want to do is step through the door of the next tour stop so I can photograph."

She sat back, resting her feet up on the coffee table. "It's like me with my music. I can't not play. I can't go a day without jotting down a lyric idea. I have notes all over the place. Music is a part of me. No one can take that away or else I'll just die. Life isn't worth living if I'm not playing music."

She sat up, and I caught the delicate wisp of her scent. She smelled sweet and earthy like she'd just taken a walk through a field of freshly cut green grass.

"Is it worth living without having someone by your side who wants what's best for you?"

"That's a tall order," she said.

"Is it?" I asked.

"When you find that something that makes you happy, it's impossible to return to a life that doesn't encourage its growth. If the person you're with doesn't agree, how is it worth it?"

I turned my head to the side to avoid seeing my confused reflection in her eyes.

"My dreams are hurting her."

"What are your dreams?"

"I want to wake up and do something purposeful with my life," I said. "I want to make a difference. I want to know that I'm adding to and not deleting from this world."

"A child is a great way to do that."

"Not for me. I crave to take pictures. I crave to sit down and edit them. I crave to tell a story with them. It's like a hunger that is eating through me. Bonnie takes my indulging in this to mean that I work too hard. She thinks because I'm not lifting heavy furniture to vacuum crumbs or taking off a layer of skin on my hands to scrub the shower or sitting down to watch a television show with her that I'm working too hard on my dreams. She thinks that one day this will cause me to crash. I know she feels this way. I can sense it."

"How so?"

"When she enters a room and sees me in front of my computer, she inhales and exhales like she's suffering an asthma attack." I just kept tossing Bonnie under the bus to smooth over the hard choice that cornered me. "She glares at me out of the corner of her eye when I take out my camera, as if it's a drug that sends me reeling like a bad mushroom trip."

"I used to feel that way whenever I'd take out my guitar."

"With me?"

She nodded.

I winced. "I'm sorry."

"You only did it because you were missing a piece of yourself."

I lay back against the couch and stared at an angel figurine Margie hung from the corner of the room, marinating her powerful statement. "I feel like a piece of me is still missing."

"It's not missing. You found it, and now you're scared because you don't know what to do with it."

I nodded at that.

She rested her arm against the back of the couch. "Do you love her?"

"I do," I said, wavering on the words.

"If you do, then why not prove to her that she's worth it?"

My gaze strayed down Becca's long torso, past her curvy hips, and down to her stylish boots. I slowly traveled my gaze back up to her waiting eyes.

Becca wanted me with Bonnie, and that killed me.

"I will."

She reached out and twirled a piece of my hair. "Of course you will. That's who you are. You put others first." She stopped twirling and stared into my eyes. "Bonnie is good for you, isn't she?"

"Of course she is." I rested in her gaze. "But, this decision on CRE8 should be an easy choice for me. I have a job offer at *Howard County Home and Garden Magazine* on the table. So, why isn't it easy for me to walk away from your opportunity?"

She picked up my camera from the coffee table and pointed it at me. Mid snap, she said, "You're afraid."

The familiar tug at my heart and the taste of bitterness on my lips surged back in me as if I had closed my eyes and reopened them to five years prior, before Becca came home to tell me life had just taken a new turn and would get even better for us. She hit it right on. My taking the project on would change my entire life. I feared Bonnie would no longer fit into it, and I didn't know how to break someone's heart for the sake of enjoying my own selfish dream. I wasn't that careless or selfish to do that to her after all she had done for me through the rocky moments of limbo. "It would change everything," I finally said.

She reached out for my hand with her empty one, cradling my camera with her other one. "This could be an incredible change."

"You say that as though my life could use a change."

"Couldn't it?"

"What is that supposed to mean?" I asked.

"If you were happy, Bonnie would be sitting in this room with us right now, joining into this conversation and not at home worrying about why you're spending so much time away from home."

"She has nothing to worry about."

She paled. "Yes. I know that. I'm just talking hypothetically."

I frowned. "Back in the day, your venture was a sure thing. You had a signed contract and paired up with someone already bringing in the crowds. You didn't approach your decision with blinders on. For me, upending our lives for something that may never see the light from my flash is risking a lot. I'm risking the trust and faith Bonnie has put into me at being a good life partner, a good future mother, and a good provider in a world where stability

211

is no longer something that's even admired."

"Is that what you're setting out to achieve? Admiration for being stable?"

I shrugged off her accusation. "Bonnie admires that side of me. It's what she loves most about me."

"You've changed so much." She sighed. "You used to dream up a life where something like this idea would happen for you. You used to dream of spending weeks touring landscapes in search of that perfect moment when you clicked the shutter just in time to capture the essence of life happening right before your camera lens. You used to dream of being able to share that moment with every single living being on the planet. Where did that person go off to?"

As she waited on me to respond, I saw my dream die. I saw it being pulled from my heart and withering away in the shock of the cold air outside of its cocoon deep inside of me. I saw its life turn brown under the darkness of fear, and its leaves fall from its weak branches. I saw the mighty trunks of what used to be life, dismantled in a rotting heap on a ground too barren to sustain such a life force.

"Why are you challenging me like this?"

She placed my camera back on the table. "Because I see your potential, and I see it shrinking away under the protective guise of a life you're trying to escape. You're wasting a golden opportunity, and for what? For the hope that you'll find this same level of joy in a copy of *Howard County Home and Garden Magazine* that someone may or may not read?"

I slapped her across the face. "How dare you?"

Her eyes flew open wide.

Silence littered the room.

She brought her hand up to her red cheek and blinked.

Finally, she looked at me. "You think everything in life should be

212

presented picture perfect. Well, it's never going to be. It's never going to be the right time." Her voice grew loud. "If you wait for that, you're going to lose the chance. It's going to disappear and you'll be left ten years from now viewing this moment as one of those times in life when you wished you would've let your pride fall to the ground."

She stood up.

"You've got a choice. Status quo or change." She clicked her tongue. "You've got a unique gift to share and you're doing a lot of people a disservice by ignoring it for fear you're going to ruin something that should already be solid."

"It is solid." I glared at her.

"Then you should have all the firm ground you need to stand on and soar."

I wanted to protest, but no worthy argument presented itself. She brushed past me, lifted my chin with her pointer finger and gazed into my eyes. "If your love is as strong as you say it is, then trust Bonnie with this. Go to her, tell her your plan, and ask her to be a part of it."

I nodded and gulped.

"All I want, all I ever wanted, was to see you fulfilled and living out your dream." She paused before dropping her finger. "This is your chance."

She walked away. I sat for a long time, remembering her words, eating them, digesting them, and putting them to work in my restless brain. I should've been grateful that she wanted to include Bonnie in the venture. Instead, her eager encouragement hurt.

I wanted her to love me still.

I wanted her to fight for me.

I wanted her to tell me that I had nothing to fear with her, that I'd be enough, and that I would always be enough.

My fear of inadequacy remained engrained, like hearty weeds in a pesticide-induced garden.

# #

I still hadn't told Bonnie about the job offer because I was stuck on CRE8 and on Becca.

My mind's eye formed a picture of what life could be like if lived within the fruitful landscape of being the photographer for the CRE8 Foundation. I'd spend my mornings rifling through photos and selecting the shots that would inspire and flatter most. Then, I'd fire up my editing software and soften harsh lines, fade insignificant details, and zero in on the reflection of creativity and expression in the eyes of countless people. I'd showcase those beautiful images on the CRE8 website and spark up all sorts of interest and awareness on a level not seen before. For every photo I'd capture, at least ten people would see it. That was the average as I figured it. Most people knew at least ten people they'd show it off to. They'd toss it on their social networking profiles, and the awareness of the foundation would grow exponentially. With Becca's clout, perhaps we could even intrigue celebrities to come out and get their CRE8 photo taken to show their support for music education throughout schools.

The purpose etched itself like a prism, gathering up all sorts of colors, hues, and shapes and casting them onto the world. The idea reigned as one that would get recognition and place more instruments in the hands of countless needy kids; kids like Charlie who harnessed talent that the world needed to hear.

The impact could be far reaching. As Becca proclaimed all the time, the importance of music on the brain had been researched and documented as critical. We could be setting the stage for the next generation of learners in

214

the country. Who knew what talent would emerge, and not just with artists, but in all categories of science, math, language and humanities.

I envisioned many meetings spent huddling over a desk of photos with Becca. Our breaths would mix with each other's, as we discussed potential photos for important promotions.

We'd have to work side-by-side, me as her equal.

She'd look to me for direction on something she knew little about. Finally, the seat I'd reserved all those years back and forfeited had opened up and offered me the chance to prove I could take action on my dreams and principles.

Bonnie would never go for it. It wouldn't matter if I told her it would cure autism, she still wouldn't like it one bit. A few years back, I had landed where Bonnie landed now. I sat in her exact seat, staring out at a world that bent and twisted into horizons with no hint of a promising sunrise on the other side. Bonnie would question her role, her place, and her confidence. She would begin to distrust me and imagine me in all sorts of wrongful positions, making the worst choices possible for our future.

She would graze on the decision of how to be supportive to me, yet fair to herself. She might even decide, like I did, to look elsewhere for her need to be satiated. Perhaps she'd start to make new friends to keep her company while I ventured on the open road, snapping photos. Maybe at first she'd sneak around as she discovered her way through the new territory, a territory that surprisingly tickled her to the core and helped her forget that her fiancée took the first step to ruin their lives.

# #

Becca sat in the center of the stage and cradled the mic between her two hands. Even though the distance from the stage obscured my view, her wispy

215

spirit took up flight as an adorable giddiness rose up in her belly, releasing its contagious vibe onto us all.

Owning her place under the spotlight, she waved to a few people in the front row. "Hey, I've got a shirt just like that," she said into the mic.

I snapped a photo of the fan blushing and pointing to the small icon above her right breast. She screamed something out and blushed ten more shades of red. Becca swept her eyes straight ahead, covering them as if shading off the blazing sun. "Anyone out there want to hear a little bit of Johnny Cash?"

The crowd flamed to life, filling the space with chants, applause, and buzz.

She placed the mic back into its holder and drew out her beloved guitar. She broke out into the classic cover "Walk the Line."

She sang from a place deep inside where emotions brewed until ready to quench the thirst of her fans. The rhythm pulsated through my body, dissolving all time and place. I bobbed up and down in the deep sea of her tranquility, hanging onto every one of her notes. Her face etched in emotions that stretched from sadness, to empathy, to regrets. The crowd mirrored those emotions. Heads swayed and bobbed, feet tapped, and people hummed and slapped their palms to their thighs. She stole the night as usual.

When she ended, she leaned forward on her stool, moved her guitar to her backside, and picked up her mic again.

"I wrote a song a few months back about hard work and dreams."

People screamed out their joy, clapping and whistling, bracing for her song "Working Girl."

"How many people here have had a dream that they let die?"

People murmured.

"Go on, raise up your hands. Let's see." She nodded to her fans. "Come on. Don't be shy."

216

Just about everyone raised up their hands, except me. I just fixed my eyes for a moment on my camera, knowing full well the words that would soon project out of her lips.

"I've let a few die, and I regret those." She strummed.

Was I one of them?

"I almost let my dream of becoming a musician die. My internal engine refused to shut off, though." She stopped strumming. "When you have a dream, you have to protect it because there are going to be people who will tell you your dream is unrealistic."

She exhaled, resting on a long pause. "That's their fear talking, not yours."

I tightened my fingers around the camera, fighting to stay there and take on the truth of her speech.

"If I had listened to everyone in my life that said being a musician was a silly venture and a pipedream, well, I'd probably be stuck sitting in a cubical, fudging numbers all day instead of sitting up here, in front of all of you nice people, getting set to play my heart out for you." A small cry hung on the edge of her voice.

The place broke out in thunderous applause.

"Don't let someone destroy your dreams. If you want to do something, go do it. Don't sit on it and say you'll do it in another month when you can better sell your ideas to people. Nope. Procrastination in this sense is the killer of dreams."

I hated that she was right. I hated that she had me questioning my life. What did she expect me to do? Did she expect me to throw away Bonnie and go live on the road with her?

She shifted on her stool and placed her mic back in its holder.

"So, what do you say you allow me to fulfill my dream right now, which is to stop flip flapping my mouth and start playing some music?"

I tore off out of the room, unable to listen to another word or strum.

Chapter Sixteen

My parents were just as eager as Bonnie to bring a child into our lives. They cradled the ideology that parenting a child was a person's primary purpose on earth. When they met Bonnie and learned she wanted children, they were willing to remortgage their house for the cause.

Bonnie and my father were out hunting for puzzles at yard sales when my father brought up their generous offer. When they returned, they spoke about the next twenty years like they had already happened and they were reminiscing. Our child would come home in a top of the line car seat and sleep in a bedroom decorated with wood carved furniture and butterfly mobiles. She'd walk by the time she turned a year old, attend private schools from kindergarten to high school, and get a full ride scholarship based on academic credentials to three of the top rated universities for medical school.

I stopped the conversation when my father said, "And we'll call her Petunia for a nickname."

"We're not adopting a baby and calling her Petunia."

My parents believed a baby completed a family. They brought my sister, Patti, and me into the world with that romantic idea. My parents married young, right out of high school. They met in second grade on the hill on top of Mulberry Street. My father climbed on his skateboard and sped down the steep, buckling road. My mother, the ever-ready caretaker, stared on in horror

219

as he whizzed by her, waving with a shit-eating grin on his handsome face. He didn't see the avalanche of bumps in front of him, only my mother's horrified face. For that split second, he worried about his crooked teeth, his weird haircut, and his high-water jeans. He wanted to grab her attention, but not for his faults, and certainly not for his clumsiness. Airborne, he flew like a ragdoll, his arms flailing and his legs wriggling under him as he braced for impact. Impact he got. He smacked into the tar and skidded down the road on his belly before flipping over and bearing more of the road burn on his back. When he finally stopped, my mother stared down at him, slapping him across his upper arm and calling him a showoff. Under the sting of pebbles cutting through his skin, he sat up, braving the blood, and told her he would marry her one day. When she asked how he knew that, he simply said because no other girl made his belly flip over.

They spent the next ten years courting, teasing, and pining after each other until finally my father's parents allowed him to take her out on a date, the day after he turned eighteen. His father forbade him to marry her, or anyone, until he turned nineteen, at which point, he was a free man to live out his life as he so desired. So, he married her the day after he turned nineteen because he followed rules like no other man I'd ever known. Patti arrived into the world ten months later on a sunny day in mid-September. Then I came along and completed their circle a year later, the day after my sister's first birthday.

Patti followed in my parents' footsteps, marrying her childhood sweetheart, Gary. My father lightened up on his father's rule a bit and allowed her to marry Gary after she turned eighteen. So, on my birthday, my sister got married. Of course, my sister, following the road of tradition much like one would follow the road to the pot of gold, got pregnant and had Tommy one month later than my parents had her.

With Patti's circle complete, all attention turned to me.

I didn't come out to my parents until I met Bonnie. So, up until then, my mother would toss out hints to me about where I might find a nice man to date. Part of the reason it took me so long to tell them I was a lesbian was that I didn't know how to tell them they'd never get to see me marry a man and birth a grandchild with him.

I didn't know how to break that news to them.

My mother hated Becca from day one. I brought her by the house for dinner one night, introducing her as my friend, and Becca said something stupid. She told my mother that she looked just like Shirley McClaine.

Big mistake. My mother didn't agree with Shirley's ideologies.

I hit her leg under the table, and she winced. My mother wiped her mouth with a cloth napkin, swallowed hard, and told Becca that was the most insulting thing someone had ever said to her.

When Becca left that night, my mother asked me where I met her. I told her Margie introduced us. With a flicker in her eye, and looking like she'd just swallowed a tablespoon of salt, my other asked me, "Are you gay?"

I spent the next several years denying that anything more than a platonic friendship existed between Becca and me.

Then Bonnie came along. Margie had invited my parents and me to her spa holiday party, and I brought Bonnie along too. I enjoyed her company, and if my parents had a problem with it, they'd have to say so in a public setting amongst a room full of gay hairstylists.

Bonnie noticed my mother standing alone in the corner of the spa next to a table of magazines. My mother flipped through an issue of *Rolling Stone*, and Bonnie took that as her cue to break the discomfort. Not realizing she was my mother, Bonnie walked up to her and asked where she bought her shoes. They were best friends before Margie's caterers served the main course.

At the end of the night, my mother whispered to me, "I like this one." She waltzed away on my father's arm and served me a wink over her shoulder.

The very next night, my parents invited her over for spaghetti.

My mother wrapped Bonnie up in a warm hug and welcomed her to the family dinner. She even offered her the prized seat with the view of the lake and the fall foliage dancing on the water ripples.

"I'm just going to go wash my hands first," Bonnie said and scooted off down to the bathroom.

My mother leaned over and whispered to me, "I like her." She passed the bread to me. "She's more like one of us than that girl, Becca."

"Like us?"

"Regular," she said.

My mother's one word description of us sat like a rock in my stomach. She swept me to the regular side of the road where grass refused to grow, where trees died, and where the ground broke apart and crumbled. What happened to the other side of the road, the extraordinary side where flowers in every color of the rainbow bloomed, where birds sang songs, and where the sun highlighted the beauty of opportunity? I wasn't good enough for that?

We chomped and poked our way through the salad and bread before my mom invited her to my father's birthday dinner only a few weeks later. By the time we sank our forks into carrot cake, she asked Bonnie if she wanted to have children one day.

Bonnie perked up like a puppy waiting for the ball to be tossed at her. "Definitely."

"How would that work, exactly," my mother asked.

"Mom?" I shot her a warning.

"Well, I don't know how these things work. Which one of you will carry the baby or would you rather adopt? Will you pick someone you both know to be the father and ask him to donate his sperm?"

I placed my hand on Bonnie's arm. "I'm sorry."

Bonnie beamed. "I think it's cute."

My father passed the whip cream to her. "This is how we roll in our family. No secrets. Just let the thoughts out and let them hang dry." He laughed, and Bonnie joined in the laughter.

That night marked the entrance of Bonnie into my *regular* family. Whatever that meant.

That night also marked the last time we spoke about babies until she got that adoption itch.

Since that spaghetti dinner, Bonnie hung with them more than me. She and my father loved to go to yard sales together on early Saturday mornings. My father would buy the newspaper and circle the good ones. Then, they'd set out by seven in the morning and come home with a car full of junk, shouldering happiness and joking about their findings.

Bonnie had turned into my daddy's little girl somewhere between passing the whipped cream and stuffing a wooden dresser in the back of his pickup truck. That marked a wonderful step in the evolution of my father's previous need to control the trajectory of Patti's life and mine.

Control he tried. Two days before I was scheduled to leave on my second to last tour stop, he invited Bonnie and me over, along with Bonnie's parents for my birthday celebration. As I applied my makeup for the party, Becca texted me. "Wishing you a great birthday, Bumbles. Eat lots of cake, but save some room in your tummy for more when we meet up next."

In just one short message, she managed to smooth over my anger and frustration, wiping away the tall defensive wall I had built up that night on the tour.

I replied with a simple, "You bet."

An hour later, I sat with my family and Bonnie's and opened gifts.

"What does it say?" Bonnie leaned in close to me.

"For our future holiday dinners." I reluctantly pulled the card off the gift and handed it to Bonnie who looked about ready to cry.

I lifted the foiled bow off the box and slid my thumb under the paper to open it. I folded the paper back and looked down at a quesadilla maker.

"We can use it next New Year's Eve," Kelly's mother said, scooting up to get a picture of my bewildered face.

"There's another gift." My mother picked it up and handed it to me. "This one is from us."

Our mother's exchanged smiles, and it turned my stomach. I felt just like someone dropped me in the middle of a television sitcom show, and we were all acting out the parts of a well-adjusted family. Everything felt plastic and make-believe.

I didn't even get the gift opened all the way when my mother said, "What's a quesadilla maker without serving bowls?" She pointed to the serving bowl picture on the box. "Look, it even matches the red of your kitchen."

"It's nice." I peeled back the gift-wrap from the serving bowl package and handed it to Bonnie.

"This is just what we wanted," she said like a child excited about a pair of roller skates. Her shoulders curled forward as she examined every square inch of the box.

My life caved into something too domestic, too prissy, and too regimented. What next? Matching sweatshirts that said I'm hers and she's mine?

My father walked over to me and handed me an envelope. "This is from all of us." He winked, and I took it from him. I held it at arm's length, afraid to open it. I just knew whatever that envelope carried would send me down a road I didn't want to go down anymore. I grasped the envelope between my hands.

Bonnie tore it out of my hands. "You're killing me." She ripped it open and revealed a check for twenty thousand dollars made out to us both.

She handed it to me without blinking, as if invisible toothpicks secured her eyes in their wide position. "Oh my God."

I stared at my mother's handwriting. Her big, loopy cursive letters screamed out things like 'We love you. We love Bonnie as our own. Go make a future. Go get us a grandkid. Go buy a house for your beautiful family and line it with a white picket fence so we can have barbeques and play volleyball on sunny Sunday afternoons.'

My parents just handed me a ticket to their version of a picture perfect life.

I forced my mouth to move. "I don't understand," I said to my parents. "What is this for?"

"Consider it an early wedding gift." My father placed his arm around my mother's waist. They smiled like two good, supportive parents would be expected to smile.

I shook my head. "No. We can't accept this."

The grandfather clock down the hall chimed. Bonnie's mother jumped as if on cue. "It's eight o'clock. Let's make a toast on the top of this happy hour to a great life for you both."

Everyone began darting around the room, gathering their wine glasses, tucking their shirts in as they shifted, and scooping up piles of love like bubbles in a bathtub. The scene sickened me. I didn't fit into it. I stood outside a glass partition and stared in on a happy family that knew exactly where they were headed. I knocked, but they didn't answer. They tuned me out and carried on with their plans to my future without seeking my input and without regard for how confused I might've been feeling at that moment in time.

Joy bloomed on everyone's face. Bonnie wore the brightest and prettiest smile of them all. Her eyes sparkled. All of her dreams were coming true. Her engine revved, waiting on her to climb aboard and get the party started. The twenty grand served as the fuel to a new journey, erasing all worry, concern, and inhibitions to failure. We could put our foot to the pedal right now and zoom off to what I used to consider the epitome of a perfect life. With our parents on board, we had nothing more to wait for. Time ticked away just as the second hand on that annoying grandfather clock ticked. The pulsating sound reminded me that if I didn't jump off the crazy train immediately, I'd most likely have to spend a lifetime suffering the consequences of not running away that very second.

Run away I did. I jumped up off the couch and headed for the kitchen. I needed water. Fast. I leaned over the sink and splashed my face with the fresh running tap water, spilling it all over my shirt. The coolness helped ward off the nausea brewing in the pit of my stomach.

My new melded family giggled, cackled and spoke over each other in rapid succession. Their words piled on top of each other's and caused my heart to beat too fast.

My life had turned into a domesticated nightmare. I wanted my eyes to open, my mind to clear, and my body to move far away from that moment that dragged on far too long. Their cackles clawed at me, scratching my skin and leaving me prickled and pained.

I needed a bright spotlight to shine down on the dark new twist in my life and brighten the path so I could see exactly how to get the hell out of its way. Like any nightmare, the end hung in the distance, unreachable. It taunted me with its hidden resolve to keep me pinned down against an imaginary mattress, clinging to wet bed sheets and screaming out in silence to deafened

226

walls that absorbed my cries and pleads.

"Kelly?" Bonnie yelled from the living room. "Where did you go?"

I shut off the water and reached for a hand towel. I buried my face in it, pleading for the chokehold to release so I could get back to a normal life. "I'll be right in. I'm just getting some water."

A cold chill enveloped me as I stared down at my engagement ring. My purpose caught up to me. I had a life waiting for me to respond to it. Quesadillas with salsa in serving bowls didn't fit into my picture any more than a new house, a new car, and a kid did.

In trying to protect Bonnie from my success, I had distanced her.

When I distanced her, I saw the reality of what we actually were versus what I had created in my vivid mind. We clung to each other in fear, hoping we would save the other from hurt. Yet, by that clinging, we wrapped ourselves in that very hurt.

Chapter Seventeen

Becca sat before us and fingered her strings, gifting us in audible sweetness. "I watched a movie recently with the brilliant Will Smith and his son Jaden. Will's character talked about fear. I'm going to botch this up, but he said something to the effect that fear is silly because what we fear has not even happened yet. Fear is premeditated. We fear a possible outcome. We play the scenario in our head, and the effect is always amplified. Isn't it?"

"Fear is useless," someone yelled.

She pointed to the person and cocked her head. "This next song I'm going to play for you is one I wrote after I freaked out over a spider."

People laughed and hooted, pumping the air with their fists.

"Fear stops a lot of people from doing the things in life they want to do. I'm going to go on the edge here and say some even fear succeeding."

She picked up a glass of water and took a swig. "You're probably thinking, *that's a little strange, Becca. Fearing success*?" She arched her eyebrow. I snapped a photo of that moment.

"We want fame, fortune, and success, yet we have no idea what that can bring into our life. Lots of great stuff, no doubt. But it's the residual leftover of a former life that burns and causes us to stop and say, hey, this success thing is scary stuff." She stretched out her words. "My life is about to change, and that scares the crap out of me."

229

Her eyes grew wide, and the fans flickered to life.

"So many people stop just short of accomplishing great things because they fear what will happen once they cross over to the other side of the road."

Her words rang a truth that ate right through any arguments of her deservedness that still lingered in the far reaches of my mind. She lifted me to higher ground and created a sense of wild abandonment in me, like I could raise a two-ton vehicle with my pinky. How did she get such a gift? Did she lift people out of defeat and gift them with the illusion of invincibility?

Her enthusiasm attached itself to me and worked as a hydraulic pedestal, raising me up so high even the clouds tickled my core. A free spirit like Becca could craft all sorts of ideals, despite how wild they were, and sprinkle them around people as if their mere presence would solve all of life's problems.

She picked at her strings and stared right at me.

"Don't run from fear. Embrace it, unless of course, this fear comes in the form of a tiger staring you down while licking its chops. Then, you're up shit's creek, my friends."

She strummed her guitar and laughed.

The crowd cheered, and the louder they got, the bigger her presence on that stage grew. Her fans sung along with her, reciting her lyrics word for word and sharing the same passion for her music.

She could really hurt me all over again if I didn't watch myself.

# #

The next morning, we visited a school to drop of more donated instruments. Becca sat with a blond boy wearing baggy jeans and a rumpled shirt that hung two sizes too big for his small frame. He showed off his red guitar to her. "My father painted it himself before he went to war."

"Do you record yourself playing it for him?"

"He died in Afghanistan."

The room hushed.

"I'm so sorry." She bowed her head.

"It's okay," he said, swallowing hard.

"Play it. I want to hear it," she urged.

He cradled it in his scrawny arms and strummed an unfamiliar melody. He closed his eyes and dove into a harmonious song that brought chills to me.

I squatted down to get a picture of him in his moment of glory when the entire classroom stopped taking in air to hear him play. I looked away from my finder to let my brain ignore the obvious details and get a grasp of the far more important underlying structure. That red guitar, with its bold shape and color, created a perfect composition. I positioned the guitar to sit front and center with the boy off to the right. I clicked just as he opened his eyes and looked my way. His face told a story in and of itself of a young boy who found power through music. His chin pointed up just so, and his eyes commanded a power similar to that of great leaders.

Later on, his teacher told us, "After his father died, he withdrew from talking, from smiling, and from completing schoolwork. His grades slipped below passing, and the principal suggested he take music lessons at the school. As soon as he started, his mood shifted. He became alert, talkative, gregarious, and his grades improved. Music saved him and pulled him from the wreckage of depression. Now he plays each song for his father. Music is his connection to him. Without this music program, who knows if he would've pulled out of the sadness?"

The picture took on a whole new meaning. In it, I saw the connection, the pride, and the love on his face. That picture was the perfect representation of the CRE8 Campaign.

"This photo makes a bold statement," Becca said later on as we sat across from each other sharing a Mai Tai served in a fish bowl. "It's saying to me, don't you dare tell me music isn't important. Take it away and see what kind of destruction you cause. This instrument is part of me. Taking it away from me is like cutting off a limb.'"

Chills erupted.

"It's showing instead of telling," I whispered.

"Exactly," Becca said.

The two of us eyed each other, nurturing the visual gift that could eventually change the way people viewed music.

As we drank, my desire for her grew. My foot kept inching closer to hers. We drank some more. We began dancing our feet around under the table, sharing long gazes over our near empty fish bowl drink, and daring the occasional glance down to each other's lips.

Three drinks later, I invited her up to my room to look at some of the edits I'd done from our last school visit. All business like, she agreed on a nod and a nonchalant smirk.

Once we got to my room, I showed her my edits. We sat on the edge of the bed and looked at them. At one point, I braved closer to her, brushing her hair away from her cheek. I moved in closer to kiss her, and she backed away. "No. You don't want to do this."

I pulled back and fell back against the mattress with my arms outstretched. My belly was full from so much liquid. She snuggled up beside me, resting her head in the crook of my arm.

She tucked me under my covers and kissed my forehead. I closed my eyes, comforted by the familiar scent of her, and fell asleep.

# #

I woke up to find her staring out the window. Her waves from the night before relaxed and fell softly past her shoulders. The sun danced along her arms and profile. I sat up, pulling the blankets up with me. "I'm sorry about last night," I said.

She turned to me and bathed me in her sweet smile. "Care to tell me what that was all about?"

I patted the bed.

She strolled over to it, not taking her soft eyes off me.

"I wanted to be sure about my decision."

She bowed her head. "Kissing each other would've just clouded your judgment. You should choose the road that'll bring you the most happiness ten years down the road."

"How do I know which one that will be?"

"The one that won't disappoint you." She ran her finger through my hair. "We both know that I can't be counted on to prevent that from happening."

Disappointment pooled into every fiber, every molecule, and every nook and cranny of my soul. "Do you ever see yourself settling down, Becca?"

"I could never drop this lifestyle into someone's lap." Her voice carried a wistfulness, reminding me of an ocean's spray on a cool, fall day; its echo always refined, yet never complete.

"I guess you're sort of stuck with it at this point." I smirked.

"I love it, honestly. I love the lights, the audience, and the rush of the moment. Being on that stage is like home to me. It's where I would want to die, playing my favorite song to an eager crowd. I tried to live without the music, and I couldn't. Life is far too boring without it. I can't be that person who sits in front of a television set for hours each night or the girl who can

233

spend her night curled up with a good book in a bathtub with Mozart playing in the background. I need the stage. Without it, my engine would just cut off and sputter. I freak out a little when I imagine my hair graying and my face wrinkling, and not having this platform anymore. By then, who's going to want to come hang with a gray-headed, eighty-year-old, right?"

"You don't see a time when you'll be ready to buy a house, get a dog, get married, have a kid or two and teach them how to play guitar in your band?"

She dropped her hands and hugged her chest. "I wish I could have that one day. It's like I have to choose one or the other, though. At least this way, I know how to deal with it all, and no one gets hurt."

"Makes sense." I forced a grin on my pained face and searched the counter for my pocketbook. "I should call Bonnie. She's probably worried about me."

"She seems like a nice person who just needs to know she's special. You gained strength when you became friends with her. You never stood up to me before then. That day you broke it off with me, you came at me with a fire in your eyes. I'd never seen such fight in them before. You stood up for yourself. I figured that girl Bonnie must have inspired you with some power talk before you arrived that night."

I fumbled for words while she stared at me. "I...she opened my eyes. You were ridiculous. You disrespected me."

"How? By living out my dream? See, that's what I mean. If *you* can't understand it, how could I ever expect anyone to?"

The sting from an old wound reopened. "You cheated on me. Admit it. You adored Kara, and I just got in the way."

"I didn't cheat," she whispered. "I would never do that to you."

Placing a hand on my shoulder, she spoke to me in a slow, delicate tone as if to ensure I understood every emotion behind every syllable. "I caved into a lifestyle that I wouldn't wish upon anyone. It can be intoxicating and fun, but it's also poisonous to anyone with a dream of living a life of comfort, security, and familiarity. I would never put someone I love through the agony of fame ever again."

"Agony? You said you loved this lifestyle?"

Her eyes softened, reminding me of the beautiful lady I fell in love with back when we were young and full of dreams. "I do. But, it's not for everyone. This isn't a normal life."

Normal. The word alone bored me.

# #

All logic pointed to taking the job at *Howard County Home and Garden Magazine*, marrying Bonnie once and for all, and adopting a baby. That life would afford me the opportunity to participate in artistic work and live a life where I wouldn't have to worry what the next bend in the road would do to my balance.

Logic and passion existed on different wavelengths, however.

I could only trust the path of logic.

Yet passion burned so bright, it blinded me from finding logic's path.

I stood before Bonnie with my unpacked suitcase from my latest trip in one hand, and my camera in the other, ready to unload my truth and free her from a life of regret. "We need to talk."

Her chin quivered and tears sprang.

"Why are you crying?"

Her lips buckled under the pressure of her emotions. She shrugged and folded over.

I dropped my suitcase and placed my camera on its top. "Stop it. Stop crying." I massaged her back.

She bowed her head lower and broke into sobs.

235

"Stop." I softened my touch even more, circling my hand to ease her. "Please don't cry."

"I don't want to lose you."

She fell feeble in my arms. I caressed her head against my chest. She sobbed more, and it tore at my heart knowing I had caused that. "You aren't losing me." I lifted her chin so I could put an end to her pain. "Guess who is starting at *Howard County Home and Garden Magazine* next Monday?"

Chapter Eighteen

I sat across from Becca as she warmed up for her second to last tour stop on the documentary. The camera crew was setting up around us for her pre show interview.

We small talked about the weather and about how Kara's single just flew to the top of the Indie charts last week.

Bracing for the inevitable, I gripped my chair and launched my final decision at Becca. "I've accepted the position at *Howard County Home and Garden Magazine*, and they need me to start on Monday."

She leaned back in her chair. "So you're not taking the CRE8 position?"

"I'm not taking the CRE8 position."

"If you're starting Monday, that means you're not going to be there for our last school tour stop?"

"They need me on Monday." I bit my lower lip.

"The school is right around the corner from your condo," Becca said. "You're just going to leave us like that?"

"I need stability. This is my shot at it. I can't live on the road and have a family at the same time."

Becca braced her hands on her quads. "So you *do* want a family now?"

"It's what people do when they grow up. They graduate college and get real jobs. We're not all folk musicians with a string of top hits falling in our laps like confetti."

"Does Bonnie realize how important this is?" Her voice rose louder.

"I promised her my full attention after this documentary."

"Doesn't she want you to live out your dreams? If she loves you like you say she does, she would accompany you on this journey and do whatever it takes to see it through for you."

"I owe her the same. We can't both simultaneously pursue our dreams. She's been there for me. I can't just turn my back on her. What kind of a selfish person would do that?"

"My point exactly. Your opportunity is right there for you. It came first. Hers is still in processing. So, why isn't she stepping up and seeing yours through first?"

"I don't have to listen to this." I picked up my camera.

"You're short changing yourself," Becca said. "You found your calling, and you're willing to turn your back on it because you're afraid of realizing your full potential."

"That doesn't make any sense."

"No?" Her eyebrows furrowed. "You're afraid of realizing your full potential because when you do, the guilt hits hard. You feel guilty that you succeeded, and at the price of everyone around you. People will view you as selfish for going after what you've always dreamed of achieving."

"I've always dreamed of landing a stable job with a stable company. That's what I'm getting."

"The Kelly I know wants more than stability."

"You don't know what I want."

She glared at me. "Then, I stand corrected." She stood up, grabbed Tangerine Twist and left me alone, dazed and wiped off balance from her sudden and unexpected fight for me.

# #

Becca picked up the mic. She fidgeted on the stool, cleared her throat, and then settled her eyes on me. "As many of you know, I started out in a duo with someone you might remember. Yes? No?" She asked the crowd.

Cheers and whistles emerged.

"Well, as you might guess, that whole time of my life blurred before me. From the moment I climbed that first stage at a house party, life would never be the same. One minute I stood on the stage in a backyard, performing under a blanket of stars and worrying about how I would pay my electric bill, and the next, I zoomed forward to stages that stood before thousands of people. I didn't know up from down, left from right, or black from white at that point. The dream of what could be danced on my taste buds like creamy milk chocolate; smooth, rich, and heavenly."

She paused and swigged some water. "I opened my eyes and it was like I had instant access to the fast track of where the real movers and shakers were going. My life transformed from nights spent watching reruns on television to parties, gigs, and crazy adventures. Like someone flipped a switch in me, I changed. Just like that." She snapped her finger.

"But then reality caught up to me. This instant fame created an egotistical monster in me. I wasn't successful. I was lucky. There's a big difference between the two."

I stopped clicking pictures.

She fingered her strings. "After suffering through a good dose of reality, I learned you can't force success. You can only turn your attention to what you love, and hope that eventually success will find you in its rightful time."

She broke into a bluesy lullaby of a song, sweeping me up into her melancholy.

# #

The night before my first day on the job, Margie called and told me that Gabby and Becca hired a photographer. I doubled over from the blow like I'd been punched, stomped on, pushed onto some backroom storage shelf, even though I tore up the contract to disengage from the journey.

"Who is she?" I asked, as if I had any right to that information.

"She's someone who worked with Kara. She photographed her new CD."

That same night, I dreamed that I scaled the steep side of a mountain, and the notches to rest my feet disappeared, leaving me with no options. A stifling panic entrapped me, and I clung to the side of a rock formation too mighty to conquer without the help of those precious notches that were so plentiful near the base. A childhood fright took over me. I couldn't raise my voice high enough to be heard. I looked down the few hundred feet to the uneven ground and wondered if I would die on its rocky, unforgiving surface. All that worrying and putting off for tomorrow crap didn't matter anymore now that I hung like a child, vulnerable to the lack of planning I'd done up until that point.

I just climbed that rocky mass assuming, as I always did, that I could move forward and all would eventually turn in my favor. Yet, there I clung, with my fingers slipping, and my feet clamoring for solid ground, shifting to find a safety that couldn't be found. I just assumed I'd be protected on the journey, never caving into the idea that my spontaneity would be the demise of me. Had I slipped into a dream? Had I stumbled upon an accurate reflection of my life?

I looked up and saw the promise of more notches. If only I could climb up a few feet, I'd be there, at the tip of hope and continuing on my journey. I wanted to spring off the rock and reach the next notch in one brave, bold leap, having full faith that I had the strength and power to do anything I set my mind to. Then a shot rang out in the distance. I looked off past the dusty open space towards a tree line, hoping to find the person who could save me from the massive, eventual fall. I saw nothing through the swirls of dust but the leaves of trees that were too beautiful to be real in such a desolate landscape. I squinted, and the dust began to sting my eyes. I heard another shot and closed my eyes to catch a better reading on where it originated. That was when I heard a child laughing and calling someone's name.

I opened my eyes and saw Bonnie lying next to me, covered in her favorite pink velour blanket, snoring gently, her hair bunching up around her neck, and her eyes closed without a wrinkle of concern.

I heard the shot again and spread my arms out in back of me, lifting my torso off the mattress. My neighbor, Bobby, laughed again, and then I heard the familiar knock of the basketball bouncing against the backboard of his net in the parking lot. His early morning ritual drove through me like rusty nails.

"Is everything okay?" Bonnie asked with one eye still sealed shut.

I settled into the room the way one would ease into a cold pool, one blink and one heartbeat at a time. "Yeah. I just had a strange dream."

She opened up her other eye. "Tell me about it."

I picked up my cell from the nightstand, unsure I wanted to open that box of questions. "I can't remember the details anymore." I leapt out of bed and headed to the bathroom.

The curious side of Bonnie wouldn't be undeterred from my rapid ascension out of the potential moment of intimacy where I could spill all that cluttered my soul to her, and she could single-handedly catch all my fears and discard them in one clean and simple swipe. "Wait," she called after me.

Her footsteps tapped out the silence I needed to comb through the stress in my head. I needed to be alone. I needed to shut myself off from her, from

Becca, from *Howard County Home and Garden Magazine*, from our potential child, from everyone. My sanity depended on my ability to stop the world from moving and just 'be' for a few moments. "I've got to jump in the shower. I can't be late for my first day."

Thirty minutes later, I emerged, and she handed me my lunch tote. "Good luck today."

I walked out the front door and the cool air hit my face, waking me up to a refreshing confidence that I could straighten everything out in my life.

My new job was in the same exact office space as when I worked for their competitor. They had taken over the office suite when my former company couldn't afford to keep their doors open at that satellite location.

I parked in the same spot that I used to park in. I walked the same path to the front door, past the potted plants that still took up their prime position along the south edge lawn, and through the double doors. The air still smelled as moldy and archaic as it always did.

I walked up to the receptionist. "Hi, I'm here for my first day."

"Your name?"

"Kelly Copeland."

She searched a list. "Ah, yes, there you are." She circled my name with a pink highlighter. "Oh you'll be working in marketing, I see. Fun bunch." She folded her hands in front of her. "Just go down the hall, take a right then a left, and you'll be in marketing."

I could walk the path with my eyes closed. I strolled by the bulletin boards that showcased important spreads. I'd stapled my fair share to that board.

When I finally got to marketing, I spotted Donna. She wore a pink button down blouse with gray pinstriped pants and a pair of heels. She wore her hair tied back in a low ponytail, and it shined more than any other fifty something year-old person's hair would. Margie sure had a magic touch.

242

She walked towards me with her arms extended out. "Welcome."

She introduced me to my new work family, same personalities as the old marketing department, just different faces. I placed my pocketbook and lunch tote on Bonnie's old desk, my new home. She'd get a kick out of that. I sat in my new chair and got acquainted with my new office digs. The light above my head crackled and twitched. The cubicle walls were grayer than I remembered. A list of employees and their extensions hung on my wall. Lila, a young graphic designer, placed a pile of back issues on my desk. "It's probably good to get acquainted with the spreads." She adjusted her shirt and scrambled off to two cubicles down.

By mid-morning, I'd flipped through every issue of *Howard County Home and Garden Magazine* for the past two years. The tech people still hadn't furnished a login to the system. So, I opened my drawers and flicked around the thumbtacks and Post-it notes, creating mental notes that I'd need to bring in some office snacks, like gum, hard candy, and maybe some almonds.

Bored, I stood up and gazed around the silent room. The tops of heads bobbed around the upper walls of cubicles. Some had curls, some spikey hair, and some were bald.

My word. What would I do with the next six hours?

Donna came by my cubicle around eleven o'clock and apologized for not being available on my first day. She recommended that I read the employee handbook. Then, she promised to meet with me after lunch to see if I had any questions.

She walked away, and I just sat there feeling numb. At eleven forty-five, my mind tripped over the school visit and buckled at the thought of the new photographer. She would snap photos of Becca while she talked with kids and passed out instruments.

I turned to the employee handbook to avoid looking at my watch any more.

At lunchtime, I opened up my tote bag and pulled out a peanut butter sandwich. That was our typical lunch when we used to work together. She also packed an apple and Fritos, my other two companions back in the day. On top of that, Bonnie placed a note. I unfolded it with care, basking on the hope that whatever it said would quell the anxiety that had settled in that morning back in the parking lot. I opened it and it read: Dear Future Mommy K, Our FUTURE starts today. Love you lots, Future Mommy B.

I stared at it, and my heart tightened. I closed my eyes to block out the blinking fluorescent bulb above me. The murmur of people chewing their bagged lunches pounded in my head. I opened my eyes and landed back on the employee extension list. Jack, Liz, and countless other names would become my new source of companionship in that beige, barren, moldy smelling building. I opened up my peanut butter sandwich and bit into it. The bread tasted stale and stuck to the roof of my mouth, lodging itself as if trying to escape the room, too.

I looked at the note again, crumbled it up, and tossed it in the trash along with my tasteless sandwich.

At two o'clock, I met with Donna, and she discussed the rules of the workplace. The workday started at eight-thirty and ended at five-thirty. I could use my five days of vacation time after my six-month probationary period, and I couldn't use them during the holiday season. Headphones and cellphones were not allowed in the cubicle. If I had no projects, I should take the opportunity to study past layouts. Oh, and I should bring in five dollars each week to participate in Bagel Wednesday. "Any questions?"

"No." I stood up, walked back to my cubicle, and thumbed through the same magazines again until the clock struck five-thirty, at which time, I bolted

244

out the door to freedom and fresh air.

I inhaled the early summer night air like I'd spent the past decade curled up in a cave with no access to oxygen.

I jumped into my car and bowed my head against my steering wheel. "It'll get better. It has to get better."

I drove out of the parking lot and sped past the building aglow with its sickening fluorescent lights.

I glanced back at the road and suddenly a car, going the wrong way down the one-way street, approached in the distance. I panicked and swerved off to the side of the road. The car in front of me continued to drive forward.

The cars hit, and an obnoxious explosion followed. My eyes zeroed in on the debris flying in the air. Metal, tires, and God only knew what else littered the road. Then, an eerie silence followed as if someone had just hit the pause button on the remote control of life. My heart stopped beating. I couldn't swallow. A high-pitched ring pierced what little part of me didn't hurt. The sun, in its lowered position, lit up the doomed scene—a pile of wrecked and twisted metal sat a couple of hundred yards from me.

My heart started to beat harder, pounding, creating a complete conflict to the void straight ahead. My legs shook. I couldn't stand on them when I exited my car. Cars lined up behind me, stopping in the middle of the typically busy road. A man ran past me towards the tangled mess, yelling out for me to call 911. I crawled up to my seat and pulled out my cell. My fingers would not work. For the life of me, I couldn't press the button to call. Another person, an older lady with cropped, silver hair emerged next to me. I handed her my cell, pleading with my eyes for her to make the call. She took it from me, stared in shock at the scene in front of her, and made the call.

I bent over at my knees, and the lady stood there, massaging my back, telling me I would be okay. Would I? Really?

"If I had been ten seconds earlier," I finally said.

"Shh. Don't think that way."

I doubled over and threw up.

The road remained closed for an hour. When the tow truck pulled the wreckage down the road, the silver-headed lady dropped her arm from around my shoulders and wished me well. The cop who took my statement reminded me to stay tuned because I would most likely be called in should the case go to court. "Are you okay to drive," the young cop asked me.

"I might just sit for a little while longer."

"Is there anyone you can call?"

I looked up and down the street, and for the first time since standing there, I realized I didn't need anyone else at that moment. "I'll be okay."

He tipped his hat to me. "Just be sure to keep your hazard lights on."

"Will do," I called after him.

I climbed back into my car and exhaled, dipping my head to the steering wheel.

Like a halogen light just went off in my brain, the reality blinded me. I'd spent my whole life trying to create a life of safety and security, only to end up on the side of the road, trembling because life didn't operate that way.

# #

I drove home once my legs stopped shaking, and when I walked into the condo, I went to the bedroom to find Bonnie. She was watching television on our bed.

I walked past her and into the bathroom.

I sat down and petted Zoey's head. She stared up at me with her sad eyes.

Could a person really be fulfilled in a life that didn't allow for growth and discovery of her purpose and destiny? To stay fresh, didn't love need space?

246

Shouldn't a person enjoy the spectacular rush of watching her partner soar to new heights, instead of forcing her to live her life on the ground when she belonged in the air?

How could love grow when restrained with fear?

I wanted my life to mean something. I wanted to leave something behind. I couldn't do that from the safety of my condo. I couldn't protect a dream that didn't belong to me and pretend to love a person I didn't love. We couldn't love each other in the way we both deserved to be loved.

I kissed Zoey's head. "I'm so sorry, girly. I'm so so sorry."

I rose and walked back into the bedroom. "Can we talk?"

She pointed the remote at the television, clicked off the news, and offered me her undivided attention.

The moment of truth had arrived like an uninvited guest would show up on Christmas morning to steal the tranquility. I pulled in my bottom lip and stared into her eyes. "Something's wrong with us," I said on the release of a pent up puff of air.

Her eyes, now unfocused and watery, moved side to side too fast to follow. Her shoulders rose and fell in successions far too exaggerated. Her chin quivered under an apparent storm of emotions churning in her innocent heart. She slid off the bed, bent over at her waist, and clutched her knees.

I braced against my strength and placed my shaky hand on her back, searching for the right words to open a dialogue that needed opening. I dug around for something, anything that would be loving and not hurt her. All I found were lies and words covered in a milky film I could no longer wipe away. We were drowning under the power of my dreams and treading a river too enigmatic to defend against. The river's will to progress and forge new territory was too powerful against my desire not to hurt us.

"I'm sorry," I whispered, massaging her back with my fingers. "I've
247

realized something today."

She pointed her pained eyes at me.

"I realized that I've been chasing success, and it's not something you can chase. It's something that happens when you finally realize you love what you do. I love contributing to a great cause. I love photographing people. I love the idea I came up with for CRE8. That's my idea. That's my dream. That's my success story. And, I'm not there to see it through."

"Well, that's not the life we talked about living," she said. "What about adopting a special needs child, getting married, and buying that house we've talked about? That's our success story, and CRE8 is not a part of that."

"That's never been my definition of my success story."

"What about ours?"

"That's yours. It's always been yours. I don't want to hold you back from that, just as much as I don't want you to hold me back from mine."

"That's selfish," she cried out.

"No," I said. "Selfish would be continuing to pretend that your dream and my dream are the same. They're not even close. They're on different sides of the spectrum. By pursuing my dreams, I'm pulling you away from yours. By pursuing yours, I'm falling farther away from mine. That kind of story doesn't end well."

Our world folded in on itself, shoving us into its creases and shutting off the circulation of our heartbeats. I changed. She changed. We'd never be able to unfold and iron out the wrinkles. I stretched us too far, and now the easy, relaxed fit of our former life had been too exposed to return to its normal comfortable shape.

We just stared at each other, caught up in our anger and judgments, each grasping onto what we wanted as if we owned it.

"I want you to be happy for me," I whispered.

Her shoulders dropped. "You're ruining everything," she whispered back.

I nodded, unable to fight off the truth in her statement. "I'm sorry."

Hurt painted a haze over her bright eyes. "You're sorry."

"I'm truly sorry."

"So, it's over for us?"

"Yes," I whispered.

She vetted a moan and pulled away from me. Then, she began her slow waltz out of the bedroom and down the hall. I stayed put, watching her small figure move like that scared child in my dreams, unable to provide her with the notch to rest in order to gain enough power to get to the next level of her journey.

I followed her down the hall and into the living room where she sat as if a book rested on her head, tall, unwavering, and defending against whatever firestorm of litter I had just tossed at our past and her future.

#

I sat in my car in the parking lot of McFadden's and called Margie. "I just broke it off with Bonnie."

"I'm so sorry. Are you okay? Do you need me to come over?"

"I'm okay. I just feel so sad for her. The last thing I wanted to do was hurt her."

"You did the right thing. You loved her as a friend, not a lover. You would have hurt her more by staying."

"I know." I bobbed my head up and down, convincing myself I had done the right thing for both of us.

"So now what?" she asked.

"Now, I start on the next leg of my journey, I suppose."

"Well, my in-law apartment is yours. Shall I leave the door open for you tonight?"

"I was hoping I wouldn't have to beg," I joked.

"It's yours for as long as you need it." She paused, then added, "I love you, kiddo."

"I love you too."

I hung up and drew a deep breath, bracing for the next step in life.

# #

I entered McFadden's pub through the back entrance. The film crew splayed their lights on Becca as they interviewed her for her final performance of the documentary. The new photographer, a girl about twenty years old with a face of freckles and strawberry blonde hair, hung back next to me, snapping photos of the scene. "Getting any good shots?" I asked.

She looked up with shy eyes. "Yeah, I think so."

"I photographed the tour up until tonight."

She just looked down at her camera.

"Can I see?" I asked.

She nodded. "Sure."

She handed me her camera, and I flipped through them. "You've got some great stuff here."

Her eyes twinkled. "Thanks."

I handed her camera back.

She fidgeted, and then she said as she walked away, "I should get some more shots."

Gabby came and stood beside me, crossing her arms over her chest. "The walls of McFadden couldn't keep you away, could they?"

I simply shrugged and stared straight ahead at Becca who was smiling and answering questions while cradling her guitar.

A few minutes later, as Becca answered her final interview question, and the crowd behind us stirred with impatient energy, Gabby turned to me. "So, how's our new photographer? Anything good that you saw?"

I leaned up towards her ear. "You could take better photos with your cellphone," I whispered. The, I walked towards Becca.

Her laughter reached out to me from behind, wrapping me in a familiar comfort.

I approached Becca with small steps. She looked up at me with her soft brown eyes. "You came," she said so low I might've missed it had I not been so engrossed in her.

I stood before her as a woman ready to shed her fears, her guilt, and her feelings of inadequacy for the sake of rising to her purpose.

"You were right."

"About?"

"The Kelly you know me to be wants more than stability."

Her cheeks reddened and brought love to her face. "Oh, Bumbles."

I moved in close to her and placed my hand on her cheek, ignoring Gabby. "I get it now. I get where I went wrong before."

Gabby rushed up to us. "This isn't the time to get all sentimental. You've got an anxious crowd out there, and Joe is pacing."

Becca rested her hand on my waist, welcoming me to continue.

"I wanted to restrict you from your dreams because they scared me." My voice broke. "They threatened us."

She traced my trembling chin with her finger.

"I feared letting go of you because I feared you'd realize you didn't need me anymore. When you did realize this..." My chin quivered. "I felt inadequate, hollow, and completely lost."

Tears brimmed in her eyes. Her chest rose and fell in quick beats.

251

I continued. "You hurt me so badly that I never wanted to experience that pain again."

Gabby tapped our shoulders. "Seriously, this has to end. You need to go on now."

"Go on," Becca said, not taking her eyes off me.

"Bonnie protected me against it. She buffered me from getting lost in you again. And now…" I cried out. "Now that I've found myself, and love myself, and understand who I am deep down inside," I paused searching for the right words, "Bonnie can't protect me anymore. I don't need her safety net anymore. It's blocking me from embracing my own journey."

"Bumbles," she said, pulling me in closer to her. "You have no idea how happy that makes me to hear this."

I lifted her chin like a woman in charge of destiny, and brushed my lips up against hers. "I love you so much," I whispered.

She responded with a passionate kiss. "I love you more," she whispered.

I embraced the moment, allowing her love to seep deep inside of me and melt the walls I'd built to keep her out.

"Promise me something?" she asked.

"Anything," I said, placing my love on each corner of her lips.

"When you take that CRE8 photo for me, you'll leave out the lines around my mouth this time?"

I pulled away, and she winked.

I punched her butt, as she moved towards an impatient Gabby.

Becca turned one last time to kiss me again. Then she tore off towards the stage, towards her fans, and towards her dream.

Gabby crossed her arms over her chest again. A warm glow smoothed over her sun-wrinkled skin. "Does this mean I can fire the new photographer?"

I folded my arms over my chest in quiet sisterhood. "Let the poor kid have one night of glory to put on her resume."

"Fair enough," she said. "I suppose we all have to start out on the journey somewhere."

One Year Later

On the anniversary of our first CRE8 campaign photo shoot, I stood in the lobby of the concert hall and looked at my Facebook newsfeed. Bonnie posted a picture of Zoey wearing her Pet Therapy vest. Cliff posed with her outside the entrance to Land View Nursing Home with a sunny grin on his face. Together, they entertained the patients, Zoey with her charm and Cliff with his brilliant piano concertos.

I 'liked' the post then put my cellphone away.

I stood in the lobby where people swarmed around me, primping and prepping, applying lip gloss and hairspray, and deciding which side of their face they should photograph. I scanned the room and my eyes met up with Becca.

She shined from across the room, incognito. Our eyes continued to remain locked, despite the occasional head popping up in our range. She tucked a piece of her hair behind her ear and grinned at me like she cradled a secret she wanted to share. Even among the chatter, laughter, and the beat of the frenetic energy waving around us in wide circles, I found my center of gravity and home within the love that danced on her face.

I couldn't predict what the next hour, the next day, the next month, or the next year would bring us. That didn't matter. I only cared about the magic we were creating right there and then. The people buzzed to life around us

255

because Becca and I joined forces and decided we were stronger together than we were apart.

We walked towards each other, bumping arms, legs, and heads, willing to risk a twisted ankle, a broken toe, even an accidental punch in the face. I'd risk my heart and my life for her. When she landed in front of me and placed her hand in mine, a feeling of love from deep inside spread outward and embraced the two of us.

We were no longer forfeiting our chance to live a magnificent life. We were living it.

We refused to place a little white flag of surrender at the foot of the mountain. No. We held hands and trudged up that path together, lifting each other to higher ground, to safer notches and to extreme heights. We ventured onward, excited to see the new view that had enriched our lives, and thus the lives of many others. We were so blessed to have woken up in time to enjoy our journeys wherever they may have been taking us.

The taste of a fruitful journey never died. It continued to blend into new flavors the longer we fed it. To thrive, doubt couldn't be part of our recipe. We had to discard it along with the scraps, never souring our taste buds with its bitterness and lack of regard for seasoned spontaneity.

Sometimes in life, the best recipes came from sprinkling in ingredients we never dared to blend before. Taking risks with spices livened things up and got us past that barrier of traditionalism where people crawled to their deathbeds from their bland and banal lives.

Who knew where the road would take us. We could end up on one that spread out before us as flat, lifeless, and straight. Or we could encounter a path that had more twists and turns than a crazy eight. I always veered towards the road where I could see exactly what life wanted to toss at me. On such a road, I could plan and defend against sudden thrusts of nature. I could assure myself that I could control most anything that crossed in front of me, because I'd always know before I ventured upon it.

That was my past.

I'd rather shrivel up and die under an extreme desert sun than end up on a road like that now.

With Becca, I never knew what would jump out in front of me and set my heart racing. We traveled along a new, unchartered and unplanned path. Hope sprinkled its brilliance on us, and offered the necessary space for something exciting to happen every time I opened my eyes.

Sure, I wouldn't get the white picket fence, the certainty of a well-planned day, or even the comfort that came from knowing where I'd be sleeping that night. The sense of purpose I'd get in return for that sacrifice, though, seemed worth it to me, if even in just that slice of time. Really, that's all that mattered.

Right that very second, my heart beat, my blood pumped, and my eyes saw every color of the rainbow. My life had purpose.

I stood at the top of that proverbial mountain and imagined waving my fist in the air like a champion, empowered, dignified, and riding along the sweet lane of purpose. Becca met my eye, and in hers, I saw respect and admiration. I saw a road leading to a clearly defined field that leveled us both, and brought us eye-to-eye as equals with our own claim to action. Our actions that could positively affect so many.

We needed each other.

We balanced each other.

We got each other.

We could now stand up against a buckling wind and laugh at it, daring it to screw with us. It wouldn't stand a chance against our will. The fog and haze lifted and showcased our love in the proper light, the light that temporarily dimmed due to our lack of foresight. Had that light revealed itself to us years earlier, would we have seen its power? Would we have known what to do with such power? Had she not gone down the lonely road to fame and found her way back and on a more grounded road, would she have given CRE8 a second thought? Would she have given the importance of CRE8 the boost it needed to light up a whole new generation to understand music's vital role in society by bringing lost kids back to a place they called home?

I doubted it.

Becca needed to tumble down the side of that mountain a few times and bruise her ego, nurse her injured heart, and learn to open her eyes to what she could do with her fame instead of what fame could do with her. I needed to trudge my way up that same mountain, clinging to the sides of those sharp rocks with little regard for comfort and safety, too. I needed to hang on to the mouths of nooks and allow fear to creep inside of me so I could harness a strength I never knew existed in me. I needed to trip over mounds of tangled weeds and sticks in search of stable ground amongst such adversity.

We needed to experience adversity at crumbling levels to bring us in touch with our values, beliefs, and statutes that would shape us into the people we had become. Without the pain, the challenge, the obstacles, we'd just be two ordinary women, lost amongst the rubble of a chaotic, restless backdrop, never knowing which step would take us down, and which would raise us up.

The spirit of adventure and unknowing could only be brought out when we decided to let go of the past, embrace the future, and take in that moment in time when anything and everything could happen.

The dance between the known and the unknown whetted our appetites and allowed passion to be resurrected, reshaped, and reenergized. It propelled us on a new pathway where the journey began new every waking day. I loved that twisting, ever-changing path.

Finally, the happy vibe threaded itself through my system. It hung out on my shoulder, sitting in my peripheral, allowing me to enjoy the unfolding of joy in simple things like the beauty of the sun's rays, the joy on a stranger's face, and the love from my sweet Becca.

I couldn't will happiness into being. Happiness naturally occurred when I stopped forcing it and simply turned to other things, waiting for it to reveal itself in its own beautiful way.

I truly had everything I needed to be happy and successful now.

NOTE FROM THE AUTHOR

As with all of my books, I enjoy giving a portion of proceeds back to the community by donating to the NOH8 Campaign www.noh8campaign.com and Hearts United for Animals: www.hua.org. Thank you for being a part of this special contribution.

A SPECIAL REQUEST

If you enjoyed reading this story, I'd be so grateful for your honest review of it. Just a sentence or two saying what you thought about *The Journey Somewhere* will help others discover it and help me to serve you better with future books!

(www.amazon.com/author/suziecarr)

www.ingramcontent.com/pod-product-compliance
Lightning Source LLC
Chambersburg PA
CBHW021955170626
46808CB00001B/171